BRODECK'S REPORT

BRODECK'S REPORT

Philippe Claudel

*Based on a translation from the French
by John Cullen*

MACLEHOSE PRESS
QUERCUS · LONDON

First published in Great Britain in 2009 by

MacLehose Press
An imprint of Quercus
21 Bloomsbury Square
London
WC1A 2NS

Copyright © Editions Stock 2007

First Published in the French language by
Editions Stock, Paris, as *Le Rapport de Brodeck*

English Translation Copyright © John Cullen 2009

The moral right of Philippe Claudel to be identified as
the author of this work has been asserted in accordance with the
Copyright, Designs and Patents Act, 1988.

A CIP catalogue reference for this book
is available from the British Library

ISBN 978 1 906694 04 3 (HB)
ISBN 978 1 906694 05 0 (TPB)

2 4 6 8 9 7 5 3 1

Printed and bound in Great Britain
by Clays Ltd, St Ives plc

For all those
who think they are nothing

For my wife and my daughter,
without whom I would not be much myself

I am nothing, I know it, but my nothing
comprises a little bit of everything.
VICTOR HUGO, *The Rhine*

1

My name is Brodeck and I had nothing to do with it.

I insist on that. I want everyone to know.

I had no part in it, and once I learned what had happened, I would have preferred never to have spoken of it again, I would have liked to bind my memory fast and keep it that way, as subdued and still as a weasel in an iron trap.

But the others forced me. "You know how to write," they said. "You've been to the University." I replied that my studies had not amounted to much – I had not even finished my courses and did not remember much about them. They did not want to hear it. "You know how to write, you know about words and how to use them, you know how they can say things. That's what we need. We can't do it ourselves. We'd get into a muddle, but you, you'll say it right, and people will believe you. Besides, you've got the typewriter."

It is very old, the typewriter. Several of its keys are broken, and I have nothing to repair it with. It is capricious. It is worn out. Sometimes, for no apparent reason, it jams, as though suddenly baulking. But I said nothing about any of that, because I had no desire to end up like the *Anderer*.

Do not ask me his name – no-one ever knew it. Almost immediately, people coined expressions in dialect and started applying them to him: *Vollaugä*, literally "Full-Eyes" (because his bulged a bit); *De Murmelnër*, "the Whisperer" (because he spoke very little, and always in a small voice that sounded like a breath); *Mondlich*, "Moony" (because he seemed to be among us, but not of us); *Gekamdörhin*, "Came-from-over-there".

To me, however, he was always the *Anderer*, "the Other". Maybe I thought of him that way because not only had he arrived out of nowhere, but he was also different, and being different was a condition I was quite familiar with; sometimes, I must admit, I had the feeling that, in a way, he was me.

As for his real name, none of us ever asked him what it was, except the Mayor perhaps, and then only once; in any case I do not believe he received an answer. Now we will never know. It is too late, and no doubt better that way. The truth can gash you so deeply that you cannot live with the wounds any longer, and for most of us, what we want to do is live. As painlessly as possible. It is only human. I am certain you would be like us if you had known the war and what it did here, and above all what came after the war, what those weeks and months were like, particularly the last of them, the period when that fellow arrived in our village and settled here, just like that, from one day to the next. Why our village? There are dozens and dozens of villages in the foothills of the mountains, lying amid forests like eggs in nests, and many of those villages are a lot like this one. Why did he choose precisely our village, so far from everything, so utterly remote?

When they informed me that they wanted me to write the report, we were all at Schloss' inn. It was about three months ago, right after . . . right after . . . I do not know what to call it. The event? The drama? The incident? Or maybe the *Ereigniës*. *Ereigniës* is a curious word, full of mists and ghosts; it means, more or less, "the thing that happened". Maybe the best way of saying that is with a word taken from the local dialect, which is a language without being one, and which is perfectly wed-

2

ded to the skin, the breath, and the souls of those who live here. *Ereigniës*, a word to describe the indescribable. Yes, I shall call it the *Ereigniës*.

So the *Ereigniës* had just taken place. With the exception of two or three ancient villagers who had stayed at home, close to their stoves, as well as Father Peiper, who was no doubt sleeping off his intake somewhere in his little church, all the men were at the inn, which is like a great cave, rather dark, and suffused with tobacco fumes and smoke from the hearth; and the men, all of them, were dazed and stunned by what had just happened, yet at the same time – how shall I say it? – relieved, because clearly, one way or the other, it had been necessary to resolve the situation. You see, they could bear it no longer.

Each was folded into his own silence, so to speak, even though there were nearly forty of them, pressed together like withies in a bundle, choking, inhaling the others' odours: their breath, their feet, the acrid reek of their sweat and their damp clothes, old wool and broadcloth impregnated with dust, with the forest, with manure, with straw, with wine and beer, especially wine. Not that everybody was sloshed; no, it would be too easy to use drunkenness as an excuse. To say that would just be a way of diluting the horror. Too simple. Much too simple. I am going to try not to simplify what is very difficult and complex. I am going to try. I do not promise that I will succeed.

Try to understand. I repeat: I could have remained silent, but they asked me to tell the story, and when they made the request, most of them had their fists clenched or their hands in their pockets, where I imagined them grasping the handles of their knives, the very knives which had just . . .

I must not go too fast, but it is hard not to, because now I keep sensing things behind my back – movements, noises, staring eyes. For some days I have been wondering if I am not changing, bit by bit, into quarry, into a tracked animal with the whole hunt, led by a pack of snuffling dogs, at its heels. I feel watched, followed, spied upon, as if from now on there will always be someone just over my shoulder, alert to my smallest gesture and reading my thoughts.

I will come back to what was done with the knives. I will perforce come back to that. But what I wanted to say was that to refuse a request made under such conditions, in that particular atmosphere when everyone's head is still full of savagery and bloody images, is impossible and even quite dangerous. And so, however reluctantly, I agreed. I simply found myself in the inn at the wrong time, that is, some few minutes after the *Ereigniës*, in one of those moments of stupefaction characterized by vacillation and indecision, when people will seize upon the first person who comes through the door, either to make a saviour of him or to cut him to pieces.

Schloss' inn is the largest of the six taverns in our village, which also boasts a post office, a haberdashery, an ironmonger's, a butcher's, a grocer's, a tripe and offal shop, a school, and a branch of a lawyers' office based in S. Over this last place, which is as filthy as a stable, preside the senile lorgnettes of Siegfried Knopf, whom they call a lawyer even though he is only a clerk. In addition, there is Jenkins' little office; he served as our policeman, but he died in the war. I remember when Jenkins left. He was the first to go. He never usually smiled, but that day he shook everyone's hand, laughing as though he were on the way to his own wedding. Nobody recognized him. When he turned the corner at Möberschein's sawmill, he waved broadly and threw his helmet into the air in a joyful farewell. He was never seen again. He has never been replaced. The shutters in his office are closed, and its threshold is now covered by a small growth of moss. The door is locked. I do not know who has the key, and I have never tried to find out. I have learned not to ask too many questions. I have also learned to take on the colour of the walls and the colour of the dust in the street. It is not very difficult. I look like nothing at all.

Schloss' inn is the only place where you can buy a few provisions after Widow Bernhart pulls down the metal shutter of her grocery at sunset. It is also the most popular of the taverns. It has two public rooms. The one at the front is the larger of the two; its walls are blackened wood, its floor is covered with sawdust, and you practically fall into it when you enter, because you have to go down two steep steps carved into the sandstone itself and worn down in the middle by the soles of the thousands of drinkers who have trodden there. And then there is the smaller room in the back which I have never seen. It is separated from the first by an elegant larch-wood door with a date engraved on it: 1812. This little room is reserved for a small group of men who meet there once a week, every Tuesday evening; they drink and smoke, either tobacco from their fields in porcelain pipes with carved stems or bad cigars from who knows where. They have even given themselves a name: *De Erweckens'Bruderschaf*, which means something like "the Brotherhood of the Awakening". A peculiar name for a peculiar association. No-one knows exactly when it was created or what its purpose is or how you get into it or who its members are – the big farmers, no doubt, maybe Lawyer Knopf, Schloss himself, and definitely the Mayor, Hans Orschwir, who owns the most property in these parts. Nor does anyone know what they get up to or what they say to one another when they meet. Some say that that room is where crucial decisions are taken, strange pacts sealed, and promises made. Others suspect that the brothers dedicate themselves to nothing more than the consumption of brandy and the playing of draughts and cards, accompanied by much smoking and jocularity. A few people claim to have heard music coming from beneath the door. Maybe Diodème the teacher knew the truth; he rummaged through everything, through people's papers and in their heads, and he had a great thirst to know things inside and out. But the poor man, alas, is no longer here to tell us what he knew.

Schloss' inn is a place I hardly ever go to because, I have to confess, Dieter Schloss makes me uneasy, with his darting mole's eyes, his bald, pink cranium, his eternally sweaty forehead, his brown teeth that give off the smell of dirty bandages. And there is another reason, namely that ever since I came back from the war, I do not seek out human company. I have grown accustomed to my solitude.

On the evening the *Ereigniës* took place, old Fédorine had sent me to the inn to get a bit of butter; we had run out and she wanted to make some little shortbreads. Normally she is the one who goes in quest of the provisions, but on that baleful evening my Poupchette was lying in bed with a bad fever, and Fédorine was at her side, telling her the story of *Bilissi and the Poor Tailor*, while Emélia, my wife, hovered nearby, ever so softly humming the melody of her song.

Since then, I have thought a great deal about that butter, about the few ounces of butter we did not have in the pantry. You can never be too aware of how much the course of your life may depend on insignificant things – a little butter, a path you leave to take another path, a shadow you follow or flee, a blackbird you choose to kill with a bit of lead or decide to spare.

Poupchette's beautiful eyes shone too brightly as she listened, rivetted to the old woman's voice, the same voice I had listened to in days gone by, coming from the same mouth – a younger version of the same mouth, but already missing a few teeth. Poupchette looked at me with her eyes like little black marbles, burning with fever. Her cheeks were the colour of cranberries. She smiled, stretched out her hands to me, and clapped them together, quacking like a duckling: "Papa, come back Papa, come back!"

I left the house with the music of my child's voice in my ears, mingled with Fédorine's murmuring: *"Bilissi saw three knights, their armour bleached by time, standing before the doorstep of her thatched cottage. Each of them carried a red spear and a silver shield. Neither their faces nor even their eyes could be seen. Things are often thus, when it is far too late."*

2

Night had dropped its cape over the village as a carter throws his cloak over the buring embers of his campfire. The houses, their roofs covered with long pinewood tiles, breathed out puffs of slow blue smoke and made me think of the jagged backs of fossilized animals. The cold was beginning to settle in, a meagre cold as yet, but we had lost the habit of it, because the last days of September had been as hot as so many baking ovens. I remember looking at the sky and seeing all those stars crowded against one another like frightened fledglings looking for company, and thinking that soon we would plunge, all of a sudden, into winter. Where we live, winter seems as long as many centuries skewered on a giant sword, and while the cold weather lasts, the immensity of the valley around us, smothered in forests, evokes an odd kind of prison.

When I came into the inn, they were there, almost all the men of our village. Their eyes so sombre, standing as still as stone, so immediately I guessed what had happened. Orschwir closed the door behind me, then came up to me. He was trembling a little. He fixed his big blue eyes on mine, as if he were seeing me for the first time.

My stomach began to churn. I thought it was going to eat my heart. Then I asked in a very weak voice – staring at the ceiling, wanting to pierce it with my gaze, trying to imagine the *Anderer*'s room, trying to imagine him, the *Anderer*, with his sideburns, his thin moustache, his sparse, curly hair rising in tufts from his temples, and his big round head, the head of an overgrown, good-natured boy – I said, "Tell me you haven't – you didn't—?" It was barely a question. It was more like a moan that escaped from me without asking permission.

Orschwir took me by the shoulders with both hands, each of them as broad as a mule's hoof. His face was even more purple than usual, and a droplet of sweat, tiny and glistening like a rock crystal, slid very slowly down the bridge of his pock-marked nose. He was still trembling, and since he was holding me like that, he made me tremble too. "Brodeck . . . Brodeck . . ." That was all he managed to say. Then he stepped backwards and melted into the crowd. Everyone's eyes were on me.

I felt like a tiny weak tadpole in the spring, lost in a great puddle of water. I was too stunned for my brain to work properly, and, oddly enough, I thought about the butter I had come to buy. I turned to Dieter Schloss, who was standing behind the bar, and I said, "I'm just here to buy some butter, a little butter, that's all . . ." He shrugged his narrow shoulders and adjusted the flannel belt he wore around his pear-shaped belly, and I believe it was at that very moment that Wilhem Vurtenhau, a rabbit-headed peasant who owns all the land between Steinühe forest and the Haneck plateau, took a few steps forward and said, "You can have all the butter you want, Brodeck, but you're going to tell the story. You're going to be the scribe." I rolled my eyes. I wondered where

Vurtenhau could possibly have come up with that word, "scribe". He is so stupid, I am sure he has never opened a book in his life, and besides, he said the word wrong; in his mouth, the *b* became a *p*.

To be able to tell stories is a skill, but it is not mine. I write only brief reports on the state of the flora and fauna, on the trees, the seasons and the quantity of game, on the water level of River Staubi, on the snowfall and the rainfall. My work is of little importance to my Administration, which in any case is very far away, a journey of many days, and which could not care less about what I write. I am not sure my reports are still reaching their destination, or, if they are, whether anyone reads them.

Since the war, the post has been quite unreliable and I think it will be a long time before the postal service functions smoothly again. I hardly ever receive money any more. I have the impression that I have been forgotten, or that they think I am dead, or indeed that they no longer need me.

From time to time, Alfred Wurtzwiller, the postmaster, walks to the city of S. and back – once a fortnight – he is the only one who can go, because he alone has the *Genähmigung*, the "authorization" – and sometimes he gives me to understand that he has brought back a money order for me and hands me a few banknotes. I ask him for explanations. He makes big gestures I cannot interpret. Sounds ground up like meat issue from his mouth, which is creased by a large harelip, and I cannot understand them either. He bashes a receipt three times with a big rubber stamp; I take up the crumpled, illegible document and the little money that comes with it. That is what we live on.

"We're not asking you for a novel." The speaker was Rudi Gott, the blacksmith. Despite his ugliness – a long time ago a horse's hoof crushed his nose and shattered his left cheekbone – he is married to a beautiful woman called Gerde who is forever posing outside the forge, as if eternally waiting for the painter destined to do her portrait. "You just have to say what happened, that's all. The way you do in your reports." Gott was clutching a big hammer in his right hand. His naked shoulders burst out of his leather apron. He was standing near the hearth. The fire burned his face, and the steel head of the tool he held gleamed like a well-sharpened scythe blade.

"Alright," I said, "I'll tell the story – that is, I'll try. I promise you I'll try. I'll write in the first person, I'll say 'I' the way I do in my reports, because I don't know how to tell a story any other way, but I warn you, that's going to mean everyone. Everyone, you understand me? I'll say 'I', but it'll be like saying the whole village and all the hamlets around it. In other words, all of us. Alright?"

There was a hubbub, a noise like a draught animal relaxing in its harness and grunting a little, and then they said, "Agreed, do it like that, but be careful. Don't change anything. You must tell the whole story. You must say everything, so that whoever reads the Report will understand and forgive."

I do not know who will read it, I thought. *Maybe they would understand, but forgiveness is another matter entirely.* I did not dare advance this point of view openly, but I thought it in the deepest part of myself. When I said yes, a sound filled the inn, the sound of relief, and fists were unclenched. Hands were removed from pockets. It was as though these men turned to stone had come to life again. As for me, I was breathing very hard. I had come within a whisker of something. I preferred not to know what.

This was early last autumn. The war had been over for a year. Mauve autumn crocuses were blooming on the slopes, and often in the morning, on the granite crests of the Prinzhornï which border our valley

10

to the east, the first snows left a fresh, dazzling white powder, soon to melt away in the hours of sunlight. It had been three months almost to the day since the *Anderer* arrived in our village, with his enormous trunks, his embroidered clothes, his mystery, his bay horse and his donkey. "His name is Monsieur Socrate," he said, pointing to the donkey, "and this is Mademoiselle Julie. Please say hello, Mademoiselle Julie." And the pretty mare bowed her head twice, whereupon the three women who were present stepped back and crossed themselves. I can still hear his small voice as he introduced his beasts to us as though they were humans, and we were all dumbfounded.

Schloss brought out glasses, goblets, bowls and cups, and wine for everybody. I was required to drink too. As if to seal a vow. I thought with terror of the *Anderer*'s face, of the room he lived in, a room I was somewhat familiar with having entered it, at his invitation, three times to exchange a few mysterious words and to drink some strange black tea, the like of which I had never drunk before. He had several books with obscure titles, some of them in languages written in a different way to ours; they must sound like sliding scree and clinking coins. Some of the books had tooled, gilt bindings, while others looked like piles of bound rags. There was also a china tea service which he kept in a studded leather case, a chess set made of bone and ebony, a cane with a cut-crystal pommel, and a quantity of other things that he kept stored in his trunks. He always had a big smile on his face, a smile that often substituted for words, which he tended to use sparingly. He had beautiful, jade-green eyes, very round and slightly bulging, which made his look even more penetrating. He spoke very little. Most of all, he listened.

I thought about what those men had just done. I had known them all for years. They were not monsters; they were peasants, craftsmen, farm workers, foresters, minor government officials – in short, men like you and me. I put down my glass. I took the butter Dieter Schloss handed me, a thick slab wrapped in glassine paper that made a sound like turtle-doves' wings. I left the inn and ran all the way home.

Never in my life have I run so fast.

Never.

3

When I got back to the house, Poupchette had fallen asleep and Fédorine was dozing beside the child's bed, her mouth slightly open, exposing her three remaining teeth. Emélia had stopped humming. She looked up at me and smiled. I could not say anything to her. I quickly climbed the stairs to our room and dived into the sheets as one dives into oblivion. I seemed to go on falling for a long time.

That night I slept only a little, and very badly. I kept circling and circling around the *Kazerskwir*. The *Kazerskwir* – that was because of the war: I spent nearly two long years far from our village. I was taken away, like thousands of other people, because we had names, faces or beliefs different from those of others. I was confined in a distant place from where all humanity had vanished, and where there remained only conscienceless beasts which had taken on the appearance of men.

Those were two years of total darkness. I look upon that time as a void in my life – very black and very deep – and therefore I call it the *Kazerskwir*, the crater. Often, at night, I still venture out onto its rim.

Old Fédorine never leaves the kitchen. It is her own private realm.

She spends the nighttime hours in her chair. She does not sleep. She declares that she is past the age of sleeping. I have never known exactly how old she is. She herself says she does not remember, and in any case, she says, not knowing did not prevent her from being born and will not prevent her from dying. She also says she does not sleep because she does not want death to take her by surprise; when it comes, she wants to look it in the face. She closes her eyes and hums a tune, she mends stories and memories, she weaves tapestries of threadbare dreams, with her hands resting on her knees in front of her, and in her hands, her dry hands, marked with knotty veins and creases straight as knife blades, you can read her life.

I have described to Fédorine the years I spent far from our world. When I returned, it was she who took care of me; Emélia was still too weak. Fédorine looked after me the way she had done when I was little. All the movements came back to her. She fed my broken mouth with a spoon, bandaged my wounds, slowly but surely put the flesh back on my bare bones, watched over me when my fever mounted too high, when I shivered as though plunged into a trough of ice, or raved in delirium. Weeks passed like that. She never asked me anything. She waited for the words to emerge of their own accord. And then she listened for a long time.

She knows everything. Or almost everything.

She knows about the black void that returns to my dreams again and again. About my unmoving promenades around the rim of the *Kazerskwir.* I often tell myself that she must make similar excursions, that she too must have some great abysses which haunt her and pursue her. We all do.

I do not know if Fédorine was ever young. I have always seen her twisted and bent, covered with brown spots like a medlar long forgotten

13

in the pantry. Even when I was a small child and she took me in, she already looked like a battered old witch. Her milkless breasts sagged beneath her grey smock. She came from afar, far back in time and far away in the geography of the world. She had escaped from the rotten belly of Europe.

It was a long time ago, I was standing outside a house in ruins from which a little smoke was rising. Was it perhaps my father's house, my mother's? I must have had a family. I was a full four years old, and I was alone. I was playing with a hoop half consumed by the fire. It was at the beginning of another war: Fédorine passed by, pulling her cart. She saw me. She stopped. She dug in her bag, brought out a beautiful, gleaming red apple. She handed it to me. I devoured the fruit like a starveling. Fédorine spoke to me, using words I did not understand, asked me questions I could not answer, she touched my forehead and my hair.

I followed the old woman with the apples as if she were a piper. She lifted me into the cart and wedged me among some sacks, three saucepans and a bundle of hay. There was also a rabbit with pretty brown eyes and tawny fur; its stomach was soft and very warm. I remember that it let me stroke it. I also remember that Fédorine stopped at a bend in the road, where broom grew along its edges, and, in my language, asked me my name. She told me hers – "Fédorine" – and pointed down at what remained of my village. "Take a good look, little Brodeck. That's where you come from, but you'll never go back there, because soon there will be nothing left of it. Open your eyes wide!"

So I looked as hard as I could. I saw the dead animals with their swollen bellies, the barns open to the four winds, the crumbled walls. There were also a great many puppets lying in the streets, some with their arms crossed, others rolled up into balls. Although they were big

14

puppets, at that distance they seemed tiny. And then I stared at the sun, and it poured burning gold into my eyes and made the tableau of my village disappear.

I tossed and turned in bed. I felt that Emélia was not sleeping any more than I was. When I closed my eyes, I saw the *Anderer*'s face, his pond-coloured eyes, his full, amaranth-tinged cheeks, his sparse, frizzy hair. I smelled his violet scent.

Emélia moved. I felt her warm breath against my cheek and lips. I opened my eyes. Her lids were closed. She seemed utterly tranquil. She is so beautiful that I often wonder whatever it was that I did to make her take an interest in me. It was because of her that I did not founder back then. When I was in the prison camp, I thought about her every minute.

The ones who guarded us and beat us were always telling us that we were nothing but droppings, lower than rat shit. We did not have the right to look them in the face. We had to keep our heads bowed and receive their blows without a word. Every evening, they poured soup into the tin bowls used by their guard dogs, mastiffs with coats the colour of honey and curled-up lips and eyes that drooled reddish tears. We had to go down on all fours, like the dogs, and eat our food without using anything but our mouths, like the dogs.

Most of my fellow prisoners refused to do it. They are dead. As for me, I ate like the dogs, on all fours and using only my mouth. And I am alive.

Sometimes, when the guards were drunk or had nothing else to do, they amused themselves by putting a collar and a leash on me. I had to crawl around like that on all fours, wearing a collar attached to a leash. I had to strut and turn round in circles and bark and hang my tongue out and lick their boots. The guards stopped calling me Brodeck and started calling me "Brodeck-the-Dog". And then they laughed their heads off.

Most of those who were imprisoned with me refused to act the dog, and they died, either of starvation or from the repeated blows the guards dealt them.

Not one of the other prisoners had been talking to me for a long time except to say, "You're worse than the guards, Brodeck! You're an animal. You're shit, Brodeck!" Like the guards, they kept telling me I was no longer a man. They are dead. They are all dead. Me, I am alive. Perhaps they had no reason to survive. Perhaps they had no love lodged deep in their hearts or back home in their village. Yes, perhaps they had no reason to go on living.

During the night, the guards at last took to tying me to a post near the mastiffs' kennels. I slept on the ground, lying in the dust amid the smells of fur and dogs' breath and urine. Above me was the sky. Not far away were the watchtowers and the sentinels, and beyond was the countryside; the fields we could see by day, the wheat, rippling with fantastic insolence in the wind, the clumped stands of birch, and the sound of the great river and its silvery water, only too close.

But I in fact was very far from that place. I was not tied to a post. I was not wearing a leather collar. I was not lying half-naked near sleeping dogs. I was in our house, in our bed, pressed against Emélia's warm body and no longer crouched in the dust. I was warm, and I could feel her heart beating against mine. I could hear her voice speaking to me those words of love she was so good at finding in the darkness of our room. For all of that I came back.

Brodeck-the-Dog came home alive and found his Emélia waiting for him.

4

The morning after the *Ereigniës*, I got up very early. I shaved, dressed, and left the house without a sound. Poupchette and Emélia were still asleep, while Fédorine was in her chair, dozing and talking a little. She spoke words without coherence or logic in a strange babble drawn from several languages.

Daylight was only just beginning to bleach the sky, and the whole village was still bound up in sleep. I closed the door very softly behind me. The grass in front of the house was drenched with whitish, almost milky dew, which quivered and dripped on the edges of the clover leaves. It was cold. The peaks of the Prinzhornï looked higher and sharper than usual. I knew that this was a portent of bad weather, and I told myself that before long snow would begin to fall on the village, enveloping it and isolating it even more.

"*Zehr mogenhilch*, Brodeck!"

I jumped as though caught in some shameful act. I knew that I had done nothing wrong, that I had nothing to feel guilty about, but I nevertheless leapt like a kid called to order by the goatherd's switch. I had not recognized the voice, even though it belonged to Göbbler, our neighbour.

He was sitting on the stone bench built against the wall of his house. He was leaning forward and supporting himself on the stick he held with both hands. I had never seen him sit on that bench before, except perhaps once or twice on one of the rare summer nights when the air is stifling and oppressive and there are no cool breezes to refresh the village.

He is a man over sixty, with a rough-hewn face; he never smiles and seldom speaks. An opaque, milky veil is slowly covering his eyes, and he cannot see further than five metres. The war brought him back to the village, although people say he occupied a position in some administration in S. for years before his return; but no-one knows exactly which administration that was, and I do not think anyone has ever asked him. Now he lives on his pension and his hen house. Moreover, he has come to resemble his roosters somewhat. His eyes move in the same way, and the skin that hangs down below his neck has ruddy patches like wattles. His wife, who is much younger than he, is called Boulla. She is fat and a great chatterer. She smells of grain and onion. They say that a great heat burns between her legs, and that it would take many buckets of water to extinguish it. She seeks men as others look for reasons to exist.

"Yes, indeed, up very early!" Göbbler repeats. "So where are you going?"

It was the first time he had ever asked me a question. I hesitated. I became confused. Words stumbled in my mouth and collided with one another, like stones in a mountain torrent. With the tip of his stick, Göbbler pushed away a snail that was calmly moving towards him, and then turned it over. It was a small snail with a yellow and black shell and a fine, delicately marked body, full of innocent grace. Caught by surprise, the creature took a few moments to withdraw its body and its fragile horns into its shell, whereupon Göbbler raised his stick and brought it down on the little mollusc, which exploded like a walnut. "Be careful, Brodeck," he murmured, without taking his eyes off the debris of the snail's shell and body, now reduced to a slimy, beige pulp. "Be careful. There's been trouble enough already."

He turned his eyes towards me. He smiled, drawing back his lips. It was the first time I had ever seen him really smile, and I got my first glimpse of his teeth. They were grey and pointy, strikingly pointy, as though he had spent many an evening filing them down. I did not reply. I almost shrugged, but I stopped myself. A great shudder ran up and down my back. I pulled my cap down over my ears, pressed the flaps against my temples, and moved away without looking at him again. There was a little sweat on my forehead. One of his cocks crowed, followed by all the others. Their cries rang in my head like a series of blows. Gusts of wind from the depths of the valley swirled around me, laden with the odours of beechnuts, of peat bogs, of heather and wet rock.

On rue des Püppensaltz, our main street, old Ohnmeist was going from door to door. Ohnmeist is an unusual dog. He gets his name from the fact that he has no master and has never wanted one. He avoids other dogs and children, makes do with very little, and goes around begging for food under kitchen windows. He accompanies whomever he fancies to the fields and sleeps under the stars, and when it is too cold, he scratches on the doors of barns; people are glad to give him a little hay to lie on and some soup to eat. He is a big, gangling beast, brown with reddish spots, about the size of a griffon but with a pointer's short, dense fur. No doubt his blood is a mixture of many breeds, and it would be a clever man who could say which ones they were. As he ambled over to sniff me, I remembered how, whenever he crossed the *Anderer*'s path, Ohnmeist would give two or three little yelps of joy and wag his tail excitedly. Then the *Anderer* would stop, remove his gloves – beautiful gloves of very fine, soft leather – and stroke the animal's head. It was very strange to see the two of them like that, the dog placid and happy, quietly accepting the *Anderer*'s caresses when ordinarily none of us could get close to the beast, much less touch him, and the *Anderer*, patting the big fellow with his bare hand and looking at him as if he

19

were a human. That morning, Ohnmeist's eyes were both bright and shifty. He walked alongside me for a while, occasionally heaving a brief, melancholy moan. He kept his head low, as if it were suddenly too heavy for him, too filled with distressing thoughts. He left me near the Urbï fountain and disappeared down the narrow street that leads to the river.

I had my own idea, which I had mulled over at length during the course of my agitated night: I had to speak to Orschwir, the Mayor. I had to see him, and he had to tell me what it was that he and the others expected of me. I was almost at the point of doubting my reason. I wondered if I had understood Göbbler's words correctly, or if perhaps I had dreamed him sitting there on his bench, or if the scene at the inn the previous night – that clamp of bodies tightening around me, that vice of faces, that request, and that promise – if all that were not made of the same stuff that formed some of my peculiar dreams.

Orschwir's house is the only one that really does have the forest at its back. It is also the biggest house in our village. It gives an impression of wealth and power, but in fact it is only a farmhouse, a large farmhouse, old, prosperous, paunchy, with immense roofs and walls whose granite and sandstone form an irregular chequerboard, and yet people think of the place as something of a chateau. What is more, I am sure Orschwir is pleased to think of himself, if only occasionally, as lord of the manor. He is not a bad man, although he is as ugly as an entire barbarian regiment. People say it was his ugliness, strangely enough, which assured his conquests in former days, when he was young and went to all the dances. People talk too much, and so often they have nothing to say. One thing that is sure is that Orschwir ended up marrying the richest girl in the region, Ilde Popenheimer, whose father owned five sawmills and three watermills. In addition to her inheritance, she gave her husband two sons, each the spitting image of his father.

The resemblance did not matter much. I speak in the past tense because as it happens they both died. Right at the beginning of the war. Their names are carved on the monument the village erected between the church and the cemetery depicting a woman swathed in great veils and kneeling on the ground; it is hard to say whether she is praying or meditating her revenge. The inscribed names include *"Günter and Gerhart Orschwir, aged 21 and 19"*. My name too was on the monument, but when I returned, Baerensbourg the road-mender rubbed it out. The job caused him a great deal of difficulty – it is always a very delicate undertaking to remove what is written in stone. On the monument I can still just read my first name. This makes me smile, but the monument gives Emélia the creeps. She does not like to pass in front of it.

According to a persistent rumour, Orschwir owes his position as Mayor to the deaths of his sons. In spite of the fact that their deaths were anything but heroic. They killed themselves at their lookout post while playing with a grenade like a couple of children. That is what they were after all, big children still, who thought the war would suddenly make men of them. The explosion could be heard in the village. It was the first explosion. Everyone ran to the little sentry box which had been built to overlook the road to the border. The post stood right in the middle of the Schönbehe pasture and atop its highest elevation, a hill sheltered by a great, brown-red boulder covered with lichen the colour of jade. Nothing much was left, either of the box or of the boys. One had died pressing both hands against his belly, trying to hold in his guts; the other's head, blown clean off by the blast, stared at us fixedly. We buried them two days later, wrapped in sheets of white linen and lying in oaken coffins which Fixheim, the carpenter, had fashioned with care. Those two were our first dead. Father Peiper, who in those days still drank only water, pronounced a sermon on the themes of chance and deliverance. Few of us understood it, but the congregation very much liked the words he chose, most of them rare or very old, and the way he sent them rolling among the pillars, the vaults, the clouds of incense, the soft light of the candles and the stained-glass windows of our little church.

I walked into the farmyard, still deserted at this hour. It is immense this yard. A whole country all by itself, bordered by handsome heaps of manure. The entrance is a large postern made of hand-turned wood, painted bright red and carved with a motif of chestnut leaves; in their midst is the motto, *"Böden und Herz geliecht"*, which means, more or less, "Belly and heart united."

I have often pondered the meaning of that phrase. Someone told me that it was Orschwir's grandfather who had the inscription added. When I say "someone", I mean Diodème, the schoolmaster, who told me about it. Diodème was my elder by several years, but we got along like two old comrades. If he had the time, he liked to accompany me as I went around collecting information for my reports, and it was a pleasure to chat with him. He was an uncommon man, who often – not always, but often – showed good sense, who knew many things, and doubtless many more than he admitted to knowing, and who had a perfect command of reading, writing and arithmetic. This last quality, in fact, was the reason why the previous Mayor appointed him as the village schoolmaster, even though Diodème was not from the village and came from another to the south of ours, about four days' walk away.

It has been three weeks since Diodème died in circumstances so strange and so poorly defined that his death made me even more alert to all the little signs I was noticing around me. Fear began to brew gently in my brain. The day after he died, I started to write this account alongside the Report the others had already assigned me to do. I am writing the two of them at the same time.

Diodème spent most of his free hours in the village archives. Sometimes I saw a light in his window very late at night. He lived alone above the school in a tiny, uncomfortable, dusty apartment. Books, documents, and the records of olden times were all the furniture he had. "What I'd like to do is to understand," he confided to me one day. "We never understand anything, or if we do, not much. Men live, in a way, as the blind do, and generally that's enough for them. I'd go so far as to say that it's what they're looking for: to avoid headaches and dizzy spells, to fill their stomachs, to sleep, to lie between their wives' thighs when their blood runs too hot, to make war because they're told to do so, and then to die without knowing what awaits them afterwards, but hoping that something is awaiting them, all the same. Ever since I was a child, I've loved questions, and I've loved the paths you must follow to find the answers. Sometimes, of course, I end up knowing nothing but the path itself, but that's not so bad; at least I've made some progress."

Maybe that was the cause of his death: Diodème wanted to understand everything, and he tried to give words and explanations to what is inexplicable and should always remain unexplored. On the day I am referring to, I could not think of anything to say to him. I think I smiled. Smiling costs nothing.

But there was another time, on a spring afternoon, when we talked about Orschwir, about his postern and the inscription carved on it. This was before the war. Poupchette was not yet born. Diodème and I had

23

been sitting on the short grass in one of Bourenkopf's stubble-fields, which lie towards the Doura valley and beyond it to the border. Before going back down to the village, we rested for a while near a wayside cross representing Jesus. He had an unusual face, the face of a Negro or a Mughal. It was the end of the day. From where we sat, we could see the whole village and cup it in one hand. Its houses looked like the little houses in children's toys. A fine sunset was gilding the roofs, which were glistening from the recent rain. Plumes of smoke rose from every dwelling, and in the distance, the slow, sluggish smoke clouds mingled with the shimmering air, blurring the horizon and making it appear almost alive.

Diodème took some pieces of paper out of his pocket and read me the last pages of the novel he was writing. Novels were his obsession; he wrote at least one a year, on whatever crumpled writing material came to hand, including strips of wrapping paper and the backs of labels. He kept his manuscripts to himself and never showed them to anybody. I was the only one to whom occasionally he read passages from his work. He read them to me, but he expected nothing in return. He never asked my opinion about the passages he read or the subjects they treated. So much the better. I would not have been able to say anything. The stories were always more or less the same: complex tales written in tortuous, interminable sentences which evoked conspiracies, treasures buried in deep holes, and young women held as prisoners. I loved Diodème. I was also very fond of his voice. Its music made me feel drowsy and warm. I would look out at the landscape and listen to the melody. Those were wonderful moments.

I never knew Diodème's age. Sometimes I thought he looked quite old. On other occasions, I persuaded myself that he was only a few years my senior. He had a noble face. His profile reminded me of a head on an ancient Greek or Roman coin, and his curly, jet-black hair, which lightly brushed the tops of his shoulders, made me think of certain heroes of the distant past who lie asleep in fairytales and tragedies and epics, and whom a magic charm sometimes suffices to awaken or destroy. Or, perhaps better than a hero, one of those shepherds of antiquity who, as is well known, are more often than not gods in disguise, come among men to seduce them, to guide them, or to bring them to ruin.

"*Böden und Herz geliecht,*" Diodème concluded, chewing on a blade of grass as the evening gradually gathered around us. "Funny motto. I wonder where the old fellow came across that. In his head, or in a book? You find some really bizarre things in books sometimes."

5

Orschwir was sitting at one end of his kitchen table, a table four metres long carved from the bole of an oak tree several hundred years old – one of those trees that stand like lords in the heart of the Tannäringen forest. A young serving girl stood beside him. I did not know her. She could not have been more than sixteen. She had a pretty, round face like that of the Virgin in certain very old paintings. She was pale, in spite of her rosy cheeks the colour of peonies. She moved so little that she might have been taken for a dressmaker's mannequin or an unusually large doll. Later, I learned that she was blind. This seemed strange, for her eyes, although somewhat fixed, appeared to see everything around her, and she moved about easily, never bumping into furniture or walls or other people. She was a distant cousin whom Orschwir had taken in; she had come originally from the Nehsaxen region, but her parents were dead, their house had been destroyed and their lands confiscated. The villagers called her *Die Keinauge*, "the no-eyed girl".

Orschwir dismissed her with a whistle, and she went soundlessly away. Then he gestured to me to approach and sit down. In the mornings he looked less ugly than usual, as if sleep had tightened his skin and softened his imperfections. He was still in his underpants. Around his waist, a leather belt awaited the trousers it was destined to hold up. He had thrown a goatskin jacket over his shoulders, and his otter's fur cap was already on his head. On the table before him was a gently steaming plate of eggs and bacon. Orschwir ate slowly, pausing occasionally to cut himself a slice of brown bread.

He poured me a glass of wine, looked at me without the least sign of surprise, and simply said, "So how are things?" Then, without waiting for a reply, he directed his attention to his last rasher of bacon, a thick chunk whose fat, rendered almost translucent by the cooking, dripped onto his plate like melted wax from a candle. He carefully carved the bacon into small, even-sized pieces. I watched him, or rather I watched his knife, which that morning he was using to feed himself as naturally as you please, and which the previous evening had no doubt been driven several times into the *Anderer*'s body.

It has always been difficult for me to speak and express my innermost thoughts in person. I prefer to write. When I sit down and write, words grow very docile; they come and feed out of my hand like small birds, and I can do almost what I will with them, whereas when I try to marshal them in the open air, they steal away. And the war did nothing to improve things. It made me even more silent. In the camp I saw how words could be used and what could be required of them. Before then, before the camp, I used to read books, particularly books of poetry.

Professor Nösel had instilled this taste in me when I studied in the Capital, and I had retained it as a pleasant habit. I never forgot to stick a volume of poems in my pocket when I set out to gather information for my reports, and often, surrounded by the great spectacle of the towering mountains with their escarpment of forest and the chequerboard pastures, as the sky above seemed to look on, contented with its own infinite expanse, I would read verses aloud. The ones I liked and read again aroused in me a kind of agreeable buzzing, like an echo of some confused thoughts which lay in the deepest part of myself, but which I was incapable of expressing.

When I returned from the camp, I put all my poetry books in the stove and burned them. I watched the flames as they consumed everything, first words, then sentences, then whole pages. The smoke that rose from the burning poems was neither better nor nobler nor more charming than any other smoke. There was nothing special about it. I learned later that Nösel had been arrested during the first raids, along with a number of professors and others whose occupation it was to study the world and explain it. He died shortly afterwards in a camp similar to mine, a camp little different from hundreds of other camps which had sprung up all over the place on the other side of the border, like poisonous flowers. Poetry had been of no use to him in the matter of his survival. Perhaps it had even hastened his demise. The thousands of verses in Latin, in Greek and other languages, which he kept in his memory like the greatest of treasures, had availed him nothing. I felt certain that he, unlike me, had refused to act the dog. Yes, that was it. Poetry knows nothing of dogs. It ignores them.

Orschwir mopped his plate with a piece of bread. "Brodeck, Brodeck, I can see you haven't had much sleep," he began, speaking softly in a tone of muffled reproach. "I, on the other hand – well, it's been a long time since I've slept so well, quite some time indeed. Before, I couldn't so much as close my eyes, but last night, I felt like I was six or seven years old again. I laid my head on the pillow, and three seconds later I was asleep . . ."

The sun had fully risen by now, and its white light came into the kitchen in oblique rays which struck the scarlet flagstones of the floor. Farm noises could be heard: animals, servants, creaking axles, unidentifiable thwacks, and snatches of conversation.

"I want to see the body." I spoke the words without realizing what I was doing. They surfaced almost of their own accord, and I let them pass. Orschwir looked surprised and upset. His face changed in an instant. He froze like a shellfish when you sprinkle it with a few drops of vinegar, and quite suddenly his features regained all their ugliness. He lifted his cap, scratched the crown of his head, stood up, turned his back to me, walked over to one of the windows, and planted himself in front of it.

"What good would that do, Brodeck? Didn't you see your fill of corpses during the war? And what does one dead man look like, tell me, if not another dead man? You must tell what happened. You mustn't forget anything, nor must you add useless details. They'll deflect you from your course, and you'll run the risk of confusing, perhaps even irritating your readers. Because you will be read, Brodeck, don't forget that; you will be read by people who occupy very important positions in S. Yes indeed, you will be read, even though I have a feeling you don't believe it . . ."

Orschwir turned around and looked me up and down. "I respect you, Brodeck, but it is my duty to put you on your guard. It is my duty as Mayor, and as . . . Please don't leave the path, I beg you, and don't go looking for what has never existed – or what does not exist any more."

He drew up his great carcass to its full height, yawned, and stretched his huge arms towards the ceiling. "Come with me," he said. "I'm going to show you something."

He was a good head taller than I was. We left the kitchen and entered a long corridor which wound its way through the entire house. I had the feeling we would never get out of that corridor; it made my head spin and filled me with dread. I knew Orschwir's house was big, but I would never have imagined it to be so labyrinthine.

It was an ancient structure that had been remodelled many times, and it bore witness to an age unconcerned with alignment or logic. Diodème told me that its oldest walls dated back more than four centuries. According to a document he had found in the archives, the Emperor stopped there in the autumn of 1567, on his way to the marches of Carinthia and an encounter with the Grand Turk. I walked behind Orschwir, who stepped out smartly, displacing a quantity of air. I felt as though I were being tugged along in his wake, drawn by his scent, a combination of leather, night, fried bacon, beard and unwashed skin. We met no-one. Sometimes we went up a few steps or down two or three others. I would be hard put to say how long we walked – a few minutes, a few hours – because that corridor extinguished all the reference points of space and time. Finally, Orschwir stopped at a large door covered with weathered green copper and square nails. He opened it, and the white light behind it dazzled me. I had to stand still for a moment with my eyes closed before I could open them again to the light. And see.

We were about to step out into the area behind the house. I had never managed to get a look at this part of Orschwir's property except from very far away, while walking up in the mountains. I knew that the sheds and outhouses back here housed the Mayor's entire fortune, and the fortune of his father before him, and that of his father's father. A pink, noisy fortune which spent its time wallowing in mud. A squealing fortune, which produced a diabolical racket all day long.

Orschwir's gold was swine. For several generations, his family had lived on and grown rich from hog fat. They had the largest pig farm for fifty kilometres around. Every morning, vehicles left the property – carrying either freshly killed carcasses or panic-stricken, squealing animals bound for slaughter – and drove to the villages, trade fairs and butchers' shops in the region. These daily rounds constituted a well-ordered choreography which not even the war had managed to disrupt. People eat in wartime, too. Some of them, at least.

For three months after the war began, there was a long period of stupefied calm when everyone gazed eastward and cocked an ear for the sound of marching boots, a speciality of the still-invisible *Fratergekeime*. (That is the word in our dialect for those who came here to spread death and ashes, for the men who turned me into an animal, men very much like us. Having gone to university in their Capital, I happened to know them well. We associated with some of them since they often visited our village, brought here by business and trade fairs, and spoke a language which is the twin sister of our own and which we understand with little difficulty.) When the calm ended and suddenly our border posts were swept aside like paper flowers scattered by a child's breath, Orschwir was not in the least worried: he went on raising, selling and eating his pigs. His door remained immaculate; no obscenities were painted on it. Although the conquerors marching in triumph through our streets bore a certain measure of responsibility for the idiotic deaths of his two sons, he had no qualms about selling them the fattest of his hogs in exchange for the pieces of silver they pulled out of their pockets in handfuls, having no doubt stolen them somewhere along the way.

In the first pen that Orschwir showed me, there were dozens of piglets a few weeks old playing on fresh straw. They chased one another, collided with one another and poked one another with their snouts, giving off little cries of joy all the while. Orschwir tossed them three shovelfuls of grain, which they rushed to devour.

In the next pen eight-month-old pigs wandered about, jostling and challenging one another. I could sense their strange, gratuitous violence and aggressiveness, and yet there was nothing in evidence to justify or explain it. They were already large, thick beasts, with drooping ears and brutish faces. An acrid stench assailed my nostrils. The straw the animals sprawled on was filthy with their excrement. Their grunts bounced off the wooden walls and battered my temples. I wanted to get out of there as quickly as possible.

Further on, in the last pen, there dozed the full-grown pigs. Immense, livid, long-loined, stretched out. They looked like so many small boats. They all lay on their sides, panting through open snouts and wallowing in black mud as thick as molasses. Some of them watched us with great weariness. Others were rummaging beneath them. One might have thought them giants changed into beasts, creatures condemned to a fearful metamorphosis.

"The ages of life," Orschwir murmured. I had almost forgotten his presence, and the sound of his voice made me jump. "First you saw innocence, then stupid aggression, and now, here, wisdom." He paused for a while and then began to speak again, slowly and very quietly: "But sometimes, Brodeck, wisdom's not what we think it is. The creatures you see before you are savage beasts. Truly savage, however much they look like beached whales. Brutes with no heart and no mind. With no memory, either. Nothing counts but their belly, just their belly; all the time they think of one thing and one thing only: keeping that belly full."

He paused and looked at me with an enigmatic smile that contrasted sharply with the heavy features of his dirty face. Breadcrumbs clung to his moustache, and his lips still glistened a little with bacon fat.

"They're capable of eating their own brothers, their own flesh. It wouldn't bother them at all – to them, it's all the same. They chew it up, they swallow it down, they shit it out, and then they start all over again, *ad infinitum*. They're never sated. And to them everything tastes good. Because they eat everything, Brodeck, without question. Everything. Do you understand what I'm telling you? They leave nothing behind, no trace, no proof. Nothing. And they don't think, Brodeck, not them. They know nothing of remorse. They live. The past is unknown to them. They've got the right idea, don't you think?"

6

I am trying to return to those moments, to get as close to them as I can, but what I would really like to do is to forget them and run away, far away, on light feet and with a brand-new brain.

I have the feeling that I am the wrong size for my life. I mean, I feel that my life is spilling over everywhere, that it was never cut to fit a man like me, that it is full of too many things, too many events, too many torments, too many flaws. Is it my fault, perhaps? Is it because I do not know how to be a man? Because I do not know how to sort things, how to take what I need and leave the rest? Or maybe it is the fault of the century in which I live, which is like a great crater; the excesses of every day flow into it, and it is filled with everything that cuts and flays and crushes and chops. My head – sometimes I think my head is on the point of exploding, like a heavy shell crammed with gunpowder.

That infamous day, the day after the *Ereigniës*, was not so long ago. And yet, in spite of everything, it is slipping through my fingers. I remember only certain scenes and certain words, very exact and very clear, like bright lights against a deep black background. And I also remember my fear, above all my fear, which I have worn like a garment ever since. I cannot cast it off; in spite all my efforts it has grown tighter and tighter, as if it has shrunk a little more each week. The strangest thing is that back in the camp, after I became Brodeck-the-Dog, I was not afraid any more. Fear no longer existed for me there; I had moved well beyond it. For fear still belongs to life. Like hyenas circling carrion, fear cannot do without life. That is what nourishes and sustains it. But I – I was out on life's margins. I was already halfway across the river.

After I left Orschwir's farm, I believe I wandered the streets. It was still quite early. My memory focused on the image of the pigs, lying on their sides and looking at me with their glaucous eyes. I tried to banish that vision, but it was tenacious. It planted roots I will never be able to destroy. Those animals, their enormous faces, their swollen bellies, and their eyes, their pale eyes examining me. And their stench, too. Good God . . . My thoughts joined hands and danced together inside my skull. Everything – the pigs, the *Anderer*'s calm, trusting face – spun in a sarabande, with no music but the solo violin of Orschwir's appalling serenity.

I found myself outside Mère Pitz's café, next to the old washhouse. I had no doubt headed there because I wanted to be certain I would not meet anyone, or any man at least. Only old women frequented the café. They would be there at any hour, but especially towards evening, drinking cups of herbal tea or little glasses of marc mixed with Dutch gin and a bit of sugar. We call drinks like these *Liebleiche*, "charmers".

To tell the truth, that café is not altogether a café. It is part of a house, a room that adjoins a kitchen. There are three little tables with embroidered tablecloths, a couple of chairs at each, a narrow chimney that draws badly, some plants in glazed ceramic pots and, on the wall, an extremely faded photograph of a young man who is smiling at the camera as he smoothes his moustache with two fingers. Mère Pitz is more than seventy-five years old. She is bent in half, as though folded at a right angle. When children pass her in the street, they call her *Die Fleckarei* – "the hinge". The young man in the photograph is her husband, Augustus Pitz, who died half a century ago.

I must be the only man in the village to occasionally set foot in Mère Pitz's place. Sometimes she helps me, and that is why I go there. She knows all the plants that grow on the plateau, even the rarest ones, and when I cannot find them in my books, I go and ask her, and we spend a few hours talking about flowers and grasses, about footpaths and under-growth, about pastures grazed by sheep, goats and cows, and also by the hungry wind which never draws breath; about all the places where she cannot go any more and has not seen for a long time.

"My wings have been clipped, Brodeck," she says. "My life was really up there, with the flocks in the high stubble-fields. Down here I suffo-cate. The air is too low. Down here it is like being a worm; you creep along the surface of the earth and eat dust. But up there . . ."

She has the finest dried plant collection I have ever seen: an entire armoire filled to bursting with large books between whose dark-brown cardboard covers she has for years and years pressed specimens of flowers and plants from the mountain. She has recorded below each one the place where it was collected, the day, the appearance of the sky, the scent of the plant, its exact colour and its orientation, all in her careful handwriting, and occasionally she has added a brief commentary that has nothing to do with the specimen in question.

"So, Brodeck, you've come to see the Great Book of Dead Things again?" That is how she greeted me when I pushed open her door and the little bells jangled. To be more precise, since she spoke in dialect, she called her herbarium *"De Buch vo Stiller un Stillie"*, which sounds softer and less tragic.

I closed the door behind me, as though someone were following me. I am sure I was pulling a hideous face and acting like a conspirator. I sat at the table deep in the corner of the room, the one that looks as if it wants to disappear. I asked Mère Pitz for something very strong and very hot, because I was shivering like an old wooden ratchet in the Easter wind. Even though the fully risen sun now reigned uncontested over the sky, I was freezing.

Mère Pitz came back quickly carrying a steaming cup, and with a gesture bade me drink. I obeyed her like a child, closing my eyes and letting the liquid take me over. My blood grew warmer, followed by my hands and my head. I loosened my jacket collar a little, and then my shirt collar too. Mère Pitz watched me. The walls moved gently, like poplar leaves, and so did the chairs, approaching the walls as though wanting to ask them to dance. "What's wrong with you, Brodeck?" she asked me. "Have you seen the Devil?"

She was holding my two hands in her own, and her face was quite close to mine. She had large green eyes, very beautiful, with flecks of gold around the edges of her irises. I remember thinking that eyes have no age, and that when you die, you still have the eyes you had as a child, eyes that one day opened upon the world and have not ever let it go.

She gave me a little shake and asked me again.

What did she know, and what could I tell her? The previous night, only men had been there at Schloss' inn, and it was with those men that I had come to an agreement. When I got home I said nothing to my women, and in the early hours of the following morning, which was not yet over, I left the house before they awakened. The others, all those others, had they not done the same with their wives, their sisters, their mothers, their children?

She went on gently pressing my hands, as if she were trying to squeeze the truth out of them. I said the words in my mind: "Nothing serious, nothing at all, Mère Pitz. Everything's normal. Last night, the men of the village killed the *Anderer*. The killing took place at Schloss' inn just like that, like a game of cards or a verbal agreement. It had been building up for a long time. Me, I arrived after it happened. I had gone there to buy some butter, and I had nothing to do with the killing. I have simply been charged with writing the Report. I'm supposed to explain what went on from the time he arrived in the village and why they had no choice but to kill him. That's all."

These words never passed my lips. They remained unspoken. I tried to let them out. They did not want to leave. The old woman stood up, went to the kitchen, and returned with a small, pink, enamel saucepan. She poured the rest of the brew into my cup and motioned to me to drink it. And I drank. The walls started swaying once more. I was very hot. Mère Pitz went away again. The next time she came back, she was carrying one of the large books that contained her dried plant collection. The label on the cover read *"Blüte vo Maï un Heilkraüte vo June"*, which can be translated as "May Flowers and June Simples". She placed the book on the table in front of me, sat down next to me and opened it. "Whatever it is that's ailing you, Brodeck, have a look at my little *Stillies* and they'll take your mind off it."

36

Then, as if he had been summoned by those words, I was aware of the *Anderer* standing behind me, adjusting his gold-rimmed eyeglasses on his kind, round, overgrown child's face, as I had often seen him do; he smiled at me before bowing his large head, adorned with frizzy sideburns, to contemplate the desiccated leaves and lifeless petals in Mère Pitz's book.

I have already noted that he spoke but little. Very little. Sometimes, when I looked at him, the image of a saint crossed my mind. Saintliness is very odd. When people encounter it, they often take it for something else, something completely unlike it: indifference, mockery, scheming, coldness, insolence, perhaps even contempt. But they are mistaken and that makes them furious. They commit a grievous crime. This is no doubt the reason that most saints end up martyrs.

7

I have to tell the story of the *Anderer*'s arrival among us, but I am afraid: afraid of waking ghosts, and afraid of the others. The men of the village, I mean, who are no longer with me the way they used to be. Yesterday, for example, Fritz Aschenbach, whom I have known for more than twenty years, failed to return my greeting when we met on the slope of the Jornetz. He was on his way down from cutting firewood; I was going up to see whether I might still be able to find some chanterelles. For a moment, his silence dumbfounded me. I stopped, turned around, and said to his back, "What's this, Fritz, no 'good morning'?" But he did not even slow his pace or turn his head. He contented himself with spitting extravagantly to one side; that was his only reaction. Maybe he was so lost in his thoughts that he did not see or hear me – but thoughts of what?

I am not crazy. I am not going crazy. Nevertheless, there is Diodème's death to consider too. (Another death! And an odd death indeed, as I shall soon describe.) Ever since my time in the camp, I have known the wolves outnumber the lambs.

The *Anderer* arrived late in the afternoon on 13 May. It will be a year ago next spring. A gentle, blond-tinged year. Evening came on tiptoe, as if unwilling to bother anyone. In the fields surrounding the village, and in the high pastures, as far as the eye could see, was a vast ocean of white and yellow. The green grass practically disappeared beneath a carpet of dandelions. The wind swayed, brushed and bent the flowers according to its whim, while above them bands of clouds hastened westward and vanished into the Prätze gap. On the stubble-fields, a few patches of snow still held out against the early spring warmth, which was gradually lapping them up, shrinking them from one day to the next, and would soon change them into clear, cold pools.

It was around five o'clock, perhaps five-thirty, when Gunther Beckenfür, who was busy mending the roof of his shepherd's hut, looked up and saw a bizarre crew making its way along the road from the border. Nothing has been seen on this road since the end of the war; no-one travels on it any more, and it would occur to no-one to travel on it.

"Coming on like a real slow train, they were." That is Beckenfür talking, in answer to my question. I write down every word he says in a notebook, literally every word. We are at his house. He has served me a glass of beer. I am writing. He is chewing on the cigarette he has just rolled for himself, half tobacco and half lichen, which fills the room with a stench of burned horn. His old father is sitting in a corner; his mother has been dead for a good while. The old man is talking to himself. The words rumble and gurgle in his mouth, where no more than two or three teeth remain, and he shakes his fragile starling's head continuously, like a money-box angel in a church. Snow has begun to fall outside – the first snow that so delights children, whose whiteness blinds. We can see the flakes drifting close to the window, like thousands of curious eyes turned on us, and then, as though frightened, rushing away in great clouds towards the street.

"They were hardly moving, as if the fellow was hauling a load of granite boundary stones all by himself. I stopped working and took a long look, just to see if I was dreaming. But no, I wasn't dreaming, I definitely saw something, even though I wasn't sure yet what it was. At first I thought it might be stray animals, and then I thought it was people who'd lost their way or vendors of some kind, because now I could see that there was something a little human about whatever it was. I remember shivering, a real shiver, and not from cold, but from remembering the war, the war and the road it came on, that shitty, goddamned road that brought the people here nothing but bad luck and trouble, and there he was, a creature in the shape of a man, with his two beasts – I couldn't yet tell what they were – there he was, coming towards the village on that very same road. He could only have come from over there, from the *Fratergekeime*, those filthy sons of infected old whores . . . Do you remember what they did to Cathor, those sick bastards?"

I nodded. Cathor was the pottery mender. He was also Beckenfür's brother-in-law. When the *Fratergekeime* arrived in the village, he tried to play games with them. He had lost. Perhaps I will write about him later.

"I was so fascinated I put down my roofing tiles and my tool. I rubbed my eyes and squinted, trying to see as far as I could. It was like a vision out of the past. I was flabbergasted. He looked like a fairground entertainer, with his fancy old-style clothes and a pair of circus animals for mounts. Like something from a variety show or a puppet theatre."

Where we live, all the horses were slaughtered and eaten a long time ago. And after the war no-one ever gave serious thought to getting new ones. The people in our village did not want horses any more. We preferred donkeys and mules. Real beastly beasts, with nothing human about them and nothing to remind us of the past. And if someone arrived on horseback, that necessarily meant that he had come from very far away and that he knew nothing of our region, or about what had happened here, or about our misfortunes.

It was not so much that riding a horse looked old-fashioned; after the war, we all seemed to go back in time. All the misery the war had sown sprouted up like seeds in a promising spring. Farm implements from days gone by – including rickety buggies and patched-up carts – were brought out of barns and mended one way or another with what-ever had not been destroyed or stolen. People still work their fields with ploughshares forged over a century ago. Haymaking has to be done by hand. Everyone has taken a step backwards, as if humanity had suffered a huge hiccough, as if human history had given man a violent kick in the backside and now we have to start all over again almost from scratch.

The apparition was moving at a slow trot, looking (according to Beckenfür) left and right, stroking his mount's neck and often speaking to the beast (Beckenfür could see his lips moving). The second animal was attached to the horse. It was an old but still robust donkey with upright pasterns. He stepped out surely, showing no sign of tiredness and never swerving, even though he had three large and apparently heavy trunks lashed to his back, as well as various sacks that dangled down on either side like strings of onions hung up in a kitchen.

"Finally, though it took a while, he got close to where I was standing. I thought he looked like some sort of genie, or maybe the *Teufeleuzeit* my father used to tell me about when I was a little boy and he wanted to scare the crap out of me. It lived in burrows all over the valley, among the foxes and the moles, and fed on lost children and fledglings. Anyway, this new arrival was wearing a bizarre melon-shaped hat that looked as though it had been planed. He doffed it and greeted me with great ceremony. Then he began to dismount from his horse, a pretty mare with a clean, shiny coat. An elegant, graceful animal she was. He let himself slide down the side of her belly very slowly, breathing hard and rubbing his own paunch, which was big and round. When his feet touched the ground, he dusted off his operetta outfit, namely a kind of frock coat of cloth and velvet which was covered with crimson braids and other frou-frous. He had a balloon for a face, with tight skin and red, red cheeks. The donkey grunted a little. The horse answered and shook her head, and that was when the odd fellow smiled and said, 'What magnificent country you live in, sir. Yes, a magnificent country . . .'

"I imagined he was pulling my leg. His animals had not moved – they were like their master, too polite. There was a lot of fine grass right under their noses, but they did not so much as give it a nudge. Other beasts would have just grazed away, but they contented themselves with looking at each other and occasionally exchanging a few words, animal words. Then he pulled out a fancy little watch on a chain and seemed surprised at the time, and that made his smile even broader. He nodded in the direction of the village and asked, 'Will I get there before night-fall?. . .'

"He did not say the name of our village. He just moved his head in that direction. And then he did not even wait for a reply. He knew very well where he was going. He knew! And really, that is the strangest part

41

about the whole thing, the fact that he wasn't just some hiker who had got lost in the mountains, he was actually *trying* to get to our village. He came here on purpose!"

Beckenfür fell silent and drained his glass of beer, his fifth. Then he stared dully at the tabletop, whose nicks and scratches formed mysterious patterns. Outside the window the snow was now falling steadily and vertically. At this rate, it would be piled up a metre high on the roofs and in the streets overnight. And then we, already on the margins of the world, would be still more cut off from it. That is often a terrible thing: for some people, isolation can lead only to fantastical ruminations, to a brain full of convoluted, unsound constructions. And when it comes to that game, I know many players who manage to perform some extraordinary feats of mental architecture on snowy winter evenings.

8

The fact remains that the *Anderer* made a couple of quiet remarks that fateful spring day, smiling the while, then got back onto his horse, left Gunter Beckenfür without another word, and continued on to the village. Beckenür stood there for a long time watching him, until he disappeared behind the Kölnke rocks.

But before he reached our village, he must have stopped somewhere. He must have done. I have worked out the timings. There is a gap between the moment when Beckenür lost the *Anderer* from sight and the instant when he passed through the village gate at dusk, watched by the eldest Dörfer boy who was hanging about, reluctant to go home, because his father was roaring drunk again and threatening to disembowel him. It is a gap that not even the indolent gait of the *Anderer*'s horse can satisfactorily explain. Upon reflection, I think he stopped near the river by the Baptisterbrücke, at the place where the road makes a curious winding turn through a field where the grass is as tender as a child's cheek. I cannot see where else he could have gone. The view is very beautiful from that spot, and if someone does not know our region, that is the place where he can experience it like a piece of fabric, for from there he can see the roofs of the village and hear its sounds and, above all, he can be amazed by the river.

The Staubi is not a watercourse that belongs to its landscape. One would expect to find here a sluggish, meandering stream, overflowing and spreading out into the meadows and bogging down among the golden-headed buttercups; one would expect slow-moving algae, as soft as wet hair. Instead, we have an impetuous, rampaging torrent which hisses, cries, collides, churns up gravel and wears down the rocks that show through its surface as it hurls water and foam into the air. A true, wild thing from the mountain savage, clear and sharp as crystal; you can see the grey flashes of trout in its depths. Untamed summer or winter, its water is cold enough to chill the inside of your skull, and occasionally, during the war, creatures other than fish were to be found floating in it, blue creatures, some of them still looking a little astonished, others with their eyes firmly closed, as if they had been put to sleep by surprise and tucked up in pretty liquid sheets.

From my conversations with him, I am certain that the *Anderer* took the time to observe our river. Staubi – it is a funny name. It has no meaning, not even in our dialect. No-one knows where it came from. Even Diodème failed to find its origin or its meaning in all the pages he read and rifled through. They are strange things, names. Sometimes you know nothing about them, and yet you are always saying them. Basically, they are like people: I mean like the ones whose paths you cross for years but never know, until one day, right before your eyes, they reveal themselves to be what you would never have imagined them capable of being.

I do not know what the *Anderer* must have thought when he saw our roofs and our chimneys for the first time. He had arrived. His journey was done. He had come here, to our village, and nowhere else. Beckenfür was the first to realize that, and later we all felt as he did. There was no mistake. Without any doubt, the *Anderer* came here of his own free will, of his own choosing, having prepared for his adventure and brought along everything he would need. His coming was not the result of a sudden impulse or passing fancy.

Even the hour of his arrival must have been part of his calculations. An oblique hour, during which the light exalts things – the mountains that watch over our narrow valley, the forests, the pastures, the walls and gables, the hedgerows, the voices – and makes them more beautiful and more majestic. Not an hour of full daylight, yet sufficiently bright to give every occurrence a unique sheen and the arrival of a stranger a distinct impact in a village of four hundred souls who were already quite busy imagining things, even in ordinary times. And conversely, an hour which by the mere fact of its ongoing attachment to the dying day arouses curiosity, but not yet fear. Fear comes later, when the windows are down and the shutters closed, when the last log has slipped beneath the ashes, and when silence extends its realm over the innermost depths of every house.

I am cold. My fingertips are like stones, hard and smooth. I am in the shed behind my house, surrounded by abandoned planks, pots, seeds, balls of string, chairs in need of reseating – an enormous clutter of more or less decrepit things. This is where life's dross is piled up. And I am here too. I have come here of my own accord. I need to be alone so that I can try to put this terrible story into some semblance of order.

We have been in this house for nearly ten years. We moved from our cabin and came here after I had managed to buy the place with money saved from my earnings and from the sale of Emélia's embroidery. When I signed my name to the contract, Lawyer Knopf vigorously shook both my hands. "Now you've really got a home of your own, Brodeck. Never forget: a house is like a country." Then he brought out some glasses and we drank a toast, just he and I, because the seller refused the drink the notary held out to him. Rudolf Sachs was his name; he wore a monocle and white gloves and had made the trip from S. especially. He looked down on us from a great height, as if he lived on a white cloud and we wallowed in liquid manure. The house had belonged to one of his great-uncles whom, as it happened, he had never known.

The cabin had been given to us when we – Fédorine, her cart and I – first arrived in the village, more than thirty years ago. We came from the ends of the earth. Our journey had lasted for weeks, like an interminable dream. We had traversed frontiers, rivers, open country, mountain passes, towns, bridges, languages, peoples, forests and fields. I sat in the cart like a little sovereign, leaning against the bundles and stroking the belly of the rabbit, which never took its velvet eyes off me. Every day, Fédorine fed me with bread, apples and bacon, which she took from large, blue canvas sacks, and also with words; she slipped them into my ear and I had to let them out again through my mouth.

And then, one day, we arrived in the village which was to become our village. Fédorine stopped the cart in front of the church and told me to get down and stretch my legs. Back in those days, people were not yet afraid of strangers, even when they were the poorest of the poor. The villagers gathered around us. Women brought us food and drink. I can remember the faces of the men who insisted on pulling the cart and leading us to the cabin, declaring that Fédorine had done enough. Then there was Father Peiper, who was still young and full of energy and who still believed what he said, and also the Mayor, Sibelius Craspach, a former medical officer in the imperial army who was now an old man with impressive white moustachios and a beribboned ponytail. They settled us in the cabin and made it clear that we could stay there for one night or for several years. The main room contained a large black stove, a pinewood bed, a wardrobe, a table and three chairs; there was also a smaller room, which was empty. The wooden walls were the colour of honey, soft and warm, and the cabin itself was warm too. Sometimes at night we could hear the murmur of the wind in the highest branches of the nearby fir trees and the creaking of the wood caressed by the warm breath of the stove. I would fall asleep thinking about squirrels and badgers and thrushes. It was paradise.

Here, in the shed, I am alone. It is no place for women, whether young or old. In the evenings, the candles cast fantastical shadows all around. The wooden beams play a dry music. I have the feeling that I am very far away. I feel, perhaps mistakenly, that nothing can disturb or reach me here, that I am safe from everyone and from all harm, entirely safe, even though I am in the heart of the village, surrounded by the others, and they are aware of everything about me, every deed I do, every breath I take.

I have placed the typewriter on Diodème's desk. After his death, Orschwir had everything Diodème owned – his clothes, his few pieces of furniture, his novels – thrown away and burned, under the pretext that it was imperative to make a clean sweep in order to welcome the

46

new teacher properly. Johann Lülli, a local boy, has replaced Diodème as schoolmaster. He has one leg that is shorter than the other and a pretty wife who has borne him three children, the youngest of them still in swaddling clothes. Lülli is not especially knowledgeable, but he is no idiot either. Before succeeding to his current position, he did the accounts for the Mayor's office, and now he draws letters and numbers on a blackboard and gets children to stammer out their lessons. He was present on the night of the *Ereigniës*. Among all those heads looking at me, I saw his red mane and his broad, square shoulders which always look as though he forgot to remove the hanger when he put on his coat.

I did not really need Diodème's desk, but I wanted to keep something of his, something he had touched and used. His desk is like him. Two handsome panels of polished walnut glued edge to edge and set on four simple legs, without airs or ornament. It has a large drawer which locks with a key, but I do not have the key. Nor have I been curious enough to force open the drawer to see if there is anything in it. I can hear no sound coming from inside when I shake the desk a little. The drawer is clearly empty.

9

I am facing the back wall of the shed. The typewriter is on the desk in front of me. It is very cold. My fingers are not alone in resembling stones; my nose, too, is as hard as a rock. I cannot feel it any more.

When I raise my eyes from the page, searching for words, I confront the wall, and then I tell myself that maybe I should not have put the desk against it. It has too much personality. It is too present. It speaks to me of the camp. I encountered a wall there much like this one.

When we arrived at the camp, the first stop for all of us was the *Büxte* – the "box". That was what the guards called it, the little stone room about a metre and a half by a metre and a half. Once inside, you could neither stand up nor lie down.

They hauled us out of the wagons with clubs and a great deal of yelling. Then we had to run to the camp. Three kilometres of rough road, accompanied by shouts and barking dogs which sometimes bit us as well. Those prisoners who fell were finished off at once, bludgeoned by the guards. We were weak; for six days we had eaten nothing and drunk very little. Our bodies were stiff and numb. Our legs could scarcely carry us.

The person toiling along at my side was a student, Moshe Kelmar. We had travelled to the camp in the same suffocating, crowded wagon, talking for six days as the big metal vice we were in advanced at a snail's pace through countryside we could not even see, while our throats became as dry as straw at the end of August, and while the great mass of humanity around us moaned and wept. There was no air and no room. There were old people, young girls, men, women. Very close to us there was a young mother and her child of a few months. A very young mother and her tiny child. I shall remember them all my life.

Kelmar spoke Fédorine's language, the ancient tongue she had laid down in me, and it came back to my lips quite suddenly and without any effort. He knew a great number of books, as well as the names of many flowers; even though he had always lived in the Capital, far from our village and far from the mountains, he even knew the valley periwinkle, which is something of a legendary flower in our region. He had never set foot in mountain country, a fact that troubled him greatly. He had the fingers of a young woman, very fine blond hair and a delicate face. He wore a shirt that had been white, a shirt made of fine linen with an embroidered front, the kind you would wear to a dance or a romantic rendezvous.

I asked him for news of the Capital, which I knew from my younger days when I was a student. Back then, people from our province had to cross the border to go to the University. Even though it was located in the *Fratergekeime*'s capital city, our region had been connected to their country for so many years under the Empire that we still felt at home there. Kelmar and I talked about the cafés where students went to drink hot wine and eat cinnamon cakes sprinkled with sesame seeds, about the promenade Elsi, a walk around a pretty lake where in the summer you could invite girls to go boating and in the winter you could skate, about the Main Library on Rue Glockenspiel, with its thousands of books in gilt bindings, and about the Stüpe canteen, where a fat woman named Fra Gelicke assumed the role of our mothers, filling our plates with heaped servings of ragout and our bowls with sausage soup. But when I asked him about some of my very favourite places, Kelmar would reply that he had not been to them for at least three years, ever since the day when he and all those designated as *Fremdër* were confined to the old part of the Capital, which had been transformed into a ghetto.

Inside the ghetto, however, there was a place he frequented and about which he talked at length, a place so dear to me that the simple fact of bringing it to mind again today makes my heart beat faster and brings a smile to my soul: the minuscule Théâtre Stüpispiel, with its tiny stage and its mere four rows of seats. The performances put on there were without doubt the worst in the city, but tickets cost next to nothing, and on cold days in November and December, the little room was as warm and as pleasant as a haystack.

One evening I went there with a friend of mine called Ulli Rätte, a fellow student and a lover of the good life whose constant laughter sounded like a cascade of copper pieces, and who was crazy about an apprentice actress. This girl, a roundish brunette, was playing a minor role in a pointless farce. I was just on the verge of dozing off when a young woman took a seat two places away from me. Her unseasonably light clothing showed that her chief reason for coming to the theatre was the same as mine. She shivered a little. She resembled a small bird – a fragile, lively tit. Her pale pink lips were slightly parted in a smile. She breathed on her small hands, turned in my direction and looked at me. An old song from the mountains says that when love knocks at the door, everything else disappears and the door is all that remains. And so our eyes spoke for more than an hour, and we left the theatre like a pair of robots; it took the cold outside to wrench us from our dream. A smattering of snow fell on our shoulders. I dared to ask her name. She gave it to me, and it was the most precious of gifts. In the course of the night, I kept murmuring that name, saying it over and over again, as if repeating it endlessly were going to make its owner appear before me by magic, the angel with the hazel eyes: "Emélia, Emélia, Emélia . . ."

Kelmar and I climbed down from the wagon at the same time. Like the others, we ran, protecting our heads with our hands. The guards yelled. Some of them even managed to laugh as they yelled. You might have thought it was one big comedy, but people were groaning, and there was a strong smell of blood. Kelmar and I were short of breath. We had eaten nothing for six days and hardly had anything to drink. Our legs were unsteady. Our joints full of rust. We ran as best we could. The road went on and on. The morning began to drop its pale light on the fields around us, even though the sun had yet to appear on the horizon. We passed a huge, twisted oak, a part of whose foliage had

50

been scorched by lightning. Shortly after that Kelmar stopped running. Just like that.

"I won't go any further, Brodeck," he said.

I told him he was crazy. The guards would soon catch up with us, I said, and then they would fall on him and kill him.

"I won't go any further," he repeated. "I can't go on living with that . . . with what we did."

I tried to grab him by the sleeve and pull him along as best I could. He did not budge. I pulled harder. A piece of his shirt came off in my hand. The guards, far off, had by now noticed something. They stopped talking and looked in our direction.

"Come on, come on, quick!" I begged him.

Kelmar calmly sat down in the middle of the dusty road. He said again, "I will go no further," very softly, very steadily, like someone saying aloud a serious decision which he has pondered for a long time in the silence of his thoughts.

The guards started walking towards us, faster and faster, and then they began to shout.

"Kelmar," I murmured. "Kelmar, come on, get up I beg you!"

He looked at me and smiled. "You'll think of me when you get back to your country, Brodeck. When you see the valley periwinkle, you'll think about the student Moshe Kelmar. And then you'll tell our story. All of it. You'll tell about the wagon and about this morning. You'll tell the story for me, and you'll tell it for everyone else . . ."

The small of my back was suddenly aflame. A second truncheon blow cut my shoulder. Two guards were upon us, shouting and striking. Kelmar closed his eyes. A guard shoved me, bellowing at me to get moving. Another blow from his club split my lip. Blood ran into my mouth. I began to run again, weeping as I went, not because of the pain, but

51

because I was thinking of Kelmar, who had made his choice. The shouting receded behind me and into the distance. I turned around. The two guards were savaging him as he lay on the ground. His body rocked from right to left, like a poor puppet attacked by wicked boys intent on the fun of breaking its every joint. And some hideous shortcut in my mind brought me to the evening of *Pürische Nacht*, the Night of Purification.

I have never found the valley periwinkle in our mountains; I have, however, seen it in a book, a precious book. It is a low-growing flower, with deep-blue petals that appear to be fused shut, as if unwilling to open. But maybe it no longer grows anywhere. Maybe Nature decided to withdraw it permanently from its great catalogue and deprive humans of its beauty because they did not deserve it any more.

At the end of the road and the end of my run was the entrance to the camp: a large gate of handsomely worked wrought iron, like the entrance to a leisure park or a pleasure garden. There were two sentry boxes, one on either side, painted pink and bright green; the guards within stood stiff and straight, and above the gate was a large, gleaming hook, like a butcher's hook for suspending entire beef carcasses. There was a man hanging from the hook, his hands tied behind his back, a rope around his neck, his eyes wide open and bulging from their sockets, his tongue thick, swollen, protruding between his lips – a poor fellow who resembled us like a brother. His skinny chest bore a placard on which someone had written in their language, the language of the *Fratergekeime* (which in the old days was the mirror of our dialect, its twin sister), *Ich bin nichts*, "I am nothing". The wind made his body sway a little. Not far off three crows watched and waited, craving his eyes like sweetmeats.

Every day, a man was hanged like that at the entrance to the camp. When we got up in the morning, each of us thought that perhaps today it would be our turn. The guards routed us out of the huts where we slept in heaps on the bare ground and lined us up outside. We stood and waited like that for a long time, whatever the weather; we waited for them to choose one of us as that day's victim. Sometimes the choice was made in three seconds. On other occasions they rolled dice or played cards, with us as the stakes. And we had to stand there close to them and wait, unmoving, in perfect ranks. Their games went on and on, and in the end the winner had the privilege of choosing. He walked though our ranks. We held our breath. We all tried to make ourselves as insignificant as possible. The guard took his time. Eventually he stopped in front of a prisoner, touched him with the end of his stick, and said simply, "*Du*". The rest of us, all the rest of us, felt a wild joy welling up from the depths of our hearts, an ugly happiness that would endure only until the following day, until the new ceremony, but which allowed us to hold on, to keep holding on.

The "*Du*" walked away with the guards. They escorted him to the gate. They made him climb a stepladder to the hook. They made him detach the previous day's hanged man, carry him down on his back, dig a grave for him and bury him in it. Then the guards made the new victim put on the placard with the words "*Ich bin nichts*", looped the rope around his neck, made him climb to the top of the ladder and then waited for the arrival of *Die Zeilenesseniss*.

Die Zeilenesseniss was the camp commandant's wife. She was young and moreover inhumanly beautiful, a beauty composed of excessive blondness and excessive whiteness. She often went for walks inside the camp, and we were ordered under pain of death never to meet her eyes.

Die Zeilenesseniss never missed the morning hanging. She approached the gate slowly, fresh-faced, her cheeks still ruddy from pure water, soap and face cream. Sometimes the wind carried her scent to us, a scent of wisteria, and ever since then I have not been able to smell the fragrance of wisteria without retching and weeping. She wore clean clothes. She was impeccably dressed and coiffed. As for us standing a few metres away from her, eaten by the vermin in the rags we wore which no longer had either shape or colour, our bodies filthy and stinking, our skulls shaved and scabby, our bones threatening to poke through every square inch of our skin, we belonged to a different world from hers.

She never came alone. She always carried an infant in her arms, a baby boy a few months old swathed in gay cloths. She gently rocked the child, whispering in his ear or humming the melody of some nursery song. I remember one of them: *"Welt, Welt von licht/ Manns hanger auf all recht/ Welt, Welt von licht/ Ô mein kinder so wet stillecht"* – "World, World of light/ Man's hand on everything/ World, World of light/ Be still, my child, my king."

The baby was always peaceful. He never cried. If he was asleep, she would awaken him with small, patient, infinitely gentle gestures, and only when he opened his eyes at last, waved his little arms, wiggled his little thighs and yawned at the sky would she signal to the guards, with a simple movement of her chin, that the ceremony could begin. One of them would give the stepladder a mighty kick and the body of the *"Du"* would drop, his fall abruptly cut short by the rope. *Die Zeilenesseniss* would watch him for a few minutes, and as she did so a smile would appear on her lips. She missed nothing and observed everything: the jumps and jolts, the throaty noises, the outthrust, kicking feet vainly reaching for the ground, the explosive sound of the bowels emptying themselves, and the final immobility, the great silence. At this point the child would sometimes cry a little, I dare say not so much from fright as from hunger and the desire to be suckled, but in any case his mother would plant a long kiss on his forehead and calmly leave the scene. The three crows would take up their positions. I do not know whether or not they were the same three every day. They all looked alike. So did the guards, but they did not peck out our eyes; they contented themselves with our lives. Like her. Like the commandant's wife. The one we privately called *Die Zeilenesseniss*. *Die Zeilenesseniss*: "the woman who eats souls".

In the aftermath, I have often thought about that child, her child. Did he die as she did? Is he still alive? If he is alive, he must be about my little Poupchette's age. How has he turned out, that little one, who for months was nourished each morning on the warm milk from his mother's breasts and the spectacle of hundreds of men hanged before his eyes? What does he dream about? What words does he use? Does he still smile? Has he gone mad? Has he forgotten everything, or does his young mind return to the juddering movements of bodies nearing death, to the strangled groans, to the tears running down hollow grey cheeks? To the birds' harsh cries?

During my first days in the camp, when I was in the *Büxte*, I talked to Kelmar constantly, as if he were alive at my side. The *Büxte* was a windowless dungeon cell. The scant light of day came in under the big, iron-bound oak door. If I opened my eyes, I saw the wall. If I closed my eyes, I saw Kelmar, and behind him, further off, much further off, Emélia, her sweet, narrow shoulders, and further still, Fédorine, weeping and gently shaking her head.

I do not know how long I remained in the *Büxte* with those three faces and that wall. A long time, no doubt. Weeks, perhaps months. But be that as it may, over there, in the camp, days, weeks and months meant nothing. Time did not count.

Time did not exist any longer.

55

10

I am still in the shed. I am having trouble calming down. About half an hour ago I thought I heard a funny sound coming from near the door, like a scraping. I stopped typing and listened. Nothing. I held my breath for a long time. No more sound. However, I was sure I had heard something and it was not my imagination, because the sound started again a little later, only now it was no longer near the door, it was along the wall. The sound moved slowly, very slowly, as if it were crawling. I blew out the candle, spun the page out of the typewriter and stuffed what I had written inside my shirt. Then I curled up in a corner behind some tools, near an old crate filled with cabbages and turnips. The sound had not stopped. It was still moving, slowly but steadily, sliding along the walls of the shed.

This went on for a long time. Sometimes the sound stopped for a while and then started again. It moved around the perimeter of the shed, always advancing at the same slow pace. As I listened to it turning around me, I felt as though I was caught in an invisible vice; an invisible hand was closing on me, slowly but surely.

The sound travelled along each of the four walls, making a complete circuit around the shed and returning to the door. I watched as the metal door handle pivoted downwards in absolute silence. I thought about all the tales that Fédorine knows by heart, stories in which objects speak, in which chateaus cross mountains and plains in a single night, when queens sleep for a thousand years, when trees change into noble lords, when roots spring from the earth and strangle people, and when springs have the power to heal festering wounds and soothe overwhelming grief.

The door opened, just barely, in the unbroken silence. I tried to shrink deeper into the corner, to envelop myself in darkness. I could see nothing. And I could no longer hear my heart. It was as if it had stopped beating, as if it too were waiting for something to happen. A hand grasped the door and opened it wide. The moon stuck its face between two clouds. Göbbler's body and bumpkinish head were outlined in light cast by the doorway. I was reminded of the silhouettes that street vendors in the Capital used to cut out; they would work in the big market on Albergeplatz, scissoring smoke-blackened paper into the shapes of gnomes or monsters.

A gust of wind rushed through the open doorway, carrying the scent of frozen snow. Göbbler stood unmoving, searching the shadows. I did not budge. I knew that he could not see me where I was, nor for that matter could I see him, but I smelled the smell of him, the odour of hen house and damp fowl.

"Not gone to bed yet, Brodeck? Are you not going to answer me? I know you're there. I saw the light under your door, and I heard the type-writer . . ."

In the darkness, his voice took on some peculiar intonations. "I'm watching you, Brodeck," he said. "Be careful!"

The door closed again, and Göbbler's silhouette was gone. For several seconds I could hear his retreating footsteps. I imagined his heavy boots of greased leather, their muddy soles leaving dirty-brown marks on the thin layer of snow.

I stayed in my corner, unmoving, for a good while. I breathed as little as I could and told my heart to be still. I spoke to it as one speaks to an animal.

Outside, the wind began to blow harder. The shed started shaking. I was cold. All of a sudden my fear gave way to anger. What did that chicken-merchant want with me? And what was he up to, anyway? Did *I* watch *his* movements, or spy on his fat wife? Had he barged into my house without knocking just to make a few veiled threats? By what right? The fact that he had joined the others in their awful deed did not make him a judge! The one real innocent among them all was me! It was me! The only one! The only one . . .

The only one.

Yes, I was the only one.

As I said those words to myself, I heard all of a sudden how dangerous they sounded; to be innocent in the midst of the guilty was, after all, the same as being guilty in the midst of the innocent. Then it occurred to me to wonder why, on that infamous night – the night of the *Ereigniës* – all the men of the village were in Schloss' inn at the same time; all of them except me. I had never thought about that before. I had never thought about it because until then I had told my-self, rather naïvely, that I was lucky not to have been there, and I had left it at that. But they could not have just happened to decide, all at the same time, to go over to the inn for a glass of wine or a mug of beer. If they were all there, it must have been because they had an appointment. An appointment from which I had been excluded. Why? *Why?*

Another cold shiver ran over me. I was still in the dark: in the dark inside the shed and in the dark about my question. And all at once the memory of the first day began to bounce around in my head like a saw in wood too green to cut. The day of my return. When I came from the camp, at the end of my long march, when finally I came into our village.

The faces of all those I encountered that day appeared before my mind's eye: first, at the gate, the two Glacker girls – the older one with a head like a garden dormouse, and her younger sister, whose eyes are buried in fat; then, in the narrow street that leads to the wine-pressing shed, Gott the blacksmith, his arms covered with red fuzz; outside her café at the corner of Ruelle Unteral, Mère Fülltach; near the Bieder fountain, Ketzenwir, hauling on a rope attached to a sick cow; at the entrance to the covered market, holding his belly in his hands and talking to Prossa the forester, Otto Mielk who, when he saw my ghostly self opened his mouth so wide that his crooked little cigar dropped from his lips; and then all the others, some of whom emerged from their houses as though from graves and formed a circle around me, surrounding me without speaking all the way to my house; and especially those who quickly withdrew into their houses and shut their doors, as if I had come back carrying a full load of trouble, or hate, or vengeance, which I intended to scatter in the air like cold ashes.

I could paint them, those faces, if I had colours and brushes and the *Anderer*'s talent. Most of all I would want to paint their eyes, in which I read only surprise at the time. Now that I seem to know them better, I realize that they contained a great many things; they were like the ponds that summer leaves behind in the drained peat bogs in Trauerprinz glade, which harbour all manner of aggressive rot, tiny maws ready to chew to bits anything that might hinder them from accomplishing their narrow destiny.

I had recently returned from the bowels of the earth. I was lucky to get out of the *Kazerskwir* alive, to climb up out of that pit, and every step I took away from it had seemed like a resurrection. My body, however, was the body of a dead man. In the places I passed through on the long road back, children fled weeping at the sight of me, as if they had seen the Devil, while men and women came out of their houses and approached me, turned in circles around me, almost touching me. Some gave me bread, a bit of cheese, a roasted potato, but others treated me like an evil being, throwing pebbles and spitting at me and calling me filthy names. None of that was anything compared to what I had left behind. I knew that for them I had come from too far away, and it was not a matter of mere kilometres. I had come from a country which did not exist in their minds, a country which had never appeared on a map, a country no tale had ever evoked, a country which had sprung from the earth and flourished for a few months, but whose memory was destined to weigh heavily for centuries to come.

How I was able to walk so far, to trample all those paths under my bare feet, I could not say. Perhaps it was simply because, without knowing it, I was already dead. Yes, maybe I was dead like the others in the camp, like all the others, but I did not know it, I did not want to know it; and maybe by refusing I had managed to elude the gatekeepers of the Underworld, the real Underworld, who had such a multitude arriving just then that they had allowed me to turn back, telling themselves that, after all, I was bound to return sooner or later to take my place in the great procession.

I walked, walked, walked. I walked towards Emélia. I was on my way to her. I was going home. I never stopped repeating to myself that I was going home to her. Her face was there on the horizon, her sweetness, her laugh, her skin, her voice of velvet and gravel, and her accent, which gave each of her words a certain awkwardness; when she spoke, she was like a child who stumbles on a stone, almost falls, regains its balance and then bursts out laughing. There was also her fragrance, a scent of infinite air, of moss and sun. I spoke to her as I walked. I told her I was coming home. Emélia. My Emélia.

To be fair, I should point out that not all those whom I met on my long road treated me like a stray dog or a plague-stricken beggar. There was also the old man.

One evening I came to a small town on the other side of the border, in the land of the *Fratergekeime*, in their country, a place which had been strangely spared and where all the houses were still standing, still intact: no scars, no yawning gaps, no collapsed roofs, no burned barns. The church, sturdy, well-preserved, overlooked a small cemetery spread out at its feet between some carefully tended vegetable gardens and an alley lined with lime trees. None of the shops appeared to have been pillaged. The Mairie was undamaged, and some handsome cows with brown coats and peaceful eyes were drinking silently from the troughs of the big fountains on their way to the milking shed. The boy in charge of the beasts was playing with a red wooden top.

An old man was sitting on a bench set against the front wall of one of the last houses on the way out of town. He seemed to be sleeping; his hands were resting on a holly-wood cane, his pipe had gone out. A felt hat covered half his face. I had already passed him when I heard him call me. He had a slow voice, a voice like a brotherly hand placed on a shoulder: "Come . . . come here . . ."

For a moment I thought I had dreamed his voice. Then he said, "Yes, I'm talking to you, young man!"

That was a funny thing for him to call me, "young man". I even felt an urge to smile. But I no longer knew how to smile. The muscles of my mouth, my lips and my eyes had forgotten how to do it, and my broken teeth hurt.

I was no longer a young man. I had aged several centuries in the camp. It had ceased to be a topic for debate. But the longer we prisoners laboured in our curious apprenticeship, the more our bodies melted away. I had left home as round as a ball, but in the camp I watched as

61

my skin got closer and closer to my bones. In the end, we all looked the same. We had become shadows, each of us indistinguishable from all the rest. We could be mistaken one for the other. A couple of us could be eliminated every day because a couple more could be added immediately and no-one would know the difference. The camp was always inhabited by the same silhouettes and the same bony faces. We were not ourselves any more. We did not belong to ourselves any more. We were not men any more. We were just a species.

11

The old man ushered me into his house, which smelled of cool stone and hay. He pointed to a handsome, polished sideboard and told me to leave my bundle there. To tell the truth it did not contain very much: two or three tattered rags I had found one morning among the ashes of a barn, and a piece of blanket that still smelled of fire.

In the front room, which had a very low ceiling and was completely covered with pine panelling, a round table stood ready, as if I had been expected. Two places had been laid facing each other across a cotton tablecloth, and in a terracotta vase there was a bouquet of fragile, heart-warming wildflowers, which moved at the least breath of air, spreading fragrances that were like memories of perfumes.

At that moment, with a mixture of sadness and joy, I remembered the student Kelmar, but the old man put a hand on my shoulder and, with a little movement of his chin, signalled to me that I should sit. "You need a good meal and a good night's sleep," he said. "Before my maid went home, she cooked a rabbit with herbs and a quince tart. They've been waiting just for you."

He went to the kitchen and returned with the rabbit, arranged on a green earthenware platter and surrounded by carrots, red onions and sprigs of thyme. I could not manage to move or say a word. The old man stood next to me and served me copiously, and then he cut me a thick slice of white bread and poured some limpid water into my glass. I could not be completely sure whether I was sitting in that house or lost in one of the numerous pleasant dreams that used to visit me at night in the camp.

My host sat down opposite me. "If you don't mind, I'm not going to join you – at my age one eats very little. But do please start."

He was the first man in a long time to address me as if I too were a man. Tears began to flow from my eyes. My first tears in a long time too. I clutched the seat of my chair with both hands, as if to keep myself from falling into the void. I opened my mouth and tried to say something, but I could not.

"Do not speak," he said. "I'm not going to ask any questions. I do not know exactly where you have come from, but I think I can guess."

I felt like a child. I made awkward, rash, incoherent gestures. He looked at me kindly. Forgetting my broken teeth, I fell upon the food as I had in the camp when the guards threw me a cabbage stalk, a potato or a crust of bread. I consumed the whole rabbit, gobbled up the bread, all the bread, licked my plate, devoured the tart. I still carried within me the fear that someone might steal my food if I ate it too slowly. My stomach felt full, as it had not done for months and months, and it hurt. I had the feeling that I was going to explode and die in that lovely house under my host's benevolent gaze; die from having eaten too much after being nearly dead from hunger.

When I had finished cleaning both plate and platter with my tongue and picking up the scattered crumbs from the table with my fingertips, the old man showed me to my bedroom. There a wooden tub filled with hot soapy water awaited me. My host undressed me, helped me step into the tub, sat me down, and bathed me. The water ran over my skin, which no longer had any colour, my skin which stank of filth and suffering, and the old man washed my body without repugnance and with a father's tenderness.

The next day, I woke up in a high, mahogany bed between fresh, starched, embroidered sheets that smelled of the wind. On every wall of the room there were engraved portraits of men wearing moustaches and jabots; some of them in military attire. They all looked at me without seeing me. The softness of the bed had made my whole body ache. Getting up was difficult. Through the window I could see the well-kept fields that bordered the town; some of them were already sown, and in others which were still being ploughed, teams of oxen pulled harrows that gouged and aerated the soil. The earth in those fields was black and light, quite the opposite of ours, which is red and as sticky as glue. The sun was close to the horizon, its jagged line broken by poplars and birches. But what I took for dawn turned out to be dusk. I had slept all night and all day, sunk in a deep sleep without dreams or interruptions. I felt heavy, but at the same time relieved of a burden whose substance I could not have described with any precision.

Clean clothes had been laid out for me on a chair, along with some walking shoes of supple, strong leather, shoes meant to last for ever. (I still wear them; they are on my feet as I write.) When I had finished dressing, I saw a man in the mirror looking at me, a man I seemed to have known in another life.

My host was sitting outside on the bench at the front of his house, as he had done on the previous day. He was smoking a pipe, sending a pleasant smell of honey and ferns into the evening air. He invited me to sit beside him. I realized then that I had not yet spoken a single word to him. "My name is Brodeck," I said.

He took a deeper pull on his pipe. For an instant, his face disappeared in the fragrant smoke, and then he repeated, very quietly, "Brodeck . . . Brodeck . . . I am very glad you accepted my invitation. I suspect you still have a long journey ahead of you before you reach home."

I did not know what to say to him. I had lost the habit of words and the habit of thoughts.

"Do not be offended." The old man spoke again. "But sometimes it's best not to go back to where you came from. You remember what you left, but you never know what you're going to find there, especially when madness has raged in men for a long time. You are still young . . . Think about that."

He scratched a match on the stone bench and relit his pipe. By that time, the sun had definitively fallen to the other side of the world. All that remained of its light were reddish traces, spreading like scrawls of fire and licking along the borders of the fields. Above our heads, floods of ink drowned the pale sky. A few bright stars were already shining through the blackness, between the streaks of the last swifts and the first bats.

"Someone is waiting for me." It was all I could say.

The old man slowly shook his head. I managed to repeat myself, but I did not say who was waiting for me; I did not say Emélia's name. I had kept it locked up inside me for so long that I was afraid to let it go, afraid it might get lost out in the open.

I stayed in his house for four days, sleeping like a dormouse and eating like a lord. The old man looked upon me kindly as I ate and served me second helpings, though he himself never swallowed a thing. Sometimes he said nothing; sometimes he made conversation. It was a one-sided conversation, with him doing all the talking, but he seemed not unhappy with his monologues. As for me, I took a curious pleasure in letting myself be surrounded by his words. Thanks to them, I felt I was returning to the language, the language behind which there lay, prostrate, weak and still sick, a humanity that needed only to heal.

Having regained some of my strength, I decided to leave one morning very early, while the sun was rising and the scents of young grass and dew rose with it and invited themselves into the house. My hair, which was growing back in patches, gave me the look of a convalescent who had survived a disease that no physician could have identified with any precision. I still had a lemony complexion, and my eyes were sunk very deep in their sockets.

The previous evening I had told the old man that I was thinking of continuing on my way, so he was waiting for me on the threshold. He handed me a grey canvas sack with leather shoulder straps. In it were two large round loaves, a hunk of bacon, a sausage and some clothes. "Take them," he said. "They are just your size. They belonged to my son, but he won't be coming back. It is no doubt better that way."

The sack I had just grasped hold of suddenly seemed very heavy. The old man extended his hand to me. "Go well, Brodeck."

For the first time his voice shook. So did his hand as I clasped it: a dry, cold, spotted hand that crumpled in my palm. "Please," he said, "forgive him . . . forgive them . . ." And his voice died, a dwindling murmur.

12

It has been at least five days since I left off writing this account. And then, a short while ago, when I took out the sheaf of pages I keep in a corner of the shed, I saw that some of them already had a little dirt and a yellow, pollen-like dust on them. I am going to have to find a more gentle hiding place.

The others suspect nothing. They are convinced that I am busy putting together the Report they asked me to write; they think I am entirely absorbed in my task. The fact that Göbbler found me in my shed very late the other evening has worked in my favour. When I bumped into Orschwir in the street the following morning, he put his hand on my shoulder and said, "It seems you are working hard, Brodeck. Keep it up." Then he went on his way. It was very early. And I paused to reflect: despite the early hour, Orschwir had already been informed that at midnight I had been in my shed, tapping on the typewriter keys. My reflections were interrupted by his voice, which once again reached my ears through the freezing dawn mist: "By the way, Brodeck, where are you going with that sack in this weather?" I stopped. Orschwir watched me steadily as he pulled his fur cap lower on his head with both hands. As he pounded his hands together to warm himself, huge streams of vapour surged out of his mouth and rose in the air.

"Am I from now on obliged to answer any question anybody asks of me?"

Orschwir managed a small smile, but his smiles greatly resemble grimaces. Then he shook his head slowly, very slowly, as he had done when I went to see him the day after the *Ereigniës*. "That is hurtful, Brodeck. It was a friendly question. Why do you feel you must be on your guard?"

My breath failed me, but I was able to shrug my shoulders in as natural a way as possible. Then I said, "I'm going to see if I can make sense of those foxes. I have to write up a short report on them too."

While Orschwir thought about what I had said, he cast several glances at my sack, as if attempting to see what was inside it.

"The foxes? Ah, of course . . . the foxes. Well, have a good day, Brodeck. Better not go too far from the village, though. And . . . keep me informed," he said. Then he turned and continued on his way.

Two weeks or so previously, several hunters and foresters had told me about the foxes. As they were beating the woods to flush out game on one of the first hunts of the season, or cutting wood in the forest, or simply coming and going, many of them had found dead foxes: young and old, males and females. At first each of them had thought they had died of rabies, which surfaces regularly in our mountains, does a little killing, and disappears. But none of the carcasses that were found showed any of the characteristic signs of the disease: tongue covered with white froth; pronounced thinness; eyes rolled back; coat dull and matted. On the contrary, the dead foxes were superb specimens and seemed to have been well nourished and in the best of health. At my request, Brochiert the butcher opened up three of them. Their bellies were filled with edible berries, beechnuts, mice, birds and green worms. The foxes' unmarked, uninjured bodies gave no indication of a struggle, so it appeared that they had not died violent deaths. And the men who found the dead animals had been surprised at their positions: they were all lying on their side or on their back, with their forepaws extended as if they were about to take hold of something. Their eyes were closed, and they appeared to be sleeping peacefully.

When I first heard about this I paid a visit to Ernst-Peter Limmat, who had been the principal of the village school for two generations of pupils, including myself. He is now over eighty and hardly ever leaves his house, but time has not succeeded in denting or damaging his brain. He spends most of his time sitting in a high-backed chair in front of his hearth, where a fragrant fire redolent of fir and hornbeam is always burning. He watches the flames, rereads the books in his library, smokes tobacco and roasts chestnuts, which he then peels with his long, elegant fingers. When I visited him, he gave me a big handful of chestnuts, and after blowing on them we ate them in small pieces, savouring their hot, oily flesh while my drenched jacket dried by the fire.

Besides having taught hundreds of children to read and write, Ernst-Peter Limmat was without a doubt the greatest hunter and woodsman in our region. With his eyes shut he could draw an accurate and detailed map of every forest, every rock formation, every mountain crest and every stream for many kilometres around.

In years gone by, when school was finished for the day, he would go for walks, greatly preferring the company of the tall firs, the birds and the springs to the company of men. If school happened to be closed during the hunting season, he would sometimes disappear for days on end. We would watch him return, his eyes gleaming with pleasure and his game bag filled with grouse, pheasant, and fieldfare. Occasionally he had a chamois slung across his shoulders, a beast he had tracked all the way to the sheer rocks of the Hörni, where in the past more than one hunter had broken his bones.

The strangest thing about Limmat was that he never ate what he killed; instead he distributed his game among the most needy in the

69

village. When I was a young boy, it was thanks to him that Fédorine and I had meat to eat now and then. As for Limmat himself, he ate nothing but vegetables, clear broths, eggs, trout and mushrooms; among these last, his preference was for "trumpets-of-death". He told me one day that this was the monarch of mushrooms, and that its sinister appearance served merely to discourage the ignorant. Trumpets-of-death adorned the inside of his house, hanging everywhere in long garlands, and as they dried they filled the place with the smell of licorice and manure. He had never married. A maid named Mergrite lived with him, a woman very nearly his own age; in the old days, wicked tongues used to say that she surely did more for him than wash his clothes and polish his furniture.

I told him about the foxes, about the discovery of numerous carcasses, about their peaceful appearance. He searched his memory in vain, unable to recall any precedents, but he promised to dive into his books and report back to me should he find any reference to similar cases in other regions, or in the past. Then our conversation turned to the winter, which was approaching with rapid strides, and to the snow, which was encroaching on the village from higher ground, slowly but surely descending the slopes of the mountains and the sides of the valley, and would soon be arriving on our doorsteps.

Like all the other old men, Limmat had been absent from Schloss' inn on the night of the *Ereigniës*, and I wondered if he had been informed of what had happened. I was not even sure whether he had known or been told about the *Anderer*'s presence in our village. I would certainly have liked to talk to him about the affair, to get it off my chest.

"I am delighted to see you have not forgotten your old teacher, Brodeck," he said. "Indeed, I am touched. Do you remember when you first came to school? I remember your arrival very well. You looked like

70

a skinny dog, with eyes too big for the rest of you. And you spoke a gibberish only you and Fédorine could understand. But you learned fast, Brodeck, very fast. Our language; and all the rest."

Mergrite came in with two glasses of hot wine. It smelled of pepper, orange, cloves and aniseed. She added two logs to the fire, sending showers of bright sparks into the darkness, and then disappeared.

"You weren't like the others, Brodeck," my old schoolteacher went on. "And I do not say that because you weren't from here, because you came from far away. You weren't like the others because you always looked beyond things . . . You always wanted to see what did not exist."

He fell silent, slowly ate a chestnut, drank a mouthful of wine, and threw the pieces of shell into the fire. "I've been thinking about your foxes. The fox is an odd animal, you know. We say foxes are sly, but in fact they are a lot more than that. Man has always hated foxes, doubtless because they are a little too much like we are. Foxes hunt for food, but they are also capable of killing just for the fun of it."

Limmat paused a while and then began to speak again in a pensive voice: "So many people have died these last years, in the war. You know that better than anyone in the village, alas. Maybe the foxes are only imitating us, who knows?"

I did not dare tell my old teacher that I could not put that sort of thing in my report. The officials in the Administration who read what I write – if what I write is read at all any more – would understand nothing, and perhaps they would think I had gone mad and decide to dispense with my services altogether, in which case the paltry sums I receive so irregularly, the money my family lives on, would stop coming altogether.

I stayed a little longer in his company. We spoke no more about foxes but about a beech tree which some woodcutters had recently felled, because it was sick, on the far side of the Bösenthal. According to them the tree was more than four hundred years old. Limmat reminded me that in other climates, on distant continents, there were trees that could live for more than two thousand years. He had already taught me that when I was a child, and at the time I thought that God, if he existed, must be quite a strange character, to allow trees to live peacefully for centuries but to make man's life so brief and so hard.

After he had presented me with two garlands of trumpets-of-death and walked me to the door, Ernst-Peter Limmat asked for news of Fédorine, and then, more gently, more gravely, he inquired about Emélia and Poupchette.

The rain had not stopped, but was mingled now with heavy flakes of wet snow. A small stream flowed down the middle of the street, making the sandstone cobbles gleam. The cold air smelled good, a combination of smoke and moss and undergrowth. I thrust the dried mushrooms into my jacket and went home.

I asked Mère Pitz the same question about the foxes. Her memory is not as good as the old teacher's, and she is surely no expert on the subject of game animals and pests, but back in the days when she used to drive her livestock to and from the mountain pastures, she covered all the local roads, paths and stubble-fields so thoroughly that I hoped she might be able to provide some sort of explanation. By tallying all the figures reported by my various sources, I had arrived at a total of eighty foxes found dead – a considerable quantity, if you think about it. Unfortunately, the old woman had no memory of ever having heard of such a phenomenon, and in the end I realized that she could not possibly care less about it. "I'd be glad if they all croaked!" she declared. "Last year they carried off my three hens and all their chicks. And they didn't even eat them! They just ripped them to shreds and disappeared. Your foxes are *Scheizznegetz'zohns*, 'sons of the damned'. They're not even worth the blade of the knife that slits their throats."

In order to speak to me, she had interrupted a conversation with Frida Niegel, a magpie-eyed hunchback who smells like a stable. She and Mère Pitz love to consider all the widows and widowers in the village and the surrounding hamlets and imagine possible remarriages. They write the names on small pieces of cardboard and for hours, as if they were playing cards, they arrange and rearrange the deck into pairs with mounting excitement, conjuring up wedding celebrations and darning the fates of their cast, all the while drinking little glasses of mulberry liqueur. I could see that I was disturbing their concentration.

In the end I concluded that the only person who might be able to shed light on the matter was Marcus Stern, who lives alone in the middle of the forest an hour's walk from the village. He was the one I was off to see on the morning I ran into Orschwir.

13

The path that leads to Stern's cabin begins its steep climb almost as soon as you leave the village. You enter the woods, go around a few hairpin bends, and in no time at all you are looking down at the roofs. Halfway along the path, a rock shaped like a table invites the walker to take a break. The rock is called the *Lingen*, the dialect name of the tiny woodland sprites that are said to gather there and dance on it by moonlight, singing songs which sound like muffled laughter. Here and there on the broad rock, small cushions of milky-green moss soften its hard surface, and the heather surrounds it with posies of flowers. It is a fine place for lovers and dreamers. I remember seeing the *Anderer* there one day in high summer – on 8 July, in fact (I make a note of everything) – at around three o'clock in the afternoon, in the very hottest part of the day, that is, when the sun appeared to have paused in its course across the sky and was pouring down its heat on the world like molten lead. I had gone there to pick wild raspberries for my little Poupchette, who is crazy about them. I wanted to surprise her when she awoke from her afternoon nap.

The forest was alive and humming with busy bees and darting wasps, with frenzied flies and horseflies buzzing around in every direction, as if seized by a sudden madness. It was a great symphony which seemed to come from the ground and the air. In the village I had not encountered a living soul.

Although brief, the climb had weakened my legs and winded me. My shirt was already soaked through, sticky and clinging to my skin. I stopped on the path to catch my breath, and that was when I noticed him: a few metres away from where I stood was the *Anderer*, with his back turned to me, contemplating the roofs of the village from his position on the rock. He was sitting on his strange, portable seat which had been an object of fascination for everyone the first time we saw him deploy it. It was a folding stool, substantial and sturdy enough to support his ample buttocks, but when collapsed and folded away it looked like a simple cane.

In that landscape, all greenery and bright yellow, his dark clothing, his endlessly long, black-cloth frock coat impeccably ironed cut a figure that hardly belonged. Drawing a little closer to him, I noticed that he was also wearing his ruffled shirt and woollen waistcoat, and gaiters on his heavy, highly-polished shoes which reflected light like the shards of a mirror.

Some twigs snapped beneath my feet, and he turned in my direction and caught sight of me. I looked, I have no doubt, like a thief, but he did not appear startled. He smiled, raising his right hand and doffing an imaginary hat in a gesture of greeting. He had very pink cheeks, and the rest of his countenance – forehead, chin, nose – was covered with white lead paste. With the black curls on either side of his balding skull providing the final touch, he looked like an old actor. Great drops of perspiration ran down his face, and he mopped it with a handkerchief whose embroidered monogram I could not read.

"May I assume that you have also come here to take the measure of the world?" he asked me in his mellifluous, mannered voice, gesturing at the countryside spread out before us. Then I noticed a notebook lying open across his perfectly round knees and saw that he was holding a graphite pencil in one hand. There were straight lines and curving lines and shadowed areas sketched on the page. When he realized what I was looking at, he closed the book and put it in his pocket.

It was the first time I had been alone with him since his arrival in the village, and the first time he had ever spoken to me. "Would you be so kind as to render me a service?" he asked, and since I made no reply and my face no doubt hardened a little, he went on, flashing the enigmatic smile that was never far from his lips. "Nothing to worry about. I simply hoped you might tell me the names of all these heights that enclose the valley. I fear that my maps may be inaccurate."

And accompanying his words with a sweep of his hand, he indicated the mountains outlined in the distance, shimmering in the torpor of that summer's day. Parts of them almost blended with the sky, which seemed intent on dissolving them. I stepped towards him, knelt down to be on his level and, starting from the east, I began to give their names: "This one, the one closest to us, is the Hunterpitz, so called because its profile looks like a dog's head. Next you have the three Schnikelkopfs, then the Bronderpitz, and after that the ridge of the Hörni mountains, with Hörni peak as their highest point. Then there is the Doura pass, the crest of the Florias, and finally, the furthest west, the peak of the Mausein, which is shaped like a man bent over and carrying a load on his back."

I stopped speaking. He finished writing the names in his notebook which he had taken out of his pocket, and then very quickly put it away again. "I am infinitely grateful to you," he said, warmly shaking my hand. A glint of satisfaction brightened his large green eyes, as if I had just presented him with a treasure. As I was about to leave he added, "I understand that you're interested in flowers and herbs. We are alike. I am an amateur of landscapes, forms, portraits. Quite an innocent vice, aside from its other charms. I have brought with me some rather rare books that I believe you would find interesting. I should be delighted to show them to you, if one day you would honour me with a visit."

I nodded but made no other response. I had never heard him talk so much. I walked away and left him on the rock.

"And you gave him all their names!?" Wilhem Vurtenhau raised his arms to heaven and glared at me. He had come into Gustav Röppel's ironmonger's, just as I was relating my encounter with the *Anderer*, some hours after it had taken place. Gustav was an old friend of mine. We were benchmates in school, sitting side by side, and when we were working out problems I would often let him copy the answers from my exercise book. In exchange for this service, he would give me nails, screws or a bit of twine, things he had managed to pilfer from the shop, which at the time was owned and managed by his father. I have just written that Gustav *was* a friend, because now I am no longer sure that is true. He was with the others at the *Ereigniës*. He did what cannot be undone! And he has not spoken a single word to me since, even though we have seen each other every Sunday after Mass outside the church, to where Father Peiper, red-faced and wobbly on his feet, steers his flock before bestowing upon them the incomplete gestures that constitute his last blessing. I do not dare to go into Gustav's shop either. I am too afraid that there is nothing left between us but a great void.

As I believe I have already mentioned, Vurtenhau is very rich and very stupid. He beat his fist on Röppel's counter, causing a box of tacks to tumble down from its shelf. "Do you realize what you have done, Brodeck?" he asked. "You have given him the names of all our mountains, and you say he wrote them down?"

Vurtenhau was beside himself. All the blood in his body seemed to have been pumped into his huge ears. In vain, I pointed out that the names of mountains are no secret, that everybody knows them or can find them in maps or books, but my observations failed to calm him. "You're not even considering what he might be up to, coming here out of the blue, nosing around everywhere the way he does, asking all his innocent questions, with his fish face and his smooth manners!"

I tried to soothe Vurtenhau by repeating some of what the *Anderer* had said to me on the subject of forms and landscapes, but that only made him more angry. He stormed out of the shop, flinging over his shoulder one last remark which at the time seemed unimportant: "Remember this, Brodeck, if anything happens, it will be your fault!" It is only now that I realize the extent of the menace contained by his words. After he had slammed the door, Gustav and I looked at each other, shrugged at the same time and then burst into loud laughter, the way we used to do in the old days when we were children.

77

14

It took me nearly two hours to get to Stern's cabin, whereas normally one good hour is enough. But no-one had cleared the track, and as soon as I passed the upper limit of the broadleaf trees and entered the forest of tall firs, the new snow became so thick that I sank into it up to my knees. The forest was silent. I saw no animal and no bird. All I heard was the murmur of the Staubi about two hundred metres below me, at the point where it rushes into a fairly sharp bend and crashes against some enormous rocks.

As I passed by the *Lingen*, I averted my eyes and did not stop. I even increased my pace, and the frigid air penetrated my lungs so deeply that they hurt. I was too afraid of seeing the *Anderer*'s ghost in the same position as before, sitting on his little stool, surveying the landscape, or maybe stretching out his arms to me in supplication. But in supplication for what?

Even had I been at the inn when the others all went mad that night, what could I have done on my own? The least word, the least gesture from me would have meant my life, and I would have suffered the same fate as his. That thought, too, filled me with terror: the knowledge that if I had been at the inn, I would not have done anything to prevent what happened, I would have made myself as small as possible and I would have looked on impotently as the horrific scene unfolded. That act of cowardice, even though it had never actually taken place, filled me with disgust. Fundamentally I was like the others, like all those around me who had charged me with writing the Report, which they hoped would exonerate them.

Stern lives outside the world – I mean, outside our world. All the Sterns have lived the way he does, for as long as anyone can remember: living in the midst of the forest and maintaining only distant relations with the village. But he is the last of the Sterns. He is alone. He has never taken a wife and he has no children. His line will die out with him.

He lives by tanning animal skins. He comes down to the village twice every winter, and a little more often in fine weather. He sells his hides as well as various objects that he carves from the trunks and branches of fir trees. With the money he buys some flour, a sack of potatoes, some dried peas, tobacco, sugar and salt. And if he has any money left over, he drinks it in *eau-de-vie* and makes the climb back to his cabin completely drunk. He never gets lost. His feet know the way.

When I reached the cabin I found him sitting on the threshold, busy binding some dead branches together to make a broom. I greeted him. Always suspicious of visitors, Stern replied with a movement of his head but said nothing. Then he got up and went inside, leaving the door open.

Many things, both animal and vegetable, were hung up to dry from the beams; the acrid, violent odours blended and clung to whoever was in the room. The fire in the hearth produced some mean little flames and a great deal of smoke. Stern dipped a ladle into a kettle and filled two bowls with thick soup, a porridge of groats and chestnuts which had no doubt been simmering since the early morning. Then he cut two thick slices of hard bread and filled two glasses with dark wine. We sat facing each other and ate in silence, surrounded by this stench, with its overtones of carrion, that many would have fled from. But I was familiar with stenches. That one did not bother me. I had known worse.

79

In the camp, after my stint in the *Büxte* and before I became Brodeck-the-Dog, for a few long months I was *De Scheizeman*, the "Shit Man". My task consisted of emptying out the latrines into which more than a thousand prisoners relieved their bowels several times a day. The latrines were large trenches a metre deep, two metres wide and about four metres long. There were five of them, and my job was to muck them out thoroughly. To accomplish this task, I had only a few tools at my disposal: a big pan attached to a wooden handle and two large tin buckets. I used the pan to fill the buckets, and then, under escort, I went back and forth to the river, into which I emptied their contents.

The pan, fastened to the handle only by a few lengths of old string, often came loose and fell into the latrine. When that happened I had to jump down, plunge my hands into the mass of ordure, and feel around for the pan. The first few times I did this, I remember puking up my guts and the little they contained. Then I got used to it. You can get used to anything. There are worse things than the smell of shit. A great many things have no smell at all, and yet they rot senses, hearts and souls more surely than all the excrement in the world.

The two guards who escorted me back and forth held handkerchiefs soaked in *eau-de-vie* over their noses. They kept a few metres away from me and talked about women, sprinkling their tales with obscene particulars that made them laugh and inflamed their faces. I stepped into the river. I emptied the buckets. And I was always surprised at the frenzy of the hundreds of little fish that arrived in a brownish whirl and wallowed in the filth, flicking their thin silvery bodies in every direction, as though crazed by their stinking food. But the current quickly diluted it, vile though it was, and soon clear water and the movements of algae were all that could be seen, as well as the reflected sunlight which struck the surface of the river and shattered it into a thousand mirrors.

80

Sometimes the guards, in their drunken euphoria, allowed me to wash myself in the river. I would pick up a round, smooth stone and use it like a bar of soap, rubbing my skin with it to remove the shit and the dirt. Occasionally I would succeed in catching some of the little fish that were still lingering about my legs, perhaps hoping for another portion. I would quickly press their bellies with two fingers to squeeze out their guts and pop them into my mouth before the guards had time to see me. We were forbidden under pain of death to eat anything other than the two litres of fetid broth we were served in the evening and the chunk of hard, sour bread we got every morning. I chewed those fish for a good long time, as though they were savoury delicacies.

Throughout that period, the smell of shit never left me. It was my only true clothing. The result was that during the night I had more room to sleep; no-one in the hut wanted to be near me. Man is made thus: he prefers to think of himself as a pure spirit, a creator of ideas and ideals, of dreams and marvels. He does not like to be reminded that he is also a material being, and that what flows out from between his buttocks is as much a part of him as what stirs and germinates in his brain.

Stern wiped his bowl clean with a piece of bread and then, with a brief whistle, summoned a slender creature out of nowhere: a ferret he had tamed which kept him company. The small animal went to him and ate from his hand. Every now and then, while it was gobbling away, it cast a curious glance in my direction; its round, gleaming little eyes looked like black pearls or ripe mulberries. I had just told Stern everything I knew about the foxes and about my visits to Limmat and Mère Pitz.

He got slowly to his feet, disappeared into the darkness on the far side of the room, and returned with several handsome fox skins bound together with a piece of hemp cord which he spread out on the big table. "You can add these to your tally," he said. "Thirteen of them. And I didn't have to kill them. I found them dead, and all in the position you describe."

Stern took a pipe and filled it with a mixture of tobacco and chestnut leaves as I stroked the fox furs, which were glossy and thick. Then I asked him what all this could possibly mean. He shrugged, pulled on his pipe which crackled merrily, and exhaled great clouds of smoke that made me cough. "I don't know anything, Brodeck," he said. "I know nothing about it. Foxes – I don't understand foxes."

He stopped talking and petted his ferret, which began to wrap itself around his arm, whimpering. Then he spoke again: "I don't know anything about foxes. But I remember my grandfather Stern talking about wolves. There were still wolves around here in his time. Nowadays, whenever I see one, if it's not a wolf ghost, it's a stray come from far away. Once old Stern told me the story of a pack, a fine pack according to him, of more than twenty animals. He liked to spy on them and stalk them a little, just to get on their nerves. And then one day they're all gone. He stops hearing them and stops seeing them. He tells himself they got tired of his little game and went off to the other side of the mountain. The winter passes. A heavy winter, lots of snow. Then spring comes. He tramps through all the forests, as though he's inspecting them, and what does he find at the foot of the big Maulenthal rocks? The remains of the entire pack in an advanced stage of decay. They were all there, every one of them, old and young, males and females, all with their backs or their skulls broken. Now, as a rule, wolves don't fall off rocks. Occasionally, one might take an accidental step into thin air, or slip, or the edge of the cliff may crumble beneath its feet, but it'll only be one. Not a whole pack."

Stern fell silent and looked me right in the eye. I said, "You mean to tell me they all fell to their deaths of their own accord?"

"I'm telling you what old Stern told me, that's all."

"But what has that got to do with the foxes?"

"Wolves, foxes, they're more or less cousins. Family. Maybe man isn't the only animal that thinks too much."

Stern's pipe had gone out. He relit it, grabbed the little ferret which was now trying to get inside his jacket, and refilled our wine glasses.

A great silence came over us. I do not know what Stern was thinking about, but I was busy trying to make what he had just told me concur with what old Limmat had said. I got nowhere. Nothing was clear; and there was nothing I could incorporate into a report that an official in S. would have accepted without scowling at it and chucking it into the stove.

The fire was dying. Stern fed it a few bundles of dried juniper twigs. We spoke for perhaps an hour longer, about the seasons and the winter, about game and woodcutting, but concerning foxes nothing more was said. Then, seeing that the light was beginning to fade from the sky and I wanted to get home before night, I bade Stern farewell. He accompanied me outside. The wind had risen and was agitating the tops of the tall firs. This caused their branches to shed some large clumps of snow, but the gusting wind broke them up into a fine powder which covered our shoulders like frozen white ash. We shook hands, and then Stern asked me, "How about *De Gewisshor*? Is he still in the village?"

I was on the point of asking Stern what he was talking about when I remembered that some had referred to the *Anderer* in that way – *De Gewisshor*, the "Learned Man", the "Scholar" – probably because that was the impression he gave. I did not answer straight away, and suddenly I felt cold. And I thought that if Stern was asking me that question, then he could not have known anything; on the infamous night of the *Ereigniës* he had not been at the inn. So there were at least two of us with no blood on our hands. I did not know what to say to him.

"He went away . . ."

"Then wait," Stern said and went back into his cabin. When he re-emerged a few seconds later he was carrying a package, which he handed to me. "He ordered this from me. It's already paid for. If he doesn't come back, you can keep it."

The package contained an unusual-looking soft hat, a pair of gloves and a pair of slippers, all in handsome marten fur, beautifully dressed and sewn. I hesitated, but in the end I stuck the package under my arm. That was when Stern looked me in the eye and said, "You know, Brodeck, I don't think there are any foxes any more. They're all dead. They're never going to come back."

And as I did not reply, not knowing what to say, he shook my hand without another word, and after a few moments' hesitation, I set off down the track.

15

As I have already related, at the moment when the *Anderer* first arrived in the village and passed through the gate with his animals, night was approaching, creeping down like a cat that has just spotted a mouse and knows she will soon have it in her jaws.

It is a strange time of day. The streets are deserted, the encroaching darkness turns them into cold, grey blurs, and the houses become shifty silhouettes, full of menace and innuendo. Night has the curious power of changing the most everyday things, the simplest faces. And sometimes it does not so much change them as reveal them, as if bringing out the true natures of landscapes and people by shrouding them in black. The reader may shrug off everything I am saying here. He may think I am describing childish fears, or embellishing a novel. But before judging and condemning, one must imagine the scene: that man, come from nowhere – for he really did arrive out of the blue, as Vurtenhau said (now and again Vurtenhau enunciates a few truths amid a great mass of idiocy) – as I was saying, one has to imagine that fellow, dressed like a character from another century, with his unusual beasts and his imposing baggage, entering our village which no stranger had entered for years, and moreover arriving here just like that, without any ado, with the greatest of ease. Who would not have been a little afraid?

"I wasn't afraid of him."

This is the Dörfer boy, the eldest, answering my questions. He was the first person in the village to see the *Anderer* when he arrived.

Our conversation takes place in Pipersheim's café. The boy's father insisted that we should talk at the café rather than in the family home. He must have decided he would have a better chance of downing a few shots in peace here. Gustav Dörfer is a small, drab creature, always bundled in dirty clothes that give off a whiff of boiled turnips. He hires himself to the local farms, and when he has a few pennies, he drinks them up. His wife weighs twice as much as he does, but their relative sizes do not keep him from beating her like a dusty rug when he is drunk, after he has wrecked their home and broken a few of the remaining dishes. He has given her five children, all of them puny and glum. The eldest is named Hans.

"And what did he say to you?" I ask Hans. The boy looks at his father, as though requesting permission to speak, but Dörfer could not care less. He has eyes only for his glass, which is already empty, and he contemplates it, clutching it with both hands and gazing at it with a look of painful melancholy. Pipersheim is watching us from behind the bar, and I signal to him to refill Dörfer's glass. Our host puts a hand to his mouth and removes the toothpick he sucks constantly, the cause of his punctured, bleeding gums and upsetting breath. Then he grabs a bottle, comes to our table and pours Dörfer another drink. Dörfer's face brightens a little.

"He asked me the way to Schloss' inn."

"Did he know the name, or were you the one who said it?"

"He knew it."

"So what did you say to him?"

"I gave him directions."

"And what did he do?"

"He wrote down what I said in his little notebook."

"And then?"

"And then he gave me four beautiful marbles. Real beauties. He took them out of a bag and said, 'For your trouble.'"

"'For your trouble'?"

"Yes. I didn't understand at first. People around here don't say that."

"What about the marbles? Do you still have them?"

"Peter Lülli won them off me. He's really good. He's got a whole bagful."

Gustav Dörfer was not listening to us. His eyes were riveted to his glass and its liquid contents, which were disappearing too fast. The boy drew his shoulders up around his ears. His forehead bore bruises and scabs and bumps and small scars, some fading, some brand-new, and his eyes, when you managed to catch and hold them for a few moments, spoke of blows and suffering, of the wounds that constituted his harsh, unalterable, daily lot.

I recalled that notebook which I had often seen in the *Anderer*'s hands. He wrote everything down in it, including, for example, the directions to an inn located only about sixty metres from where he was standing. The longer his sojourn among us, the larger his little notebook began to loom in people's minds, and while his producing it on every possible occasion had at first seemed like no more than an odd compulsion, a comical tic good for smiling at or gossiping about, it quickly became the object of bitter recriminations.

I particularly remember a conversation I overheard on 3 August, a market day. It was coming to an end, and the ground was littered with spoiled vegetables, dirty straw, pieces of string, crate fragments and other objects which seemed to have been left in the market square by the receding waters of an invisible tide.

Poupchette loves the market, and so I take her there with me almost every week. The little animals in their pens – kids, bunnies, chicks, ducklings – make her clap her hands and laugh. And then there are the smells, of fritters and frying and hot wine and roasting chestnuts and grilled meat, and also the sounds, voices of every pitch and timbre mingling together as though in a giant basin: the cries, the calls, the chatter of the vendors hawking their wares, the prayers of those selling holy icons, the feigned anger essential to successful bargaining. But what Poupchette looks forward to most of all is when Viktor Heidekirch arrives with his accordion and begins to play, filling the air with notes that sound sometimes like laments and sometimes like cries of joy. People make way for him and form a circle around him, and suddenly the buzz of the market seems to die out, as if everyone were listening to the music, as if it had become, for the moment, more important than everything else.

Viktor turns up at every party and every wedding. He is the only person in the village who knows music, and just about the only one in possession of a working musical instrument. I believe there is a piano in the back room of Schloss' inn, the one in which *De Erweckens'-Bruderschaf* meets, and there may be some brass instruments in there as well. Diodème affirmed that there were, having seen them, so he said, one day when the door was not completely closed, and when I teased him about being so well informed, declaring that he must know the room very well and suggesting that maybe he was, in fact, a member of the brotherhood, his face darkened and he told me to shut up. Viktor's accordion and his voice are also a part of our local collective memory. That day, he made the women weep and the men's eyes go red with his rendition of "Johanni's Complaint", a song about love and death whose origins are lost in the mists of time. It tells the story of a young girl who loves but is not loved in return, and who, faced with the prospect of seeing the ruler of her heart in another woman's arms, prefers to step into the Staubi at twilight on a winter's day and lie down for ever in the cold, fast-moving water.

> *When de abend gekomm Johanni schlafft en de wasser*
> *Als besser sein en de todt dass alein immer verden*
> *De hertz is a schotke freige who nieman geker*
> *Und ubche madchen kann genug de kusse kaltenen*

Sometimes Emélia comes with us. I take her arm. I lead her. She lets herself be guided and her eyes gaze at things only she can see. On the day of the conversation I now want to record, she was sitting on my left, humming her song and moving her head back and forth in a gentle rhythm. Poupchette, on my right, was chewing on a sausage I had just bought for her. We leaned against the largest of the columns that support the entrance to the covered part of the market. A few metres away from us old Roswilda Klugenghal, who is half madwoman and half vagrant, was digging around in some garbage looking for vegetables and offal. She found a twisted carrot, held it up for inspection, and talked to it as if it were an old acquaintance. At that moment I heard voices coming from the other side of the column, voices that I recognized at once.

They belonged to four men: Emil Dorcha, a forester; Ludwig Pfimling, a stable-boy; Bern Vogel, a tinsmith; and Caspar Hausorn, a clerk at the Mairie. Four men who were already quite excited as they had been drinking since dawn, and the market's festive atmosphere had served only to whip up their spirits. They spoke loudly, sometimes stumbling over words, but the tone of their conversation was very clear and I quickly realized who its subject was.

"Did you see him? Like a weasel, he is, always sniffing around at everything," Dorcha said.

"That fellow's nothing but *rein schlecht*, 'pure bad'," Vogel added. "Mark my words – bad and depraved."

"He's never hurt anybody," Pfimling pointed out. "He goes for walks, he looks about him, he smiles all the time."

"'Outside smiles hide inside wiles' – you forget the proverb. Besides, you're so stupid and near-sighted, you wouldn't see anything wrong even with the Devil himself!"

The speaker was Hausorn, and he had spat out his words as though they were small pebbles. He continued in a milder tone: "He must have come here for some purpose. Some purpose that isn't very clear and doesn't bode well for us."

"What do you think it is?" Vogel asked him.

"I don't know yet. I'm racking my brains. I don't know what it is, but a chap like him is bound to have something up his sleeve."

"He writes everything in his notebook," Dorcha said. "Did you not all see him a little while ago, sitting in front of Wuzten's lambs?"

"Of course we saw him. He stayed there for minutes on end, writing things down and looking at the lambs the whole time."

"He wasn't writing," Pfimling said. "He was drawing. I saw him, and I know you say I don't see anything, but I saw him drawing. And he was so absorbed in what he was doing that you could have eaten off the top of his head and he wouldn't have noticed. I walked up behind him and looked over his shoulder."

"Drawing lambs?" Dorcha asked, his eyes on Hausorn. "What is that supposed to mean?"

"How should I know? Why should I have all the answers?"

The conversation came to a halt. I imagined it was over for good, not to be resumed, but I was mistaken. After a while a new voice began to speak, a very low, very serious voice I could not identify. "There aren't many lambs around here, not among us, I mean . . . Maybe all those things he draws are symbols, like in the church Bible, and it is a way for him to say who is who and who has done what and how recently, so he can report it when he goes back to where he came from . . ."

I felt a shiver run down my back and scour my spine. I did not like the voice or what it had said, even if the exact meaning of his words remained obscure.

"But then, if he is using his notebook for what you suggest, it must not ever leave the village!"

This last remark was Dorcha's; his was a voice I recognized.

"Maybe you're right," the other voice said. I still could not make out whose it was. "Maybe that notebook should never go anywhere. Or maybe the person it belongs to is the one who cannot leave, not ever . . ."

After that, nothing. I waited. I did not dare move. Then, after a few moments, I leaned to one side and sneaked a look around the column. No-one. All four had left without my hearing. They had disappeared into thin air like the veils of fog snatched off our mountain crests by the southern breeze on April mornings. I even wondered whether I had dreamed the things I had heard. Poupchette pulled on my sleeve. "Home, Papa? Home?"

Her little lips were shiny with sausage grease, and her pretty eyes gleamed merrily. I gave her a big kiss on the forehead and put her on my shoulders. Her hands held on to my hair and her feet beat against my chest. "Giddyap, Papa! Giddyap!" I took Emélia's hand and pulled her to her feet. She did not resist. I hugged her against me, I caressed her beautiful face, I planted a kiss on her cheek, and the three of us went home like that, while my head still resounded with the voices of the faceless men and the threats they had made, like seeds that asked for nothing but time to grow.

Gustav Dörfer eventually passed out on the table in the café, less from drink than from weariness, no doubt: weariness of body, or weariness of life. His boy and I had long since stopped talking about the *Anderer* and had changed the subject. It turned out, to my surprise, that he had a passion for birds, and he questioned me about all the species I described in my reports to the Administration. And so we talked about thrushes and their close relatives, fieldfares, and about other birds as well: grey partridges, known as March greys, which as that name indicates return to us around the beginning of spring; crossbills, which abound in the pine forests; wrens, titmice, blackbirds, ptarmigans, capercaillies and mountain pheasants, blue soldiers, whose unusual name stems from the colour of their breast feathers and their propensity for fighting; crows and ravens, bullfinches, eagles and owls.

Inside that head of his, which was covered with lumps, the child – he was about twelve – had a brain filled with know- ledge, and his face lit up when he talked about birds. By contrast, his pupils became dull and lifeless when he turned towards his father and remembered his presence. Our conversation had made the boy forget it for a while. Hans paused and contemplated his father, who was snoring open-mouthed with one side of his face flattened against the old wood of the tabletop, his cap askew, and white saliva dribbling from between his lips.

"When I see a dead bird," Hans Dörfer said to me, "and I pick it up in my hand, tears come to my eyes. I cannot stop them. Nothing can justify the death of a bird. But if my father copped it all of a sudden, right here, right next to me, I swear I'd dance around the table and buy you a drink. I swear it!"

16

I am in our kitchen. I have just put the marten fur cap on my head. I am also wearing the slippers, and I have slipped on the gloves.

An odd sensation of warmth comes over me, bringing with it a comfortable drowsiness, like the state you enter when you drink a glass or two of hot wine after a long walk on a late autumn afternoon. I feel good and, of course, I am thinking about the *Anderer*. I am not saying that wearing clothes destined for him, items that he himself ordered (how did he manage to meet Stern, who as I have said comes to the village so rarely? And how did he know that Stern could sew animal skins?), has made me capable of seeing into his thoughts and penetrating the small world of his mind. But having said that, I still feel that I am getting closer to him in some way, that somehow I am back in his presence, and that maybe he will give me a sign or a look which will help me learn a little more.

I must confess to being totally at a loss. I have been charged with a mission that far exceeds my capabilities and my intelligence. I am not a lawyer. I am not a police officer. I am not a storyteller. The present account, should anyone ever read it, will prove that I am not: I keep going back and forth, leaping over time like a hurdle, getting lost on digressions and maybe even, without wishing to, concealing what is essential.

When I read the pages of my account thus far, I see that I move around with my words like tracked game on the run, sprinting, zigzagging, trying to throw the dogs and hunters in hot pursuit off the scent. This jumble contains everything. I am emptying my life into it. Writing is a relief to both my heart and my stomach.

With the Report I have been ordered to write up by the others, things are different. My tone is neutral and impersonal. I transcribe conversations almost *verbatim*. I pare everything down. A few days ago, Orschwir informed me that I will have to present myself in the village hall next Friday at sunset. "Come and see us on Friday, Brodeck," he said. "You can give us a reading . . ."

He came to my house in person to tell me that. He lowered his great bulk onto the chair that Fédorine had pulled up for him, without thanking her or even greeting her, took off his cap of otter's fur and refused the glass held out to him. "Don't have time, thanks. I've got work to do. We have thirty pigs to slaughter this morning, and if I'm not there, my workers are liable to make a mess of them . . ."

We heard footsteps above our heads. This was Poupchette, who was scurrying around up there like a little mouse. Then there were other footfalls, slower and heavier, and a distant voice, Emélia's, humming her song. Orschwir tipped his head back for a moment, and then he looked at me as if he were about to say something, but he changed his mind. He took out his tobacco pouch and rolled himself a cigarette. A great silence settled over us, hard as stone. Having announced that he was needed at his farm, Orschwir chose to linger for no apparent reason. He took two or three puffs on his cigarette, and an aroma of honey and yesterday's alcohol permeated the air in the kitchen. Orschwir does not smoke any old thing; he smokes a rich man's tobacco, very blond and finely cut, which he orders from far away.

He gave the ceiling another look and then turned his appalling face to me. No more sounds could be heard, neither the footsteps nor Emélia's voice. Fédorine was ignoring us. She had finished grating some potatoes and was rolling them in her hands, shaping them into little pancakes called *Kartfolknudle*; later she would fry them in oil and strew them with poppy seeds before serving them to us.

Orschwir cleared his throat.

"Not too lonely?"

I shook my head.

He seemed to reflect, took a deep drag on his cigarette, and began wheezing and choking. His skin turned as red as the wild cherries that ripen in June, and tears filled his eyes. At length the coughing subsided.

"You need anything?"

"Nothing."

Orschwir rubbed his two cheeks with one large hand, as if he were shaving them. I wondered what he could possibly be trying to say to me.

"Alright then, I'll be off."

He pronounced these words hesitantly. I looked into his eyes, hoping to see what was behind them, but he soon looked away.

I heard myself responding to him, but my words sounded so strange and threatening that they hardly seemed to come from me: "It really is convenient for you to behave as if they didn't exist. As if they are not here, neither one of them. That suits you just fine, doesn't it?"

The result of this sally was that Orschwir fell completely silent. I saw him trying to ponder what I had just said, and I could tell that he was turning my words over and over in his mind, taking them apart and putting them back together, but his efforts apparently came to naught for he leapt suddenly from his chair, took his cap, jammed it down over his head and left the house. The door closing behind him made its little noise, a high meow. And all at once, thanks to that simple little sound, I was on the other side of that door and it was two years ago, the day of my return home.

From the moment I entered the village, everyone I passed stared at me goggle-eyed and opened their mouths wide without producing a single word. Some of them went running home to spread the news of my return, and all of them understood that I should be left alone, that they should not ask me any questions yet, that all I wanted to do was to stand outside the door of my house, put my hand on the knob and push the door open, to hear its little noise, to enter my home once more, to find there the woman I loved, who had never left my thoughts, to take her in my arms, to squeeze her so tight it hurt, and to press my lips against hers at last.

Ah, the vision of those last few metres culminating in that embrace, how often had I gazed upon it in my dreams! That day, when I opened the door, my door, the door to my house, my body was trembling and my heart was pounding as though about to burst through my chest. I could not catch my breath, and I even thought for a moment that I was going to die there, that I was going to step over the threshold and die from too much happiness. But suddenly the face of *Die Zeilenesseniss* appeared to me, and my happiness stiffened and froze. It was a little as though someone had shoved a big handful of snow between my shirt and my naked skin. But why, at that precise moment, did that woman's face come floating up out of limbo to dance before my eyes?

In the last weeks of the war, the camp became an even stranger place than it had been before. Unceasing, contradictory rumours shook it like windy blasts, alternately hot and cold. Some recent arrivals murmured that the conflict was nearing its end and that we, who walked bowed down and looked like corpses, were on the winning side. This news restored to our eyes, the eyes of the living dead we had become, a gleam long since extinguished, but this fragile light could not last. The guards let their confusion show for only a few seconds before quickly and brutally dispelling it: apparently determined to affirm that they were still our masters, they attacked the first one of us they got their hands on, kicking him, beating him with truncheons and rifle butts, and driving him down into the mud as though trying to make all trace and remnant of him disappear. Nevertheless, their nervousness and the worried expressions on their faces led us to conclude that something tremendous really was happening.

The guard who was my master stopped paying much attention to me. Whereas every day for weeks on end he had amused himself by putting a leather collar around my neck, attaching a braided leash to it and parading around the camp, with me proceeding on all fours and him following behind, upright on his two legs and secure in his convictions, now I never saw him any more except at mealtimes. He came furtively to the kennel that served as my bed and poured two ladles of soup into my bowl, but I could tell that this game no longer amused him. His face had become grey, and two deep wrinkles I had never seen before now furrowed his forehead.

I knew that he had been an accountant before the war and that he had a wife, three children – two boys and a girl – and a cat, but no dog. He was an innocuous-looking fellow with a timid manner, shifty eyes, and small, well-groomed hands which he washed methodically several times a day while whistling a military tune. Unlike a great many of the other guards he did not drink, and he never visited the windowless huts where female prisoners (whom we never laid eyes on) were made available to them. He was a pale, reserved, ordinary man who always spoke in an even tone, never raising his voice, but who had twice, before my eyes and without a second's hesitation, bludgeoned prisoners to death for forgetting to raise their caps to him. His name was Joss Scheidegger. I have tried hard to banish that name from my memory, but the memory does not take orders. The best you can hope for is to deaden it a little from time to time.

One morning there was a great deal of commotion in the camp: noises of every sort, shouted orders, questions. The guards scuttled about in all directions, gathering their kits together, loading multifarious objects onto carts. There was a new stink in the air, a sour, pregnant smell that surpassed the stench rising off our poor bodies: fear had changed sides.

In their great agitation, the guards ignored us completely. Before, we had existed for them as slaves, but that morning we no longer existed at all.

I was lying in the kennel, keeping warm among the mastiffs and watching the curious spectacle of our keepers preparing to make a rapid exit. I followed each movement. I heard every call and every order, and none of them concerned us any more. At one point, when most of the guards had already abandoned the camp, I saw Scheidegger heading for a hut near the kennels. It was where the offices of the prison census authority were located. He was only in the hut for a moment and emerged with a leather pouch, which seemed to contain documents. One of the dogs saw him and barked. Scheidegger looked towards the kennel and stopped in his tracks. He appeared to hesitate, darting glances all around, and having determined that no-one was watching he walked quickly to my kennel, knelt on the ground beside me, dug in his pocket, took out the little key that was so familiar to me, and with shaky hands opened the lock on my collar. Then, not knowing what to do with the key, he suddenly threw it to the ground as if it were burning his fingers. "Who is going to pay for all this?"

It was a shabby, undignified question – an accountant's question – and as Scheidegger asked it, he looked me in the eye for the first time, perhaps expecting me to give him an answer. His forehead was covered with sweat and his skin was even greyer than usual. What did it mean, his gesture? Was he hoping for forgiveness? From me? He stared at me for several seconds, imploring, fearful. Then I started to bark. My barking was prolonged, lugubrious, melancholy, instantly echoed and extended by the two mastiffs. Scheidegger, terrified, leapt to his feet and ran away.

In less than an hour there was not a single guard left in the camp. Silence reigned. Nothing could be heard, and no-one could be seen. Then, tentatively, one by one, shadows began to emerge from the huts, not yet daring to take a proper look around and not saying a word. An unsteady, incredulous army, faltering figures with sallow skin and hollow cheeks, began to fill the streets of the camp. Soon the former prisoners had come together in a compact, fragile crowd, still silent, which took the measure of its new circumstances by drifting aimlessly from one place to another, dazzled by the freedom none of them dared to utter.

Something incredible happened as this great tide of suffering flesh and bone turned the corner and moved towards the group of huts that had housed the guards and their commanders. Everything came to a dead halt. Those in front raised their hands without a word, and everyone stopped short as though frozen to the spot. Yes, it was an incredible sight: standing alone, facing hundreds of creatures who were gradually becoming men once again, was *Die Zeilenesseniss*. Completely alone. Infinitely alone.

I do not believe in fate. And I no longer believe in God. I do not believe in anything any more. But I must admit that there seemed to be more than mere chance in that meeting between a throng of people in extreme misery and the person who was the living symbol of their tormentors.

Why was she still there when all the guards had left? She too must have left, and then she had come back in haste, doubtless to fetch something she had forgotten. The first thing we heard was her voice. Her ordinary voice, sure of itself, animated by her sense of her power and her privilege; the voice of authority which had sometimes given the order to hang one of us and sometimes sang nursery rhymes to her child.

I did not understand what she said – I was standing quite far away – but I could tell that she was speaking as though nothing had changed. I am certain she did not know that she was alone in the camp; she did not know she had been abandoned. I am certain she thought there were

99

still guards nearby, ready to execute the least of her orders and to beat us to death if she desired them to do so. But no-one answered her call. No-one came to serve her or to help. No-one in the crowd facing her made a move. She kept on talking, but little by little her voice changed. The words came faster at the same time as their intensity decreased, and then her voice exploded and became a howl before fading away.

Today, I picture her eyes. I picture the eyes of *Die Zeilenesseniss* when she began to realize that she was the last of them, that she was alone, and that perhaps – yes, perhaps – she would never leave the camp, that for her, too, it would become a tomb.

I was told that she began to strike the men at the head of the crowd with her fists. No-one returned her blows; instead they made way for her. And so she gradually moved deeper into the great river of walking dead, unaware that she would never emerge from it, for the waves closed in again behind her. There was no outcry, no complaint. Her words disappeared with her. She was swallowed up, and she met an end in which there was no hatred, an end that was almost mechanical – a fitting end, in short, an end in her own image. I truly believe, even though I could not swear it, that no-one laid a hand on her. She died without suffering a blow, without a word addressed to her, without even so much as a glance cast upon her, she who had felt such contempt for our glances. I imagine her stumbling at some point and falling to the ground. I imagine her stretching out her hands, trying to catch hold of the shadows as they moved past her, over her, over her body, her legs, her delicate white arms, over her stomach and her powdered face; shadows that paid her no attention, that did not look at her, that did not come to her help and yet did not attack her; moving shadows that simply passed, passed, passed, treading her underfoot the way one treads upon dust or earth or ashes.

The next day I found what remained of her body. It was a pitiful thing, swollen and blue. All her beauty had vanished. She looked like a *Strohespuppe*, a "straw fairy", one of those large dolls children make by stuffing old dresses with hay; *Strohespuppen* are paraded through the village on the feast of St John and then, as night falls, tossed into a great fire while everyone sings and dances to the glory of summer. Her face was not there any more. She no longer had eyes or a mouth or a nose. In their place I saw a single wound, enormous and round, inflated like a balloon, and attached to it was a long mane of blond hair tangled with clumps of mud. It was by her hair that I recognized her. Previously, when I had crept along the ground acting the dog, her hair had appeared to me like filaments of sunlight, blinding and obscene.

Even in death she kept her fists so tightly clenched that they resembled stones. Part of a prettily worked golden chain dangled from one hand. At the end of that chain, no doubt, there was a medal, one of those delicately engraved medals that represent a male or female saint and are hung around infants' necks when they are baptized. Perhaps that medal was the very reason why she had returned; perhaps she had noticed it was missing from her child's small, soft chest. She had come back into the camp, supposing she would leave it again very quickly. She cannot have known that once you abandon Hell, you must never go back there. But in the end there is no difference between dying from ignorance and dying beneath the feet of thousands of men who have regained their freedom. You close your eyes, and then there is nothing any more. And death is never difficult. It requires neither a hero nor a slave. It eats what it is served.

17

"Beer leaves no stain, nor does *eau-de-vie*, whereas wine . . . !"

Father Peiper had launched into a litany of complaints. He stood at his stone sink in his shirt and underpants, scrubbing his white chasuble with a large brush and a bar of soap. "And right on the cross, to boot! If I can't get this out, simpletons and zealots will see it as a symbol! We're already weighed down with symbols! We traffic in symbols! There's no point adding to them!"

I watched him work and said not a word. I was sitting in a corner of his kitchen on a rickety chair with a frowsy straw bottom. The air in the room was hot and heavy and reeked of dirty dishes, hardened cooking fat and cheap wine. Hundreds of empty bottles stood about the place; dozens of them held burning candles whose fragile flames stretched towards the ceiling.

Peiper stopped scrubbing his vestment, tossed it with a gesture of vexation into the stone sink and turned around. He looked at me and started, as if he had forgotten my presence. "Brodeck, Brodeck," he said. "A drink?"

I shook my head.

"You don't need it yet. Lucky you . . ."

In his quest for a bottle with some wine still in it, he shifted a great many empties, producing a crystalline, incoherent music before finding the one he sought. He grabbed it by the neck as though his life depended on it and poured himself a glass. Lifting it up with both hands, he raised it to eye level, smiled, and said in a solemn voice heavy with irony, "This is my blood. Take and drink ye all of it." Then he downed the contents in one gulp, slammed the glass on the table and burst into loud laughter.

I had just come from the village hall where, in compliance with Orschwir's demand, I had gone to discuss the progress of my Report.

Night had fallen suddenly on the village that evening, like an axe striking a chopping block. Over the course of the day, huge clouds had moved in from the west and stalled over our valley. Blocked by the mountains as though caught in a trap, they had begun to gyrate madly and then, at around three o'clock in the afternoon, a glacial north wind had arrived and split them wide open. Their gaping bellies released a great deal of dense snow, a deluge of stubborn, numberless flakes serried like the resolute soldiers of an infinite army and clinging to everything they touched: roofs, walls, paving stones, trees. It was 3 December. All the snowfalls of previous weeks had been mere tokens, and we knew it; the snow that came down that day, however, was no laughing matter. It was the first of the big snows. It would be followed by others whose company we would have to endure until spring.

Outside the village hall, *Zungfrost* – "Frozen Tongue" – had lit two lanterns and placed them on either side of the door. With the aid of a large shovel, he was piling the snow into two mounds, clearing a path like a trench between them. His clothes were covered with snowflakes which clustered and clung to him in a way that was reminiscent of feathers, so that he looked like a large fowl.

"Hello, *Zungfrost*!"

"Hel . . . hel . . . hello, Bro . . . Brodeck! It's real . . . real . . . real . . . really com . . . com . . . coming down!"

"I'm here to see the mayor."

"I . . . I know. He . . . he . . . he's waiting for you upstairs."

Zungfrost is younger than me by a few years. He is always smiling, but he is not simple-minded. In fact, if you look closely at his smile, it could just as easily be a grimace. His face froze one day long ago; his face, his smile and his tongue all froze. He had been a child of seven or eight at the time, and we were in the depths of another frigid winter. All the village children, both young and not so young, had gone to a bend in the Staubi where the river was frozen over. We slid around on the ice. We shoved one another. And then someone – it was never clear who – threw *Zungfrost's* afternoon snack, a slice of bacon stuffed into a chunk of bread, far out across the ice. The boy watched his bread skidding across the surface, getting further and further away, until it stopped about a metre or two from the far bank. Then he began to cry, shedding big, silent tears as round as mistletoe berries. The rest of us laughed and then someone yelled, "Stop crying! Just go and get it!" There was a silence. We all knew that the ice would be thin where the bread had come to rest, but nobody said anything. We waited. The boy hesitated; then, maybe out of defiance, to show that he wasn't afraid, or maybe because he was very hungry, he began to move across the ice, crawling slowly on all fours. Everyone held his breath. We all sat down on the riverbank, pressing against one another, and watched the boy as he advanced like a cautious little animal. We could tell he was trying to make himself as light as possible, even though he was not very heavy to begin with. The closer he got to his snack, the more our little group of spectators recovered from our original amazement, and we began to cheer him on, beating out a rhythm which grew faster and faster. At the moment when he stretched out his hand towards the bread and bacon, everything went awry. The ice beneath him suddenly withdrew, like a tablecloth whipped off a table, and he disappeared into the waters of the river without a sound.

A forester named Hobel happened to be passing not far away, and it was he, alerted by our cries, who pulled the boy out of the river some minutes later with the help of a long pole. The child's face was as white as cream. Even his lips had turned white. His eyes were closed and he was smiling. Some of us thought he had to be dead. But he was wrapped in blankets and his skin rubbed with alcohol, and several hours later he came to. Life returned to his veins and blood ran into his cheeks. The first thing he asked for was his afternoon snack, but in the asking he stumbled over every word, as if the cold, flowing river had frozen his mouth and his tongue had remained enclosed and half dead beneath a caparison of ice. He received his nickname that day, and thereafter no-one ever called him anything other than *Zungfrost*.

When I reached the landing, I could hear voices coming from the council room. My heart began to beat a little faster. I took a deep breath, removed my hat, and knocked at the door before entering.

The council room is huge. I would even say it is too big for the little that goes on in it. It is something out of another era, from a time when a community's riches were measured in proportion to its public buildings. The ceiling is improbably high. The whitewashed walls are covered with ancient maps and framed parchments upon which sloping, intricate scripts record laws, leases and duties dating back to a time when the village was dependent upon the lords of Molensheim, before its freedom was accorded by an imperial charter of 1756 and it was released from all servitude. From each of these documents hang shrivelled ribbons with wax seals.

Ordinarily, the members of the village council sit on either side of the Mayor along a large table, facing several rows of benches set out to accommodate the citizens who come to hear the council's deliberations. That evening the table was there, but the benches had been shoved into a corner of the room and piled atop one another in monumental disorder. The only objects in front of the big table were a single chair and a tiny desk.

"Come on in, Brodeck, we're not going to eat you . . ." That was Orschwir, addressing me from his position at the centre of the table. His words elicited muffled laughter from his companions, apparently an expression of their self-assurance and complicity. There were two of them. On the Mayor's left, Lawyer Knopf was stuffing tobacco into his pipe as he looked at me over the smudged lenses of his spectacles. The chair on Orschwir's right was empty, but Göbbler occupied the next seat but one. He nodded in my direction, turning his head to the side; since his eyes betrayed him more and more with each passing day, he had apparently decided to try to see people and things with his ears instead. My blood ran cold at the sight of him.

"Are you going to sit down or not?" Orschwir said. The warmth in his voice sounded forced. "You are among friends, Brodeck. Make yourself at home. You have nothing to fear."

I was on the point of asking the Mayor the reason for my neighbour's presence, and for that of Lawyer Knopf; Knopf may have been a village notable, but he was not a member of the council. Why were he and Göbbler there and nobody else? Why precisely those two? What offices did they hold? What were their functions? What qualified them to sit behind the large table?

Just as my brain was boiling with all these questions, I heard the door open behind me. A broad smile lit up Orschwir's face. "Come in, please," he said respectfully, addressing the newcomer whom I could not yet see. "You haven't missed anything. We were just about to get started."

Halting steps, punctuated by taps of a cane, resounded in the room.

The new arrival was approaching, but still I could not see him. The sounds at my back came closer. I did not want to turn around. He paused a few paces from me, and then I heard him say, "Hello, Brodeck." I had heard that voice say hello to me hundreds and hundreds of times. My heart stopped beating; I closed my eyes; my hands felt clammy. A bitter taste flooded my mouth. The steps resumed behind me, elegant and slow. Then there was the sound of a chair scraping the floor, followed by silence. I opened my eyes again. Ernst-Peter Limmat, my old schoolmaster, was sitting in the chair on Orschwir's right and looking straight at me.

"Have you lost your tongue, Brodeck? Come on! We're all here! Read us what you've written so far."

As he spoke these words, Orschwir rubbed his hands together the way he did after concluding a shrewd business deal. It was not my tongue that had gone missing. That was not what I had so suddenly lost. It was something else: another piece, perhaps, of faith and hope.

My dear old teacher Limmat, what were you doing there, sitting behind that table like a judge in a tribunal? So you too, you knew?

18

The faces. Their faces. Was this another of those agonizing dreams, like the ones that used to take hold of me at night in the camp and fling me into a world where nothing was familiar? Where am I? Will this all come to an end some day? Is this Hell? What wrong have I done? Emélia, tell me. Why is this happening? Because I left you? Yes, it's true: I left you.

I wasn't there. My darling, forgive me, please forgive me. You know they took me away. You know there was nothing I could do. Speak to me. Tell me what I am. Tell me you love me. Stop that humming, I beg you, stop it. Stop droning that tune. It breaks my head and my heart. Open your lips and let words come out. I can hear everything now. I can understand everything. I am so tired. I am so insignificant, and there is no light in my life without you. I am dust. I know that I am dust. I am useless.

This evening I have drunk a little too much. It is the middle of the night. I am not afraid of anything any more. I must write everything down. They could be coming. I am waiting for them. Yes, I am waiting for them.

In the council room, I read the few pages – ten at the most – on which I had recorded witness statements and reconstructed events. I kept my eyes on the words, never once looking up at my audience of four who sat there and listened. I kept slipping off the chair whose seat was tilted forward, and the desk was so small that my legs barely fitted under it. I was distinctly uncomfortable, but that was what they wanted: they wanted me to be ill at ease in that vast room, in that trial-like setting.

I read in a lifeless voice, an absent voice. I had not yet recovered from the surprise – and the bitter disappointment – of encountering my former schoolmaster there. My mouth uttered the words, but my thoughts were elsewhere. Memories of him resurfaced in my mind, some of them very old: my first day at school, when I stepped inside the door and saw his eyes turn towards me, big eyes of a glacial blue, the blue of deep crevasses; and the times – how I had loved them! – when I stayed after school and he helped me progress in my studies, helped me make up for the time I had lost, coaching me with patience and kindness. His voice was less solemn during those sessions. We were alone together and he spoke to me gently, patiently corrected my mistakes, encouraged me. I remember back then, when I was still a little boy, I would lie awake at night trying to remember my father's face. I would often catch myself giving him the schoolmaster's features, and I also remember that the image was pleasant and comforting.

A short while ago, when I got home, I took down the mushrooms, the trumpets-of-death that Limmat had given me the other day when I visited him to talk about the foxes, and threw the garlands into the fire.

Fédorine opened one eye and noticed what I was doing. "Are you crazy?" she asked. "What's wrong with them?"

"With them? Nothing. But the hands that strung them together are not exactly clean."

In her lap was a ball of coarse wool and some knitting needles. She said, "You're speaking Tibershoï, Brodeck."

Tibershoï is the magic language of the country of Tibipoï, the setting of so many of Fédorine's tales. Elfs, gnomes and trolls speak Tibershoï, but humans can never understand it.

I did not reply. I grabbed the bottle of *eau-de-vie* and a glass and went out to the shed. It took me several minutes to free the door from all the snow piled up against it. And snow was still falling; the night was full of it. The wind had stopped and the snowflakes, left to their own devices, came down in unpredictable, graceful swirls.

There was a long silence in the council room when I finished reading what I had written. It was a question of who would speak first. I raised my eyes to them, which I had not done since I had begun to read. Lawyer Knopf was sucking on his pipe as though the fate of the world depended on it. He could not produce more than a wisp of smoke, and this seemed to irritate him. Göbbler was apparently asleep, and

109

Orschwir was writing a note on a piece of paper. Limmat alone was looking at me and smiling. The Mayor raised his head. "Good," he said, "very good, Brodeck. It's most interesting and well written. Keep going, you're on the right track."

He turned towards the men on either side of him, seeking their assent or authorizing them to state their opinions. Göbbler dived in first. "I was expecting more, Brodeck. I hear your typewriter so much. It seems to me you write a great deal, and yet the Report is far from being finished . . ."

I tried to hide my anger. I tried to reply calmly, without showing surprise, without challenging Göbbler's observation or even his presence. I surely would have liked to tell him that he would do better to direct his attention to the fire burning in his wife's nether regions than to my compositions. I replied that writing this sort of report did not come naturally to me, that I had difficulty finding the right tone and the right words, that collating the statements of the people I had interviewed, putting together an accurate account, capturing the truth of what had gone on during the last few months constituted an arduous task. Yes, I was constantly at my typewriter, but I laboured, I revised, I crossed out, I tore up, I started again, and that was the reason why I was not working faster.

"I didn't mean to upset you, Brodeck. What I said was just a passing comment. I apologize," Göbbler said, feigning embarrassment.

Orschwir seemed satisfied with my justifications. He turned once more to the others. Siegfried Knopf appeared happy because his pipe was working again. He gazed at it with benevolent eyes and stroked its bowl with both hands, without paying the least heed to the people around him.

"Perhaps you have a question, Schoolmaster Limmat?" the Mayor

110

asked respectfully, turning towards the old teacher. I felt the sweat spring to my forehead, as it had done when he quizzed me in front of the whole class. Limmat smiled, allowed some time to pass, and rubbed his long hands together.

"No, not a question, Monsieur le Maire, but rather a remark, a simple remark . . . I know Brodeck well. I've known him a long time. I know he will conscientiously perform the task we have entrusted to him, but . . . how shall I say it . . . he is a dreamer, and I use that word in no bad sense – I think dreaming is a wonderful and positive thing, but in this particular case he mustn't make a muddle of everything, he mustn't mix up dreams and reality or confuse what exists with what never took place. I exhort him to pay attention. I exhort him to stay on the straight road and not to let his imagination govern his thoughts and his sentences."

For hours after the meeting, I kept going over Limmat's words in my mind. What were they supposed to mean? I had no idea.

"We won't keep you any longer, Brodeck. I imagine you are in a hurry to get home." Having said these words, Orschwir rose to his feet and I immediately followed suit. I bade farewell to the others with a small movement of my head and began to walk rapidly to the door. This was the moment that Lawyer Knopf chose to rouse himself from his reverie. His old nanny-goat's voice caught up with me: "That's a handsome cap you've got there, Brodeck. It must be really warm. I've never seen anything like it . . . Where did you get it?"

I turned. Lawyer Knopf was approaching me, hopping a little on his crooked legs. His eyes were fixed on the *Anderer*'s cap, which I had just replaced on my head. Knopf was now quite close to me, and he reached for the cap with one claw-like hand. I felt his fingers running over the fur. "Very special, and what fine work! Beautiful! Just the thing for the weather that's on the way. I envy you, Brodeck."

111

Knopf trembled a little as he stroked the cap. I could smell his tobacco-laden breath, and I saw a delirious light dancing in his eyes. Suddenly I wondered whether he had not perhaps gone mad. Göbbler came over to us and said, "You didn't answer Lawyer Knopf's question, Brodeck. He wants to know who made your cap for you."

I hesitated. I hesitated between silence and the few words I could fling at them like knives. Göbbler was waiting. Limmat joined us, clutching the lapels of his velvet jacket around his skinny neck.

In the end I summoned up a confident tone and said, "Göbbler, you'll never believe me, but be that as it may, I'm going to tell you the absolute truth. But remember that it's a secret, and please don't repeat it to anyone. You see this cap? Just imagine, the Virgin Mary made it for me and the Holy Ghost delivered it!"

Ernst-Peter Limmat burst out laughing. Knopf laughed too. Göbbler was the only one who scowled. His nearly dead eyes searched for mine, as if he wanted to gouge them out. I left the lot of them standing there and went out of the door.

Outside the snow had not stopped falling, and the path that *Zungfrost* had cleared an hour previously had already vanished. The village streets were deserted. Halos quivered around the lanterns that hung from the gables. The wind had got up again, but only slightly, and it made the snowflakes flutter in every direction. Suddenly I felt a presence against me: *Ohnmeist* was trying to bury his cold muzzle in my trousers. Such familiarity surprised me. I began to wonder whether the dog might not be mistaking me for someone else, for the *Anderer*, the only other person with whom it had taken such liberties.

We trudged along side by side, the dog and I, surrounded by the smells of the snowy cold and the pinewood smoke that came down from the chimneys in gusts. I no longer remember exactly what I thought

112

about in the course of that strange promenade, but I know that suddenly I found myself very far from those streets, very far from the village, very far from those familiar, barbaric faces. I was walking with Emélia. We were holding on to each other, arm in arm. She was wearing a coat of blue cloth with embroidered sleeves and a border of grey rabbit fur around the collar. Her hair, her most beautiful hair, was coiled up under a little red hat. It was very cold. We were very cold. It was our second evening. I gazed hungrily at her face, at her every gesture, her small hands, her laughter, her eyes.

"So you're a student, you say?"

She had a delicious accent which slid over her words and gave each of them, the pretty ones as well as the ugly ones, a discreet emphasis. We were circling the lake for the third time, walking along the Elsi Promenade. We were not alone. There were other couples like us, groups of two people who looked at each other a great deal, speaking little, laughing for no reason, and falling silent again. With the three pennies I had borrowed from Ulli Rätte, I bought a sizzling hot *crêpe* from the vendor whose stall was next to the skating rink. He poured a generous extra spoonful of honey over it and held it out to us, saying, "For the lovers!" We smiled, but we did not dare look at each other. I offered the *crêpe* to Emélia. She seized it as though it were a treasure, tore it in half and handed me my portion. Night was falling, and with it the icy air that turned Emélia's cheeks even rosier and made her hazel eyes shine all the more brightly. We ate the *crêpe*. We looked at each other. We were at the very beginning of our life.

With a long, drawn-out whine, *Ohnmeist* brought me back to the village. He rubbed his head against me one more time and then went away, taking little steps and wagging his tail as if waving me good-bye. I followed him with my eyes until he disappeared behind the woodshed

113

that stands next to the workshop in Gott's smithy. He had probably found shelter there for the winter.

I had not noticed how much distance the dog and I had covered. We had gone all the way to the end of the village, almost as far as the church and the cemetery. The snow was falling as thickly as before. I could not see the edge of the forest, even though it began barely thirty metres away. When the church came into view I was reminded of Father Peiper, and the light in his kitchen window made me decide to knock on his door.

19

Peiper had listened, regularly refilling his glass. As for me, I had let it all out. I had gone on at length. I had said almost all of it. Save that I did not talk about the pages I am writing alongside the Report, but I talked about everything else. I revealed all my doubts and fears. I told him how odd it felt to have fallen into a trap and to be unable to understand who had woven it, who was holding the cords, why I had been pushed into it, and especially how I might get out of it. When finally I stopped, Peiper let pass a little while in silence. Talking had done me good.

"Who are you confiding in, Brodeck? The man, or what is left of the priest?"

I hesitated, simply because I had no idea what my response should be. Peiper sensed my confusion and said, "I'm asking the question because the two are not the same. You know they aren't, even though you no longer believe in God. I'm going to help you a bit, and I'll start by telling you something in confidence: I scarcely believe in God any more myself. I spoke to Him for a long time, for years and years, and throughout those years He really seemed to listen to me, and to respond as well, with little signs, with the thoughts that came to me, with the things He inspired me to do. And then, that all stopped. I know now that He does not exist, or He has gone away for ever, which amounts to the same thing. So there it is: we are alone. Nevertheless, I go on with the show. I play my part badly, no doubt, but the theatre is still standing. It does no-one any harm, and there are some elderly souls in the audience who would be yet more alone and yet more abandoned if I closed the place down. Every performance gives them a little strength you see, the strength to go on. And there is another principle I have not repudiated: the seal of confession. It is my cross to bear. I shall bear it to the end."

All at once, he grabbed my hand and squeezed it tightly. "I know everything, Brodeck. Everything. And you cannot even imagine what that *everything* means."

He stopped talking, having just realized that his glass was empty. He rose trembling to his feet and cast anxious looks at the bottles that stood about the room. He lifted five or six before finding one that still held a little wine. He smiled and clasped the bottle to him as you would embrace a loved one you are happy to see again. He returned to his chair and filled his glass. "Men are strange. They commit the worst crimes without a second thought, but afterwards they cannot live with the memory of what they have done. They have to rid themselves of it. And so they come to me, because they know I'm the only person who can give them relief, and they tell me everything. I'm the sewer, Brodeck. I'm not the priest; I'm the sewer-man. I'm the man into whose brain they can pour all their filth, all their shit, and then they feel relieved, they feel

115

unburdened. When it's over, they go away as though nothing has happened. They're all new and pristine. Ready to start afresh. They know that the sewer has closed over what they dumped into it and will never repeat what it has heard to anybody. They can sleep in peace, Brodeck, and at the same time I am awash, I am overflowing, I cannot take any more, but I hold on, I try to hold on. I shall die from this build-up of horrors in me. You see this wine? It's my only friend. It puts me to sleep and makes me forget for a little while the great, vile mass I carry around within me, the putrid load they have all entrusted to me. I am not telling you this because I want your pity. I just want you to understand. You feel alone because you must write about hideous things; I feel alone because I must absolve them."

He stopped, and in the manifold, flickering light of the candles, I distinctly saw his eyes fill with tears.

"I didn't always drink, Brodeck, as you well know. Before the war, water was my daily beverage, and I knew that God was at my side. The war . . . maybe the peoples of the world need such nightmares. They lay waste to what they have taken centuries to build. They destroy today what they looked up to yesterday. They legitimize what was forbidden. They give preferential treatment to what they used to condemn. War is a great broom that sweeps the world. It is where the mediocre triumph and the criminal receives a saint's halo; people prostrate themselves before him and acclaim him and fawn upon him. Why must men find life so gloomy and monotonous that they long for massacre and ruin? I have seen them jump up and down on the edge of the abyss, walk along its crest and look with fascination upon the horror of the void, where the vilest passions hold sway. Destroy! Defile! Rape! Slash! If you had seen them . . ."

With a sudden gesture, the priest grabbed my wrist and squeezed it.

116

"Why do you think they tolerate my incoherent sermons and my drunken Masses, my cursing and raving? Why do they all come to church? Why hasn't anyone asked the Bishop to recall me? Because they are afraid, Brodeck. It's as simple as that: they are afraid of me and of all the things I know about them. Fear is what governs the world. It holds men by their little balls. It squeezes them from time to time, just to remind their owners that it could annihilate them if it so desired. I see their faces in my church when I'm in the pulpit. I see them through their masks of false calm. I smell their sour sweat. I smell it. That isn't holy water running down the cracks of their arses, believe me! They must curse themselves for having told me so much . . . Do you remember when you were an altar boy, Brodeck? Do you remember serving when I said Mass?"

I was a very young boy, and Father Peiper made a great impression on me. He had a deep, silky voice, a voice not yet worn down by guzzling wine. He never laughed. I wore a white alb and a bright-red collar. I closed my eyes and inhaled the incense, believing God would enter me more readily if I did that. My happiness, my bliss was without flaw. There were no races, no differences among men. I had forgotten who I was and where I had come from. I had never thought about the tiny piece of flesh missing from between my thighs and no-one had ever reproached me for it. We were all God's people. I stood at Father Peiper's side at the altar in our small church. He turned the pages of the Holy Book. He brandished the host and the chalice. I rang the little bells. I presented him with the water and the wine and the white linen cloth he used to wipe his lips. I knew there was a Heaven for the innocent and a Hell for the guilty. Everything seemed simple to me.

"He came to visit me once . . ." Peiper's head was bowed down, and his voice had become lifeless. I thought he was talking about God again.

"He came, but I don't think I was capable of understanding him. He was so . . . different. I could not . . . I was not able to understand him."

And then I realized that the priest was talking about the *Anderer*.

"It could not have ended any other way, Brodeck. That man was like a mirror, you see. He did not have to say a single word. Each of them saw their reflection in him. Or maybe he was God's last messenger before He closes up shop and throws away the keys. I am the sewer, but that fellow was the mirror. And mirrors, Brodeck – mirrors can only be smashed."

As if to underline his words, Peiper took the bottle in front of him and hurled it against the wall. Then he took another, and another, and another one after that, and as each bottle shattered, sending thousands of glass shards to all corners of the kitchen, he laughed, he laughed like one of the damned and shouted, *"Ziebe Jarh vo Missgesck! Ziebe Jarh vo Missgesck! Ziebe Jarh vo Missgesck!"* – "Seven years of bad luck! Seven years of bad luck! Seven years of bad luck!" Then, suddenly, he stopped, clutched his face in his hands, threw himself forward onto the table and sobbed like a child.

I stayed with him for a while without daring to move or say a word. He sniffled twice, very loudly, and then there was silence. He remained in his chair, his upper body sprawled on the table, his head hidden between his arms. The candles burned themselves down and went out, one by one, and the kitchen gradually grew dark. Peaceful snores emanated from Peiper's body. The church bell sounded ten o'clock. I left the room, closing the door very gently behind me.

Once outside, I was surprised by the light. The snow had stopped falling and the sky was almost entirely clear. The last clouds were still attempting to cling to the Schnikelkopf peaks, but the wind, now blowing from the east, was busy tidying them up, tearing their remnants into small strips. The stars had donned their silver apparel. As I raised my head to look at them, I felt as though I were plunging into a sea both dark and glittering, its inky depths studded with innumerable bright pearls. They seemed very near. I even made the stupid gesture of stretching out my hand, as if I might seize a handful of them to put inside my coat as a present for Poupchette.

Smoke rose straight up from the chimneys. The air had become very dry again, and the cold had formed a hard, sparkling crust on the mounds of snow piled up in front of the houses. I felt in my pocket for the pages I had read to the others a few hours earlier; they were just a few thin sheets of very light paper, but they seemed heavy and hot. I contemplated what Peiper had told me about the *Anderer*, and I found it difficult to distinguish between the ravings of a drunkard and the words of a man accustomed to speaking in parables. Above all I wondered why the *Anderer* had visited the priest, especially considering that our new neighbour quite conspicuously avoided the church and never went to Mass. What could he and Peiper have had to talk about?

As I passed Schloss' inn, I saw that a light was still burning in the main room. And then – I don't know why – I felt a sudden urge to go inside.

Dieter Schloss was behind the bar talking to Caspar Hausorn. They were both leaning forward, so close to each other that you would have thought they were going to kiss. I called out a greeting that made them jump, and then I went over to the table in the corner next to the fireplace and sat down.

"Do you have any hot wine left?"

Schloss nodded. Hausorn turned in my direction and made a curt movement with his head that might have passed for a "good evening". Then he leaned towards Schloss' ear once more, murmured something the innkeeper seemed to agree with, picked up his cap, finished his beer in one swallow, and left without giving me another look.

It was the second time I had been at the inn since the *Ereigniës*. And, as on the previous occasion, I found it hard to believe that this very ordinary place was where a man had been put to death. The inn looked like any other village inn: a few tables, chairs and benches; shelves holding one-litre bottles of wine and *eau-de-vie*; large, framed mirrors so covered with soot they had not reflected anything for years; a cabinet for the chess and draughts sets; sawdust on the floor. The rooms were upstairs. There were just four of them. Three of them had not been used for a long time. As for the fourth, the biggest and also the most handsome, it had been occupied by the *Anderer*.

On the day after the *Ereigniës*, after my visit to Orschwir, I had stayed in Mère Pitz's place for nearly an hour in an effort to recover my wits, to settle my mind and my heart, while the old woman sat beside me, turning the pages of a volume of her dried plant collection and providing a running commentary on all the flowers pressed inside the book. Then, when my head had finally cleared, I thanked her, left the café and went straight to the inn. I found the door locked and the shutters closed. It was the first time I had ever seen Schloss' inn like that. I knocked on the door with rapid, heavy blows and waited. Nothing. I knocked again even harder, and this time a shutter opened a little way and Schloss appeared at the window looking suspicious and fearful.

"What do you want, Brodeck?"

"I want to talk to you. Open up."

"This may not be the best time."

"Open up, Schloss. You know I have to write the Report."

The word had emerged all by itself from my mouth. Using it for the first time felt utterly strange, but it had an immediate effect on Schloss.

He closed the shutter, and I heard him hurrying downstairs. A few seconds later he was unbolting the big door. He opened it and said, "Come in, quick!"

He closed the door behind me so swiftly that I could not stop myself asking him if he was worried that a ghost might slip inside. He said, "That's no joking matter, Brodeck," and crossed himself twice. "What do you want?"

"I want you to show me the room."

"What room?"

"Don't pretend you don't understand. The room."

Schloss hesitated. He seemed to be considering my request. Then he said, "Why do you want to see it?"

"I want to see it right now. I want to be thorough. I don't want to forget anything. I have to tell the whole story."

Schloss ran his hand over his forehead, which was gleaming as though he had rubbed it with lard. "There's not a lot to see, but if you insist . . . Follow me."

We climbed the stairs to the upper floor. Schloss' immense body took up the whole width of the staircase, and every step bent under his weight. He was breathing hard. When we got to the landing he reached into one of the pockets in his apron, took out a key and handed it to me, saying, "I'll let you do it, Brodeck."

I had to make three attempts to insert the key in the lock before I could turn it. I could not control my shaking hand. Schloss backed off a little way and tried to catch his breath. Finally there was a little click, and I pushed the door open. My heart was like a hunted bird's. I was afraid of seeing that room again, afraid of encountering a dead man, but what I saw surprised me so much that my anxiety vanished at once.

The room was absolutely empty. There was no furniture, no objects, no clothes, no trunks; all that remained was a big wardrobe bolted to the wall. I opened the double doors, but the wardrobe too was empty. There was nothing in the room at all. It was as if the *Anderer* had never occupied it. As if he had never existed.

"What happened to all his baggage?"

"What are you talking about, Brodeck?"

"Don't take me for an idiot, Schloss."

The room smelled of damp wood and soap. The floor had been copiously wetted down and scrubbed. In the place where the bed used to stand, I could make out a big stain where some of the bare larch-wood planks were darker than the rest.

"Was it you who washed the floor?"

"Somebody had to do it . . ."

"And what's that stain?"

"What do you think it is, Brodeck?"

I turned back to Schloss.

"What do you think . . . ?" he repeated wearily.

20

I got up very late this morning, with a hammer at work inside my head. I believe I drank far too much last night. The bottle of *eau-de-vie* is all but empty. My mouth is as dry as tinder, and I have no idea how I found the way to my bed. I wrote late into the night, and I remember being unable to feel my fingers towards the end because the cold had numbed them.

I also remember that the keys on the typewriter were sticking more and more. The window pane was covered with frost shaped like fern fronds, and I was so drunk I thought the forest was on the march, preparing to surround and smother the shed, and me with it.

When I finally got out of bed, Fédorine asked no questions. She brewed an infusion for me, a concoction in which I recognized the aromas of wild thyme, pennyroyal and houseleek. She said simply, "Drink this. It is good for what you've got." I did as she said, as I used to do when I was little. Then she set down before me a basket that Alfred Wurtzwiller had brought a little earlier in the day. It contained potato soup, a loaf of rye bread, half a ham, apples and leeks – but no money. This was not my usual delivery. When the Administration in S. deigned to show that it had not completely forgotten me, I would receive a money order, along with three or four stamped, re-stamped, signed and countersigned official documents attesting to the payment thereby made. But in this basket there was only food. I could not help drawing a connection between the food basket and the previous evening's audience in front of the Mayor and the others. This was how they were paying me. They were paying me a little. For the Report. For what I had already written and, more importantly, for what I had not written.

Then Fédorine bathed Poupchette in the tub. My darling clapped her hands and slapped the hot water, laughing and shouting, "Li'l fish! Li'l fish!" I took her in my arms, pressing her against me, wet as she was, and kissed her soft, warm, naked skin which made her laugh all the more. Behind us at the window, with her eyes raised to the distance and the white immensity of the valley, Emélia hummed her song. Poupchette started to struggle and I put her down. She scooped up a handful of suds, ran to her mother and threw them at her. Emélia turned to look at the child but kept on humming. Her dead eyes settled for a few moments on Poupchette's pretty smile, and then she stared out at the whiteness again.

I feel weak and useless. I am trying to write things down, but who is going to read them? Who? I would do better to take Emélia and Poupchette in my arms, sling old Fédorine across my back, along with a bundle of provisions, clothes, and a few beautiful keepsakes, and go far away from here. Start again. Start all over again. In the old days, Nösel used to say this was mankind's distinguishing feature: "Man is an animal that always begins again." Nösel spoke in slow sentences, a Roman orator, his two hands flat on his wide desk, and after each pronouncement he left a great silence which each of us could fill as he chose.

"Man is an animal that always starts again." But what is it he is always starting? His mistakes, or the fragile scaffolding whose construction sometimes allows him to climb close to heaven? Nösel never said, maybe because he knew that life itself, the life we had not yet fully entered, would eventually make us understand. Or maybe because he simply had no idea, or because he was untroubled by doubts, or because he had fed on books for so long that he had forgotten the real world and those who dwelled in it.

Last night Schloss brought me my hot wine and then sat down uninvited at my table. I knew he wanted to say something to me, but I had nothing to say to him. I was too absorbed in what Father Peiper had told me. Moreover, I wanted to drink my glass of hot wine and feel the fire reviving my body, and that was all. I was not looking for anything else. My head was teeming with unanswered questions and hundreds of tiny pieces of a vast mechanism I had yet to invent in order to assemble them . . .

"I know you don't like me very much, Brodeck," Schloss suddenly murmured. I had forgotten he was there. "But I'm not the worst, you know."

The innkeeper seemed even larger and sweatier than usual. He was twisting his fingers and gnawing his plump, cracked lips. "I did what I was told, that's all. I don't want any trouble, but that doesn't stop me from thinking . . . Look, I'm just a simple man. I'm not as intelligent as you are, but whatever you might think, I'm not vicious either. I'm not the worst. It's true, I served drinks to the *Fratergekeime* while they occupied the village. But what else could I have done? Serving drinks is my business. I wasn't going to get myself killed for refusing to serve a glass of beer. I have always regretted what happened to you, Brodeck, I swear, and I had nothing to do with it, believe me . . . and as for what they did to your wife . . . my God . . ."

I nearly spat in Schloss' face when he mentioned Emélia's name, but what he said after that stopped me.

"I loved my wife too, you know. That might seem strange to you because, as you may remember, she wasn't particularly beautiful, but now that she's no longer here I feel as if I am living only half a life. Nothing is important any more. If Gerthe had been here during the war, who knows? Maybe I wouldn't have served the *Fratergekeime*. I felt strong when she was around . . . Maybe I would have spat in their faces. Maybe I would have grabbed the big knife I use to cut onions and stuck it in their bellies. And then, if she had been here, maybe . . . maybe *De Murmelnër* would still be alive, maybe I would have got myself killed before letting anything happen to him under my roof . . ."

I felt my stomach churning. A touch of nausea. The hot wine was not agreeing with me. It was not warming my insides; it was nibbling at them, like a little animal in my stomach trying to get a bite of everything within reach. I looked at Schloss as if for the first time. It was as if a bank of fog had dissolved, bit by bit, and behind it an unsuspected, oddly harmonious landscape could be seen. At the same time I wondered whether Schloss might be trying to hoodwink me. It is always easy to regret what has happened after the event. Regret costs nothing. It allows you to wash your hands and your memory, to cleanse them thoroughly and make them pure and white. But all the same, what Peiper told me about confession and the sewer – that was quite something! Every man in the village must have passed through his confessional in the end, and Schloss was probably not the last of them. And then I remembered all too clearly his behaviour and his expression on the night of the *Ereigniës* – he had not exactly hung back. He did not appear to disapprove then of the crime committed within his walls, whatever he might say to me now. He had not given the impression of a man gripped by the terror and horror of what had just taken place.

I was not sure what to think. I am still not sure what to think. That is without a doubt the camp's great victory over its prisoners; over those that died, and the other ones like me it did not kill, that is. Those who came out of it alive, all of us still carry a part of it deep down inside ourselves, like a stain. We can never again meet the eyes of other people without wondering whether they too harbour a desire to hunt us down, to torture us, to kill us. We have become perpetual prey, creatures who, whatever we do, will always look upon the dawning day as the start of a long ordeal of survival and upon nightfall with an odd feeling of relief. Disappointment and disquiet ferment within us. I think we have become, and will remain until the day we die, a reminder of humanity destroyed. We are wounds that will never heal.

"You might not know that we had a baby before the war," Schloss went on. "It was when you were away, studying at the University, and

Fédorine might not have written to you about it. The baby didn't live long – four days and four nights. It was a boy. The midwife, old Paula Beckenart, may she rest in peace, said he looked just like a little Schloss. She helped him out of Gerthe's belly on 7 April. Outside, the birds were chirping and the larch buds were growing as big as plums. The first time Paula placed him in my arms, I thought I would not know how to hold him. I was afraid I would squeeze him too tight or smother him with my big hands, and I was afraid of dropping him. I imagined him breaking apart like crystal. Gerthe laughed at me, and the little one hollered and waved his arms and legs. But as soon as he found Gerthe's breast, he began to suck her milk and did not stop, as if he wanted to empty her entirely. I had asked Hans Douda to make a cradle from the trunk of a walnut tree. It was a fine piece of wood that he had been saving to make a wardrobe, but when I put the gold coins on his workbench the deal was done."

Schloss had big, dirty fingernails. As he was telling me about his child he made an effort to clean them without looking at them, but they stayed black.

"He really filled that cradle. He beat the bottom of it with his little feet as hard as he could. He made a pretty noise, like the sound of axe blows coming from deep in the forest. Gerthe wanted to call him Stephan, but I preferred Reichart. To tell the truth we had been caught off guard; we had both persuaded ourselves that the baby would be a girl. We had a name ready for the little girl who never came: Lisebeth, because Lise was my mother's name, and Gerthe's mother was Bethsie. But when the little man made his appearance and the midwife held him up in the air, we had no name for him. Throughout the four days of his short life, Gerthe and I squabbled constantly over his name, laughing the whole time. I would say 'Reichart'; she would reply 'Stephan'. It became a game, a game that always ended in hugs and kisses. And so when the child died, he didn't have a name. He died nameless, and I've blamed myself for that ever since, as though it was part of what killed him."

Schloss fell silent and bowed his head. He stopped moving altogether, as though he had ceased to breathe. My mouth tasted of cinnamon and cloves, and the gnawing in my stomach had not let up.

"Sometimes at night I dream about him. He reaches out to me with his tiny hands, and then he leaves, he goes away, as if there is some force carrying him off, and there is no name I can call out, there is no name I can say to try to hold him back."

Schloss had lifted his head and spoken these last words with his eyes fixed on mine. His eyes were big, overflowing; they took up too much space; I felt as though they were crowding me out. He was surely waiting for me to say something, but what? I knew well that ghosts can cling stubbornly to life and that sometimes they are more present than the living.

"One morning I woke up and Gerthe had already got out of bed. I had not heard a thing. She was kneeling perfectly still beside the cradle. I called out to her. She did not reply. She did not even turn her head. I got up and went over to her, crooning the names Stephan, Reichart . . . Gerthe leapt to her feet and pounced on me like an animal gone crazy, trying to hit me, tearing at my mouth, scratching my cheeks. I looked into the cradle and saw the baby's face. His eyes were closed and his skin was the colour of slate."

I do not know how long I stayed with Schloss after he told me that. Nor do I recall whether he went on talking about his child or simply sat there in silence. The fire in the hearth died down. He did not add more wood. The flames went out, and then the few embers. It got cold.

At some point I stood up and Schloss accompanied me to the door. He clasped my hand for a long time, and then he thanked me. Twice. For what?

On the way home my head was buzzing; I had the feeling that my temples were banging together like cymbals. I found myself saying Poupchette's name aloud, again and again: "Poupchette, Poupchette, Poupchette, Poupchette . . ." It was like throwing little stones into the air, pebbles of sound that would bring me home quickly. I could not help thinking about Schloss' dead baby, about all the things he had told me, about the few hours the child had spent in our world. Life is so strange. Once you have plunged into it, you often wonder what you are doing here. Maybe that is why some, perhaps a little cleverer than the others, content themselves with opening the door a crack and taking a look around, and when they see what is inside, they want nothing more than to close that door again as fast as possible.

Maybe they are the ones who are right.

21

I want to go back to the first day, or rather to the first evening: the evening when the *Anderer* appeared in our village. I have given an account of his meeting with the eldest Dörfer child, but I have not described his arrival at the inn a few minutes later. My account is based on the statements I took from three different eyewitnesses: Schloss himself, Menigue Wirfrau, the baker, who had gone to the inn to drink a glass of wine, and Doris Klattermeier, a young girl with pink skin and hay-coloured hair, who was passing by when the *Anderer* arrived. There were other witnesses both inside and outside the inn, but the three named above related the events in almost exactly the same way – apart from one or two small details – so I thought it best to look no further.

The *Anderer* had dismounted to speak to the Dörfer boy, and he walked the rest of the way to the inn, leading his horse by the reins while the donkey followed a few paces behind. He tethered the animals to a ring outside and then, instead of opening the door and walking in like everyone else, he knocked three times and waited. This was such an unusual thing to do that he had to stand there for quite some time. "I thought it was a prankster," Schloss told me. "Or some child!" In short, nothing happened. The *Anderer* waited. No-one opened the door to him, nor did he open it himself. A few people, among them young Doris, had already gathered to observe the phenomenon: the horse, the ass, the baggage and the oddly attired fellow standing outside the door of the inn with a smile on his round, powdered face. After a few minutes he knocked again, and this time the three blows were harder and sharper. Schloss said, "At that point I realized something out of the ordinary was going on, and I went to see."

So Schloss opened the door and found himself face to face with the *Anderer*. "I nearly choked! Where had this fellow come from, I thought – the circus or a fairytale?" But the *Anderer* gave him no time to recover. He lifted his funny hat to reveal his very round, very bald pate, made a supple, elegant gesture of salutation and said, "I greet you, Monsieur. My friends" – here he indicated the horse and the donkey – "and I have come a great distance and find ourselves quite exhausted. Would you be kind enough to offer us the hospitality of your establishment? In exchange for our payment, of course."

Schloss is convinced that the *Anderer* said, "Greetings, Monsieur

Schloss," but young Doris and Wirfrau both swear that this was not the case. Schloss was no doubt so stunned by the strange apparition and its request that he lost his bearings for a few moments. He said, "I did not know how to answer him at first. It had been years since we had had any visitors, except for the ones you know about! And besides, the words he used . . . He spoke in *Deeperschaft*, not in dialect, and my ear wasn't used to hearing that."

Menigue Wirfrau told me that Schloss hesitated for a few moments, looking at the *Anderer* and scratching his head, before he replied. As for the *Anderer*, it seems he stood motionless, smiling as if all this were perfectly normal and time – which was falling drop by drop into a narrow pipe – was of no importance. Doris Klattermeier remembered that his donkey and his horse did not move either. She shivered a little when she told me that, and then she made the sign of the cross, twice. To most of the people in our village, God is a distant being composed of books and incense; the Devil, on the other hand, is a neighbour whom many of them believe they have seen at one time or another.

At length Schloss uttered a few words. "He asked the stranger how many nights he planned to stay," said Wirfrau. When I went to see him he was kneading dough, naked from the waist up, and his chest and the rims of his eyes were covered with flour. He seized the big wad with both hands, lifted it, flipped it over, flung it into the kneading trough and repeated the process. He spoke without looking at me. I had found a place to sit between two sacks and the woodpile. The oven had been humming for a good while, and the little room was hot with the smell of burning wood. Wirfrau continued: "For a while the fellow seemed to be thinking the question over, smiling the whole time. He looked at the ass and the horse, and it was as if he was asking them their opinion. Then he answered in his funny voice, 'I should think that our sojourn will be rather extended.' I am sure Schloss did not know what to say, but he did not want to look like a fool either. So he shook his head several times, and then he invited the stranger in."

Two hours later, the *Anderer* was lodged in the room which Schloss had dusted in haste. His bags and trunks had been brought upstairs and his horse and donkey given beds of fresh straw in a stable just next door to the inn, the property of Père Solzner who is about as likeable as a whack in the head with a club. At the stranger's request, a basin of fresh, pure water and a bucket of oats were placed close to the animals. He went over to make sure they were well accommodated, taking the opportunity to brush their flanks with a handful of hay and whisper in their ears some words no-one could hear. Then he handed Père Solzner three gold pieces, the equivalent of several months' food and shelter for the beasts, and on his way out of the stable he bade them farewell and wished them a good night.

In the meantime the inn had filled with people, many of whom had come to gaze upon this wonder with their own eyes. Although not curious by nature, I must confess that I myself was one of them. The news had flashed along the streets and into our houses at lightning speed, and there were thirty or more of us in the inn by the time the lukewarm night had settled on the roofs of the village. For all that, our curiosity remained unsatisfied, because the *Anderer* went up to his room and stayed there. Downstairs the discussion was vigorous, as was the consumption of beverages. Schloss did not have enough hands to keep up with all the drinkers. He must have said to himself that the arrival of a traveller was, when all was said and done, a good thing. He did as much business on that day as he would have when there were fairs or funerals. Menigue Wirfrau could not stop describing the arrival of the

Anderer – his outfit, his horse and his donkey – and after a while, since everyone stood him a drink to loosen his tongue, he began to embellish his account, stumbling on every word.

But every now and then we could hear footsteps upstairs, and the room would fall silent while everyone held his breath. Our eyes were fixed intently on the ceiling, as if in an effort to pass through it. We imagined the visitor. We gave him form and flesh. We were trying to enter into the labyrinth of his brain when some of us had not even set eyes on him yet.

At one point Schloss went upstairs to ask him if everything was alright. We tried to overhear their conversation, but in vain; even those who leaned their big ears into the stairwell caught nothing. When Schloss came back down, he was immediately surrounded.

"Well?"

"Well what?"

"What did he say?"

"He said he wanted a 'collation'."

"A 'collation'? What's that?"

"A light meal, he said."

"What are you going to do?"

"What he's asked me to do!"

Everyone was curious to see what a "collation" looked like. Most of the crowd followed Schloss into his kitchen and watched as he prepared a large tray on which he put three thick slices of bacon, a sausage, some marinated gherkins, a bowl of cooked cream pudding, a loaf of brown bread, some sweet and sour cabbage and a large piece of goat's cheese, together with a jug of wine and a mug of beer. As he passed through the crowd of his customers, he carried the tray reverently, and everyone made way for him in silence, as though for the passage of a holy relic.

Then Wirfrau's voice broke the spell: he was still describing the *Anderer*'s arrival at the inn. No-one was listening to him any more, but because of the state he was in, this escaped his notice. Similarly, a short while later, he failed to observe that he had confused his kneading-trough with his bed; after preparing his dough in the latter, he went to sleep in the former. The following day brought him a raging hangover, and we had a day without bread.

When I returned home, Fédorine was waiting for me: "What is going on, Brodeck?"

I told her what I had learned. She listened to me attentively, shaking her head. "That's not good. None of it. Not good."

They were just a few simple words, but they irritated me, and I asked her curtly why she had said them.

"When the flock has finally settled down, it must not be given any reason to start moving again," she replied.

I shrugged. I was in a light-hearted mood. I was – I have thought about this until today – I was probably the only person in the village who welcomed the arrival of a stranger. I considered it a sign of rebirth, a return to life. For me, it was as though an iron door that for years had sealed the entrance to a cave had now been opened wide, and the air of that cave had suddenly taken in the wind and the beams of a bright sun. But I could not imagine that sometimes the sun grows bothersome, that its beams, which light up the world, inadvertently illuminate what people are trying to hide.

Old Fédorine knew me like a pocket she had put her hand into several thousand times. She planted herself in front of me, looked me straight in the eye and stroked my cheek with one trembling hand. "I am very old, my little Brodeck, so very old," she said. "I won't be around for much longer. You must be careful. You have already come back once from a place people don't come back from. There is never a second chance. Never. And don't forget that you have other souls in your charge. Think about them, both of them . . ."

I am not very tall, but only then did I grasp how small Fédorine was. She looked like a child, a child with an old man's face; a bent, wizened, thin, fragile creature with crumpled, wrinkled skin, a creature a puff of air could have swept away like a drift of dust. Her eyes shone despite the milky cloud obscuring them, and her lips moved. I took her in my arms and pressed her against me for a long time, and I thought of birds, little lost birds, weak, sick or disconsolate sparrows that cannot keep up with their fellows in the great migrations; towards the end of autumn you can see them, with their feathers drooping and with panic in their hearts, perching on roofs or in the lower branches of trees, waiting resigned for the cold that will kill them.

I gave Fédorine several kisses, first on her hair, then on her forehead and cheeks as I did when I was a child, and I recognized her smell, a smell of wax, of stoves, of clean cloth, the smell that has sufficed, almost since my life began, to bring a peaceful smile to my lips, even in my sleep. I held her against me like that for a long time while scenes from the past flashed through my mind at lightning speed. My memory juxtaposed disparate instances, creating a bizarre mosaic whose only effect was to make me more aware of times that had fled away for ever, moments that would never return.

Fédorine was there; I clasped her to me and I could talk to her. I inhaled her smell; I felt her beating heart. It was as if mine were beating in her body. Again I remembered the camp. The only thoughts that occupied our minds there were of death. We lived in perpetual consciousness of our death, and this was, no doubt, the reason why some of us went mad. Even though every man knows he will die one day, he cannot live for long in a world that offers him nothing but the consciousness of his own death, a world pervaded by death and conceived solely for that purpose.

"Ich bin nichts" read the placard worn by the hanged man. We were well aware that we were nothing. We knew it all too well. Each of us was a nothing. A nothing handed over to death. Its slave. Its toy. Waiting and resigned. Oddly enough, although I was a creature of nothingness, inhabiting and inhabited by nothingness, this fact never succeeded in frightening me. I did not fear my own death, or if I feared it, it was with a sort of fleeting, animal reflex. By contrast, the thought of death became unbearable when I associated it with Emélia and Fédorine. It is the death of others, of loved ones, not our own, which eats away at us and can destroy us. And that is what I have had to struggle against, with their faces and features defying its black light.

22

At the beginning, our village welcomed the *Anderer* as if he were some kind of monarch. Indeed, there was something like magic in the whole affair. People around these parts are not open by nature. That can no doubt be explained, at least to some extent, by our landscape of valleys and mountains, of dense forests and hemmed-in vales, and our climate of rains and mists, of frosts and snowstorms and unbearable hot spells. And then, of course, there was the war, which did not improve matters. Doors and hearts were closed even more firmly and padlocks were carefully affixed, concealing what was within from the light of day.

But at first, as soon as the extraordinary surprise of his coming among us had passed, the *Anderer* succeeded, however involuntarily, in radiating a charm with the power to cajole even those who had been the least welcoming. Everyone wanted to see him – children, women and old folk included – and he happily entered into the spirit of the game, smiling at one and all, lifting his hat to the ladies and inclining his head to the men. However, he never spoke a word, and if there had not been people who had heard him speak on the day he arrived, we might have thought him a mute.

He could not walk in the streets without being followed by a small band of laughing, idle children to whom he gave small gifts that seemed to them treasures: ribbons, glass marbles, lengths of gilded string, sheets of coloured paper. He pulled all these out of his pockets, as if they were forever full of such things; one might have believed there was nothing else in his baggage.

When he went into Pére Solzner's stable to visit his two mounts, children came and watched him from the door, not daring to enter, nor did he invite them to do so. He greeted his horse and his donkey by name, always addressing them formally, stroking their coats and slipping lumps of yellow sugar (which he took from a little garnet-coloured velvet bag) between their grey lips. The children watched the spectacle with open mouths and staring eyes, wondering which language it was that he used when he murmured into the animals' ears.

To tell the truth, he spoke more to his horse and his donkey than he did to us. Schloss had received instructions to knock on his guest's door at six o'clock every morning, but not to enter the room, and to place the tray on the floor outside the door. There were always the same items arranged on the tray: a round brioche – for which the *Anderer* paid Wirfrau in advance – a raw egg, a pot of hot water and a large bowl.

"He can't be drinking hot water with nothing in it!" The man who uttered this cry of disbelief one evening was Rudolf Scheuling, who had drunk no liquid other than *schnick* since he was twelve years old. In fact what the *Anderer* drank was tea, strong tea that left large brown stains on the rims of cups. I tasted that tea once when he invited me to his room to chat for a while and to show me some books. It left a taste of leather and smoke in my mouth, along with a hint of salt meat. I had never drunk anything like it.

For lunch he went down to the large room at the inn. There were always a few curious people who had come along just to look at him, and especially to observe his manners, his refined table manners: the distinguished way in which he held his fork and knife, of sliding his knife into the breast of a chicken or the flesh of a potato.

In the very beginning, Schloss made a real effort to search his memory for recipes worthy of the visitor, but he soon gave up at the request of the *Anderer* himself. Despite his rotund figure and his red cheeks, he ate almost nothing. His plate was never empty at the end of a meal; half the food was untouched. By contrast, he drank one large glass of water after another, as if permanently afflicted by a raging thirst. This conduct moved Marcus Graz, a beanpole as lean as a stray dog, to remark that it was a blessing that the *Anderer* did not piss in the Staubi, as he would have surely caused it to overflow its banks.

In the evening he would take only a bowl of soup, and even then it was light fare – more a broth than a soup – and after that he would bow to whoever was at the inn and go upstairs to his room. The light in his window shone late into the night. Some even said they had seen it all night long. In any case, people wondered what he could be doing up there.

Early on in his time among us, he spent a good part of each afternoon walking through the streets of the village, methodically, as if he were drawing up a grid or carrying out a survey. No-one really noticed, because to see what he was doing you would have had to follow him all the time, and only the children did that.

Dressed like something out of a dusty old fable full of obsolete words, he would trudge along, slightly slew-footed, with his left hand on a handsome cane with an ivory pommel and his right clutching the little black notebook which came and went beneath his fingers like some peculiar tamed animal.

Sometimes he took one of his animals out for a breath of air. He chose either the horse or the donkey, never both at the same time, and he would lead whichever it was by its bridle, patting its sides as they walked down to the banks of the Staubi, a little upriver from the Baptisterbrücke, where the grass was fresh and thick and the grazing good. He himself would set his large backside on the riverbank and remain quite still, watching the current and the bright eddies as if he expected a miracle to rise up out of them. The children would stop some distance behind him, a little higher up on the slope. They all respected his silence, and not one of them threw a stone into the water.

The first event took place two weeks after the *Anderer*'s arrival in our village. I think it was the Mayor's idea, even though I could not swear it. I have never asked him, because it is not important. What *is* important is what happened that evening, the evening of 10 June.

By then everyone in the village was aware that the *Anderer* was only a transient presence within our walls, but it also seemed clear that he was preparing for an extended sojourn. During the day of 10 June news spread that the village, led by the Mayor, was going to welcome its visitor in a fitting manner. There would be a speech, some music and even a *Schoppessenwass*, which is the dialect word for a kind of large table

139

laden with glasses, bottles and food, traditionally set up on certain popular occasions.

Zungfrost had been at work since before dawn, building a small platform (which looked rather more like a scaffold, to tell the truth) near the covered market. His hammer blows and his screeching saw could be heard even before the sun had started to gnaw away at the blackness of the night; the sound dragged many an onlooker from his bed. By eight o'clock everyone had heard the news. By ten, there were more people in the streets than on a market day. In the afternoon, *Zungfrost* began to paint some large, shaky letters on a wide paper banner that hung above the platform. They turned out to be an expression of welcome: *"Wi sund vroh wen neu kamme*, an odd formulation which had issued from Diodème's brain. As *Zungfrost* was finishing his job, two pedlars, alerted to the opportunity in some unfathomable way, arrived and began to offer the villagers who had gathered around the market holy trinkets, rat poison, knives, skeins of thread, almanacs, seeds, pictures and felt hats. I knew the pedlars, having often encountered them on mountain roads or forest paths. The two were father and son, both dirty as earthworms and with hair as black as ink. People called them *De Runhgäre*, "the Runners", because they were capable of covering considerable distances in a very few hours. The father greeted me. I asked him, "Who told you there was a celebration today?"

"The wind."

"The wind?"

"The wind can tell you a great deal if you know how to listen."

He looked at me mischievously as he rolled himself a cigarette. "Have you been back to S.?"

"I don't have authorization. The road's still closed."

"So what do you live on? The wind?"

"No, not the wind. The night. When you know it well, the night's a fairy cape. All you have to do is put it on and you can go wherever you want!"

He burst out laughing, and his laughter exposed his four remaining teeth, planted in his jawbone like the memories of trees on a desolate hill. A little way off, Diodème was absorbed in watching *Zungfrost*, who was putting the finishing touches to his letters. Diodème gave me a small wave, but only later, when we were side by side and the ceremony was about to begin, did I ask him the question that had been troubling me a little: "Was it you who had the idea?"

"What idea?"

"The sentence on the banner."

"Orschwir told me to."

"Told you to what?"

"To come up with something, some words . . ."

"Your sentence is pretty odd. Why didn't you write it in *Deeperschaft*?"

"Orschwir didn't want me to."

"Why not?"

"I don't know."

Right then and there I did not know either, but later I had a chance to reflect. The *Anderer* was a mystery. Nobody knew who he was. Nobody knew where he came from or why he was here. And nobody knew whether he understood them when they spoke in dialect. The sentence painted on the banner was perhaps an attempt to discover the answer to this last question. An extremely naïve attempt to be sure, and in any case it failed in its purpose, for that evening, when the *Anderer* passed the platform and saw the inscription, he paused briefly, ran his eyes over the words, and then continued on his way. Did he understand what he read there? No-one knows; he never mentioned it.

Although it is possible that Diodème had not intended to be ambiguous, the slogan he came up with sounded odd. It means – or rather, it *can* mean – different things, because our dialect is like a springy fabric: it can be stretched in every direction.

"Wi sund vroh wen neu kamme" can mean "We are happy when a new person arrives." But it can also mean "We are happy when something new comes along," which is not the same thing at all. Strangest of all, the word *vroh* has two meanings, depending on the context: it can be equivalent to "glad" or "happy", but it can also mean "wary" or "watchful", and if you favour this second sense, then you find yourself faced with a bizarre, disquieting statement which nobody perceived at the time, but which has not stopped resounding in my head ever since; a kind of warning pregnant with small threats; a greeting like a knife brandished in a fist, the blade twisting a little and glinting in the sun.

23

In the afternoon of that same day, I took Emélia and Poupchette along with me. We climbed all the way to Lutz's cabin. It was formerly a shepherd's refuge, but it has not been used for two decades. The surrounding pastures have gradually been overgrown with rushes and meadow buttercups, and the grass has retreated before the advancing moss. Some ponds have appeared; at first they were merely puddles, but now they have transformed the place into a kind of ghost, the ghost of a meadow not yet completely metamorphosed into a marsh. I had already written three reports in an effort to understand and explain this transformation, and each year around the same time I returned to the spot to measure the extent and nature of the changes. The cabin is west of the village, about a two-hour walk away. The path leading to it is no longer as clearly defined as it once was, when the tread of hundreds of pairs of clogs gave it renewed depth and form each year. Paths are like men; they die too. Little by little they get cluttered and then overwhelmed; they break up, they are eaten by grass, and in the end they disappear. When only a few years have passed all that remains is a dim outline, and most people eventually forget that the path ever existed.

Poupchette was riding on my shoulders, chattering to the clouds. She spoke to them as if they could understand her. She told them to get a move on, to suck in their big bellies, and to leave the sun alone in the wide sky. The air coming down off the mountains gave a fresh pinkness to her cheeks.

I was holding Emélia's hand. She was walking along beside me at a good pace. Sometimes her eyes were turned to the ground and sometimes they stared off towards the far horizon, which was serrated by the jagged peaks of the Prinzhörni. But I could tell that her gaze never really came to rest on her surroundings, whether near or far. Her eyes seemed like butterflies, wondrous moving objects flitting here and there for no apparent reason, as though blown by the wind, by the transparent air, but with no thought as to what they were doing or what they saw. She marched on in silence. No doubt the quickened rhythm of her breathing prevented her from humming her eternal song. Her lips were slightly parted. I clutched her hand and felt her warmth, but she noticed nothing. Perhaps she no longer knew how much the person at her side loved her.

When we reached the cabin, I sat Emélia down on the stone bench by the door with Poupchette next to her. I told Poupchette to be good while I made my rounds and recorded my findings. I assured her I would not be long, and I promised that after I had finished we would sit there and eat up the *Pressfrütekof* and the apple and walnut cake that Fédorine had wrapped for us in a big white cloth.

I began to make my measurements. I soon found the landmarks on which I based my findings each year, namely various large stones that had once enclosed the sheepfold and marked property boundaries. By contrast, I had some trouble locating the sandstone trough that stood almost exactly in the centre of the pasture. The trough was carved from a single block, and when I saw it for the first time as a child, it had seemed to me like some kind of vessel abandoned there on solid ground, a ship made by the gods and now an encumbrance to men, who were neither clever enough to make use of it nor strong enough to move it.

Eventually I found the trough in the middle of a big pond whose surface area, curiously enough, had tripled in the course of a year. The mass of stone was completely submerged and almost hidden from sight. Glimpsed through the transparent prism of the water, the trough no longer put me in mind of a vessel, but rather of a tomb. It looked like a primitive, heavy coffin long since emptied of any occupant, or perhaps – and this thought sent a shiver down my spine – awaiting the man or woman destined to lie in it for ever.

I jerked my eyes away and looked for the silhouettes of Poupchette and Emélia in the distance, but all I could see were the crumbling cabin walls. My girls were on the other side, invisible, vanished. I left my measuring instruments on the edge of the pond and ran like a madman back to the cabin, calling out their names, seized by a deep, violent, irrational fear. The cabin was not far away, but I felt as though I would never reach it. My feet kept slipping on the slick earth. I sank into soggy holes and quagmires, and the soft, wet ground, which made sounds like the groans of the dying, seemed determined to suck me in. When I finally got to the cabin, I was exhausted and out of breath. My hands, my trousers and my hobnailed boots were covered with black mud that reeked of beechnuts and waterlogged grass. I could not even shout out their names any more, even though I had run so hard to reach them. And then I saw a small hand appear around a corner of the wall, reach for a buttercup, pick it off its stem, and move on to another flower. My fear disappeared as swiftly as it had overcome me. Poupchette's face came into sight. She looked at me. I could read the astonishment in her eyes. "Dirty Papa! All dirty, Papa!" She began to laugh, and I laughed too. I laughed very hard, very, very hard. I wanted everyone and everything to hear my laughter: all the people in the world who wished to reduce me to an ashen silence, and all the things in the world that conspired to swallow me up.

Poupchette was proudly holding the bouquet of buttercups, daisies and forget-me-nots she had gathered for her mother. The flowers were still quivering with life, as if they had not noticed that they had just passed the gates of death.

Emélia had strayed from the cabin, walked to the edge of the pasture and stopped on a sort of promontory, beyond which the slope splits and shatters into broken rocks. Her face was turned towards the vast landscape of plains spreading out beyond the border, an indistinct expanse that seemed to doze beneath wisps of fog. Emélia was holding her arms away from her body, as though she were preparing to take flight, and her slender silhouette stood out against the distant, pale, blueish background with a grace that was almost inhuman. Poupchette ran to her mother and flung herself against her thighs, trying in vain to get her short arms around them.

Emélia had not moved. The wind had undone her hair, which streamed in the wind like a cold, brown flame. I approached her with slow steps. The wind carried her perfume towards me, as well as snatches of her song which she had started humming again. Poupchette jumped up and managed to grab one of her arms. She pressed the flowers into her mother's hand. Emélia made no effort to hold on to the bouquet; her fingers remained open, and one by one the flowers blew away. Poupchette dashed about right and left trying to catch them, while I kept moving very slowly towards Emélia. Her body, outlined against the sky, seemed to be suspended in it.

Schöner Prinz so lieb / Handsome prince so dear

Zu weit fortgegangen / Gone too far away

Schöner Prinz so lieb / Handsome prince so dear

Nacht um Nacht ohn' Eure Lippen / Night after night without your lips

Schöner Prinz so lieb / Handsome prince so dear

Tag um Tag ohn' Euch zu erblicken / Day after day without seeing you

Schöner Prinz so lieb / Handsome prince so dear

Träumt Ihr was ich träume / Do you dream what I dream

Schöner Prinz so lieb / Handsome prince so dear

Ihr mit mir immerdar zusammen / You and me, together for ever

Emélia was dancing in my arms. We were with other couples under the bare trees of January, drunk on youth in the golden, misty light of the lanterns in the park, gliding along to music from the little orchestra that played beneath the pavilion. The musicians, bundled up in fur clothing, looked like strange animals. It was the instant before our first kiss, preceded and brought on by a few moments of vertigo. It was in another time. It was before the turmoil. That song was playing, the song of our first kiss, a song in the old language that had passed through the centuries as a traveller crosses frontiers. In dialect it is called "*Schon ofza prinzer, Gehtes so muchte lan*", a love song blended with bitter words, a song of legend, the song of an evening and a lifetime. Now it is the dreadful refrain inside which Emélia has locked herself up as if inside a prison, and where she lives without really existing.

I held her tight against me. I kissed her hair, the nape of her neck. I whispered in her ear that I loved her, that I would always love her, that I was there for her, close to her, all around her. I took her face in my hands, I turned it towards me and then, as the tears ran down her cheeks, I saw in her eyes something like the smile of a person far, far away.

24

Making our way back into the village, we were caught up in the excitement of that particular day, 10 June. On the square, men and women were beginning to form up; congregating in this group and then another, becoming a crowd.

For a long time now I have kept away from crowds. I avoid them. I know that everything – or almost everything – has stemmed from them. I mean the bad things, the war and all the *Kazerskwirs* it opened up in the brains of so many. I have seen how men act when they know they are not alone, when they know they can melt into a crowd and be absorbed into a mass that encompasses and transcends them, a mass comprising thousands of faces fashioned like theirs. They can tell themselves that the fault lies with whoever trains them, exhorts them, makes them dance like a slowworm around a stick, and that crowds are unconscious of their acts, of their future, of their course. This is all false. The truth is that the crowd itself is a monster. It begets itself, an enormous body composed of thousands of other conscious bodies. Furthermore, I know that there are no happy crowds. There are no peaceful crowds either. Even when there is laughter, smiling, music, choruses, behind all that there is blood: vexed, overheated, inflamed blood, stirred and maddened in its own vortex.

Indications of what was to come were evident a long time ago when I was in the Capital, where I had been sent to complete my studies. My going there was Limmat's idea. He shared it with the Mayor at the time, Sibelius Craspach, as well as with Father Peiper. All three agreed that the village needed at least one of its young people to advance his education beyond the rest, to go out and see a bit of the world before returning home to become a schoolmaster, a health practitioner, or perhaps a successor to Lawyer Knopf whose powers were beginning to fail; his legal work and his advice had of late astounded more than one client. And they had chosen me.

In a way you could say it was the entire village that sent me to the Capital. Limmat, Craspach and Father Peiper may have had the idea, but just about everybody pitched in and supported me. At the end of each month *Zungfrost* would make a collection, going from door to door, ringing a little bell and repeating the words: *"Fu Brodeck's Erfosch! Fu Brodeck's Erfosch!"* – "For Brodeck's studies! For Brodeck's studies!" Everyone gave according to his means and inclination. The donation might be a few gold pieces, but it could also be a woollen overcoat, a cap, a handkerchief, a jar of preserves, a small bag of lentils or some provisions for Fédorine, because while I was in the Capital I could not do any work to help her. So I would receive little money orders along with some strange parcels. My landlady, Fra Haiternitz, panting from having climbed the six flights of stairs to my room, would hand me these with a suspicious look, all the while chewing a wad of black tobacco which stained her lips and turned her breath into the fumes of Hell.

In the beginning, the Capital gave me a headache. I had never in my life heard such noise. The streets were like furious mountain torrents, ferrying along an intermingled throng of people and vehicles amid a racket that made me dizzy and often drove me to flatten myself against a wall to avoid being swept away by the uninterrupted flood. I lived in a room whose rusty window would not open more than an inch. There was hardly room for anything except my straw mattress, which I folded up every morning. A board placed on top of the folded mattress served as my desk. Apart from some luminous days in high summer or in the dead of winter, the city was permanently imprisoned beneath a fog of coal smoke which issued from the chimneys in lazy clouds that wrapped themselves around one another and then hung in the air for days and nights, deflecting the sun far beyond us. My first days of city life seemed unbearable. I never stopped thinking about our village, nestled in the valley's conifer forest as in a lap. I even remember crying as I lay in bed.

The University was a large baroque building which, three centuries earlier, had been the palace of a Magyar prince. Looted and wrecked during the revolutionary period, it was then sold to a prosperous grain merchant who converted it into a warehouse. In 1831, when the great cholera epidemic raged throughout the country like a dog tracking debilitated prey, the warehouse was requisitioned and served as a public hospital. Some people were treated there. Many died there. Much later, towards the end of the century, at the instigation of the Emperor the place was turned into a university. The wards were cleaned and furnished with benches and rostrums. The morgue became the library and the dissecting room a sort of lounge, where the professors and those students who were from influential families could sit in large armchairs of tawny leather, smoking their pipes, conversing and reading newspapers.

Most of the students came from middle-class families. They had pink cheeks, slender hands and clean fingernails. All their lives they had eaten their fill and worn good clothes. There were only a few of us who were virtually penniless. We could be spotted right away, identified by the scoured look the mountain air had given our faces, by our clothes, by our gauche manners, by our obvious and enduring fear of being in the wrong place. We had come from far away. We were not from the city or even from the countryside around it. We slept in badly heated attic rooms. We never, or very rarely, went home. Those who had families and money paid us little attention. But for all that, I do not believe they were contemptuous of us. They simply could not imagine who we were, or where we came from, or the desolate, magnificent landscapes we had grown up in, or what was our day-to-day existence in the great city. They often walked past us without even seeing us.

After several weeks I stopped being frightened of the city. I became unaware of its monstrous, hostile aspect and saw only its ugliness. And it was easy for me to forget that for hours on end because I loved plunging myself into my studies, into books. To tell the truth I hardly ever left the library, except to go to the lecture halls where the professors gave their classes. I found a companion in the person of Ulli Rätte, who was the same age and had likewise been more or less dispatched to the University by his village in the hope of his returning with an education that would contribute to the greater good. Rätte came from a far corner of the country, the border region around the Galinek hills, and he spoke a rasping language full of expressions I did not know. In the eyes of many of our fellow students, Rätte's strange tongue proved him either an eccentric or a savage. When we were not in the University library, in class or in our rooms, we would walk together through the streets, talking about our dreams and our future lives.

Ulli had a passion for cafés but not enough money to frequent them. He often dragged me along just to contemplate them, and the mere sight of those places – where blue gas and wax candles burned, where women's laughter rose to the ceiling amid clouds of cigar and pipe smoke, where the men wore elegant suits, fur coats during the winter months and silk scarves when the weather was fine, where waiters impeccably girdled into white aprons seemed to us like soldiers of an inoffensive army – sufficed to fill him with a childlike joy. "We're wasting our time on books, Brodeck," he would say. "This is where the real life is!"

Unlike me, Ulli took to the city like a fish to water. He knew every street and all the tricks. He loved the dust of the city, its noise, its soot, its violence, its vastness. He liked everything about it.

"I don't think I'll go back to my village," he often told me. It was no use my pointing out that his village was the reason why he was there or reminding him that it was counting on him; he brushed aside all that with a word or a backhanded wave. "A bunch of brutes and drunkards – that's all there is where I come from. You think they sent me here out of charity? They're motivated by self-interest, nothing else! They want me to return home stuffed with knowledge, like a force-fed animal, and then they'll make me pay for it for the rest of my life. Don't forget that. It's ignorance that triumphs always, Brodeck: not knowledge."

151

Although cafés occupied his thoughts more than University class-rooms, Ulli Rätte was far from stupid. Some of the things he said deserved to be printed in books, but he tossed them off as though they were of no importance, as though he were making fun of them and himself as soon as he said them; and then he would burst out laughing. His laugh was half bellow and half melody, and passers-by never failed to turn their heads when they heard it.

25

That conflict between knowledge and ignorance, between solitude and multitude – that is what made me leave the city before I had completed my studies. The great, sprawling urban organism was suddenly shaken by gossip, by rumours that had sprung from nothing: two or three conversations, an unsigned article a few lines long in a daily newspaper, the patter of a busker in the market-place, a song of unknown origin whose ferocious refrain was taken up in the twinkling of an eye by every street singer.

More and more often one ran into public gatherings. A few men would stop under a streetlight and speak among themselves; soon they would be joined by others, and by others after that. In a few minutes, the group would have swelled to forty – forty bodies pressed together, their shoulders a little hunched, moving about from time to time or assenting crisply to a point made by one of the speakers, though exactly which one was never clear. Then, as if blown away by a gust of wind, their silhouettes would in a moment disperse in all directions, and the empty pavement would begin its monotonous waiting once more.

Remarkable and contradictory news reached the Capital from the eastern frontier. On the other side of the border, it was said, entire garrisons were on the march, surreptitiously and by night, and witnesses reported troop movements of a scope hitherto unknown. It was also said that people on this side could hear machines at work over there digging ditches, tunnels, trenches and secret works. It was even said that recently perfected weapons of diabolical power and range were being prepared for deployment, and that the Capital was full of spies, waiting to set it ablaze when the time came. Meanwhile, hunger was tormenting citizens' bellies and ruling their minds. The oven-like heat of the two preceding summers had grilled the vast majority of the crops that grew in the fields surrounding the city. Every day, emaciated bands of farmers and their families flocked to the Capital; their bewildered eyes settled on everything they saw, as if they were about to steal it. Drab little children with yellowish complexions clung to their mother's skirts. Barely able to remain upright, youngsters would often fall asleep on their feet, leaning against a wall, and many a mother who could go on no longer sat on the ground with a sleeping child lying across her lap.

At this same time Professor Nösel would be talking to us about our great poets. Centuries and centuries ago, when the Capital was yet nothing more than a big market town, when our forests were full of bears and wolf packs, aurochs and bison, when hordes of tribesmen from the distant steppes were spreading fire and terror, these men fashioned the countless verses of our fundamental epic poems. Nösel could read Ancient Greek, Latin, Cimbrian, Arabic, Aramaic, Uzbek, Kazakh and Russian, but he was incapable of looking out of his window, or of lifting his nose from his reading as he walked home to his apartment in rue Jeckenweiss. He was a man most learned in books, and yet blind to the world.

Then the first demonstration took place. One day, after waiting in vain for someone to hire them, about a hundred men, most of them farmers who had lost everything and unemployed workers, left the Albergeplatz market, where those looking for day labour usually gathered. Walking at some speed and shouting, they made for the Parliament. Outside the building they came up against the soldiers on duty, who managed to disperse them without violence. The demonstrators passed Ulli and myself on our way to the University. They formed a somewhat noisy procession, nothing more, like students parading to celebrate their diplomas, except that the taut, ashen faces and the eyes glittering with dull resentment were not those of students.

"They'll get over it soon enough!" Ulli mocked. He grabbed me by the arm to haul me along to a new café he had discovered the previous evening which he wanted to show me. From time to time as we walked, I turned to catch a glimpse of those men disappearing down the street, like the tail of a giant serpent whose invisible head had grown larger still in my imagination.

The phenomenon repeated itself the following day and for six days after that; the only difference was that each time the marchers were more numerous and their grumbling louder. Women, perhaps their wives, joined the ranks of the farmers and workers, along with some protesters who came out of nowhere and had never been seen before. They looked like herdsmen or shepherds, except that they wielded neither sticks nor staffs for driving animals, only shouts and words. Soon there was daily bloodshed when the soldiers positioned outside the Parliament building laid into a few skulls with the flats of their swords. Newspaper headlines began to appear about the growing numbers of demonstrators, but the government remained strangely mute. On a Friday evening eight days after the demonstrations began, a soldier was seriously injured when someone threw a cobblestone. A few hours later the entire city was placarded with an announcement declaring that all gatherings were forbidden until further notice and that any demonstrations would be put dowm with the uttermost firmness.

This volatile mixture was ignited at dawn the following day, when the swollen body of Wighert Ruppach was found near the church of the Ysertinguës. An unemployed typographer known for his revolutionary opinions, he was said to have had a hand in instigating the very first demonstrations. It was true that many people had spotted his bearded, half-moon face at the head of the mob and heard his baritone voice shouting for bread and work. The police quickly established that he had been clubbed to death, and that he had been last seen in one of the numerous low dives that served black wine and moonshine in the slaughterhouse district, where he was emerging half-drunk and walking with difficulty. Robbed of his papers, his watch and every penny in his pocket, Ruppach had doubtless been the victim of one of his drinking companions, or of some criminal whose path he had crossed – or so went the explanation given by the police. But the city, which was beginning to show signs of fever, responded to the official story with growls and threats. Within a few hours Ruppach achieved the status of a martyr, the victim of a senile governing power which could not feed its children or protect them from the foreign menace that swelled with impunity along its borders. In Ruppach's death, people thought they recognized a foreigner's hand, or the hand of a traitor. By that point, the truth mattered little. Few citizens were disposed to hear it. Over the course of the previous week, the majority had stuffed their heads with plenty of powder, they had plaited a lovely fuse, and now they had their spark.

Everything exploded on the Monday, after a Sunday which most citizens had dedicated to fleeing the city. It seemed deserted, abandoned, emptied by a strange and sudden epidemic. Emélia and I had gone for a walk on Sunday evening, pretending not to notice that everything around us pointed to an imminent event of an unprecedented kind.

We had known each other for five weeks. I was entering another world. I had suddenly discovered that both the earth and my life could move to rhythms different from those I had previously known, and that the soft, regular sound of a beloved's breathing is the sweetest you will ever hear. We always walked the same streets and passed the same places. Somehow, without meaning to, we had marked out a pilgrimage that traced the first days of our love. Our walk led past Théâtre Stüpispiel, then down Avenue Under-de-Bogel to the promenade Elsi, the music pavilion, the skating rink. Emélia asked me to tell her about my studies, about the books I was reading, about the country I came from. "I would very much like to know it," she said.

She had been in the Capital for a year, having arrived with no treasure but her two hands, which knew how to do delicate embroidery, sew complicated stitches and make lace as fragile as threads of frost. One evening, when I inquired about her family and the place she had come from, she told me, "Everything behind me is darkness. Nothing but darkness," and what she said took me back to my own past, my distant childhood, to death, to houses destroyed, to crumbled walls, to smoking ruins – some of it I remember a little, and some things Fédorine has related to me. And so I began to love Emélia also as a sister, a fellow being risen from the same depths as my own, a fellow being who, like me, had no other choice but to keep her eyes fixed straight ahead.

On the Monday morning I attended Nösel's lecture in the Hall of

Medals. I have never understood why it has that name. It was a low-ceilinged, completely undecorated room whose waxed walls reflected a little of our blurred images. The topic of that day's class was the rhythmic structure of the first part of *Kant'z Theus*, the great national poem that has been passed down from generation to generation for almost a thousand years. Nösel was speaking without looking at us. I believe the truth is that he spoke mostly to himself when he lectured, carrying on an odd conversation for solo voice without much concern for our presence and even less for our opinions. As he expounded passionately upon pentasyllables and hexameters, he applied cream to his hair and moustache, filled his pipe, methodically scratched at little constellations of food particles on his jacket lapels and cleaned his fingernails with a pocket knife. Barely ten of us were paying attention to him; most of the others were dozing or examining the cracks in the ceiling. Nösel stood up, went over to the blackboard, and wrote two verses that are still in my memory because the old language of the poem resembles our dialect in so many ways:

> *Stu pekart in dei mümerie gesachetet*
> *Komm de Nebe un de Osterne vohin*

> They shall arrive in a murmur
> And shall disappear into fog and earth

At that moment, the door of the lecture room opened violently and slammed against the wall, making an enormous, reverberating din. We all snapped our heads around and saw bug-eyed faces, gesticulating arms, and mouths screaming at us: "Everybody outside! Everybody outside! Vengeance for Ruppach! The traitors will pay!" There were no more than four or five individuals in the doorway, students no doubt – their features seemed vaguely familiar – but we heard behind them the rumble of a considerable crowd, pushing and supporting those in the front line. Then they disappeared as suddenly as they had come, leaving the door open like the hole in a stone sink, and almost all the students in the room, who a few seconds earlier had been seated all around me, were sucked out through that hole as though by some imperious physical force. There was a great racket of overturned chairs and benches, shouts, insults, cries and then, suddenly, nothing. The wave had rolled on and was now getting further and further away, carrying with it brutality to spread through the city.

There were only five of us left in the Hall of Medals: Fritz Schoeffel, an obese fellow with very short arms who could not climb three steps without gasping for air; Julius Kakenegg, who never spoke to anyone and always breathed through a perfumed handkerchief; Barthéleo Mietza, who was as deaf as a post; me and, of course, Nösel himself, who had observed the entire scene with one hand raised, still holding the chalk. He mildly shrugged and went on with the class as if nothing had happened.

26

All of that strange day I spent within the walls of the University. I felt protected there. I did not want to leave. I heard dreadful sounds coming from outside, followed by great silences which dragged on and on, giving rise to an uneasiness as intense as that which was caused by the noise. I stayed in the library the whole afternoon. I knew Emélia was safe at her place, the furnished room she shared with another embroiderer named Gudrun Osterick, a ruddy-faced young woman with hair like sheep's wool. The previous evening I had promised them I would not venture out.

I do not remember much about the book I was trying to read during those bizarre hours in the library. It was the work of a physician, Docteur Klaus Reinhold Maria Messner, on the spread of the plague through the centuries. The book contained tables, charts and figures, as well as striking illustrations that contrasted with the scientific detachment of the inquiry, for they illuminated it with a sort of macabre and precious romanticism. One of the illustrations that I found particularly unsettling showed a narrow, poor, city street. The roadway was made up of uneven cobblestones, and the doors of all the houses were wide open. Dozens of fat and hirsute black rats ran from the houses, their features contorted, as three men dressed in long, dark robes, their heads hidden by peaked hoods, piled stiff corpses onto the bed of a handcart. In the distance, plumes of smoke streaked the horizon, while in the foreground, as if wishing to escape from the picture, a child in rags sat on the ground with his face in his hands. Curiously, none of the three men paid any attention to him, perhaps already considering him as good as dead. The only creature contemplating him was a rat. Standing on its hind legs, it seemed to be addressing a malicious, ironic question to the child's hidden face. I stared at the picture for a long time, wondering what its engraver's true purpose had been and why the author had wanted it reproduced in his book.

At around four o'clock, the daylight suddenly grew dim. Snow clouds had filled the sky and they began to dump their load on the city. I opened one of the library's windows. Big flakes stroked my cheeks and melted.

I saw silhouettes coming and going in the streets, walking at a normal pace; the city seemed to have regained its normal appearance. I collected my jacket and left the University. I did not know then that I would never set foot in it again.

To return to my room, I had to cross Place Salzwach, go down Avenue Sibelius-Vo-Recht, make my way through the Kolesh quarter – the oldest part of the city, a maze of narrow streets lined by innumerable shopfronts – skirt Parc Wilhem, and walk past the lugubrious buildings that housed the thermal baths. I stepped out briskly with my head down. I passed many shadows walking in the same way, and then a group of apparently drunk men who were talking loudly and laughing a lot.

In Place Salzwach and on Avenue Sibelius-Vo-Recht the snow was already beginning to settle, and the pedestrians left black tracks as they scurried along like insects. In these parts of the city one could have believed that nothing had happened, that the Capital had gone about a very ordinary Monday, and that the untimely emptiness of the streets was due to nothing more than the cold, the bad weather, and the night itself, which had fallen a little too early.

But to realize that none of that was true, one had only to enter the labyrinthine Kolesh quarter. What I noticed first was a sound. The sound of glass, of broken glass beneath my feet. I was on a narrow street littered with broken glass, and glinting shards, here and there half-buried by snow, covered the ground as far as my eyes could see. I could not help imagining that someone had scattered precious stones by the handful all through the Kolesh quarter. The thought gave the small street a new dimension, sparkling, marvellous, magical, like the setting of a fairytale; my task was to discover the plot and find the princess. But that first vision vanished as soon as my eyes focused on the shop windows that gaped like the jaws of dead animals, their looted interiors, the smashed barrels spilling out marinated herrings, dried meats, gherkins and wine, the befouled market stalls, the strewn merchandise. The sounds of groaning and weeping mingled with the crunch of footsteps on the glass carpet. I could not tell where the human sounds were coming from; there was not a living creature in sight. By contrast, three corpses, their heads grotesquely swollen and bruised from the blows they had received, were stretched out in front of a tailor's shop. Stuck on the door which was hanging from its frame by a single remaining hinge was a piece of paper with the words "*Schmutz Fremdër*", "dirty foreigner". (The word *Fremdër* is ambiguous, as it can also mean "traitor", or more colloquially, "gangrene", or "filth".) It was crudely written in red paint which had run on many of the letters, making them look as though they were dripping blood. Rolls of cloth had been piled up anyhow and someone had tried to set them on fire. Shards of glass were still attached to the window jambs, forming a star with incredibly slender, fragile rays.

That inscription, "*Schmutz Fremdër*", was to be seen in many places, usually accompanied by another: "*Rache für Ruppach*", "Revenge for Ruppach". My mind's eye kept returning to the three corpses. Dizziness overcame me, and the vision of those dead bodies called up confused images from my memory, images of other corpses sprawled out like puppets, with no trace of humanity left in their features. I became again the little boy who had wandered amid the ruins, abandoned among the debris and the rubble, surrounded by small fires, and not knowing whether he was the plaything of an unending nightmare or a victim of the times, which had decided to toy with him like a cat with a mouse. At the same time as those fragments of my past life appeared before me, I could also see every detail of the engraving in Docteur Messner's volume – the plumes of smoke, the countless rats, the child, the robed men, the heap of corpses – and it was as though this awful spectacle in the narrow street, the memories of my childhood, and the details of the illustration in Docteur Messner's book were superimposed on one another, and therefore triply horrible. I staggered and almost fell, but then I heard someone calling me; I heard a voice calling me, a weak, broken voice like the thousands of glass shards on the ground.

There was an old man crouched in a doorway a little further on. He was painfully thin, and his long white beard tugged his face downwards, making it look still thinner. He trembled as he stretched out an arm towards me. I hurried to his side, and while he kept repeating the same words – "Madmen. Madmen. They've gone mad. Madmen" – in the old language that was Fédorine's native tongue, I tried to help him to his feet.

"Where do you live?" I asked him. "Do you live on this street?"

His eyes looked into mine for a few seconds, but he did not seem to understand my questions and took up his litany again. His clothes were ripped in many places; his right hand was covered with blood and hung useless at his side. I put my arms around his waist to lift him, but I had scarcely managed to prop him against the door when voices erupted behind us.

"They're still moving! They're taunting us! They're on their feet, and our Ruppach is dead!"

Three men were coming towards us. They carried long clubs and I could make out two intertwined letters, "WR", on the black armbands they wore on their left sleeves. They were talking loudly and guffawing. The peaks of their caps cast a shadow over their features, but I thought I recognized one of the faces. Fear gripped me and my thoughts became confused. At first I thought they might be drunk, and yet they did not smell of alcohol. Anger and hatred are sufficient to scramble human brains, and they can do so even more thoroughly than *eau-de-vie*. Alas, I was able to verify this observation later on several occasions in the camp.

The old man kept up his droning. I do not think he had even noticed the presence of the other three. One of them placed the end of his club against the old man's chest and said, "You will repeat after me: 'I am a *Fremdër*, a worthless piece of shit!' Now! Say it!"

But the old man neither heard nor saw him. I said, "I don't think he understands you. He's hurt . . ."

The words had sprung unbidden to my lips, and I immediately regretted them. The stick moved to my chest.

"Did you say something? Did you dare to say something? Who are you, with that nasty mug? You stink like a *Fremdër* too!" And he struck me a blow on my side that knocked the wind out of me. At that moment one of his comrades, the one I had thought looked familiar, intervened and said, "No, I know him. His name is Brodeck."

He brought his face quite close to mine, and all of a sudden I recognized him. He was a third-year student who, like me, frequented the library. I did not know his name, but I remembered that he often consulted tomes on astronomy and spent a lot of time studying star charts.

"Brodeck, Brodeck," repeated the one who was apparently the leader. "That's a real *Fremdër* name! And look at this faggot's nose! The nose is what gives them away! And their big eyes popping out of their heads, so they can see everything, so they can take everything!" He kept shoving his club into my ribs as if I were a stubborn animal.

"Leave him alone, Felix! The old guy's the one we want. He's one of them, for sure, the old bastard, and that's his shop over there, I know it! He's a real crook! He gets rich off giving credit!"

The third member of the group, who had not yet spoken, now made himself heard: "He's mine! It's my turn! You've already bashed up two apiece!"

He had stayed in the shadows until then, but now he came rushing up and I could see that he was just a boy, a child in fact, maybe thirteen years old, hardly more. He had fresh, delicate skin, his teeth gleamed in the dark, and he was smiling like a lunatic.

"Well, how about that, tiny Ullrich wants a piece of the action! But you're too tender, little brother. The milk's still running out of your ears!"

The old man must have fallen asleep. His eyes were closed and he had stopped talking. The boy gave his older brother a furious shove, prodded me to one side with the end of his club, and stationed himself in front of the feeble mass crouched on the ground. There was a great silence. The night had become as thick as mud. A gust of wind swept through the narrow street, kicking up a bit of snow. Nobody moved. I must be dreaming, I thought, or maybe I am on the stage at Théâtre Stüpispiel, taking part in one of their many incomprehensibly grotesque and sometimes atrocious spectacles that always end in farce. But then the boy suddenly sprung into action. He raised his club above his head and brought it down on the old man with a yell. The victim did not cry out, but he opened his eyes wide and began to tremble, as if he had been flung into an icy river. The child struck him a second blow, this time on the forehead, then a third on a shoulder, then a fourth and a fifth . . . He did not stop, and he laughed as he swung his club. His comrades urged him on, clapping their hands and chanting "*Oy! Oy! Oy! Oy!*" to give him a rhythm. The old man's skull split open with a sharp sound like a hazelnut cracked between two stones. The child kept on striking, harder and harder, still laughing like a madman, but gradually,

164

even though his blows did not stop and he continued to laugh as he looked upon what was left of his victim, with his comrades still clapping time, his blood-spattered face changed. The horror of what he had just done seemed to penetrate his veins, spread out to his limbs, his muscles, his nerves, invade his brain, and wash away all its foulness. His blows slowed and then stopped. Horrified, he stared at his club, which was covered with blood and fragments of bone, and then at his hands, as if they did not belong to him. Then his eyes returned to the old man whose face was now unrecognizable, the closed eyelids hideously swollen, each as big as an apple.

The child dropped his club abruptly, as if it were burning his palm. He was seized by a sudden spasm and vomited a quantity of yellow liquid in two heaves; then he ran away, and the night absorbed him into its belly as his two comrades laughed uproariously. The leader, his brother, shouted after him: "Nice work, little Ullrich! The old guy got what he deserved! Now you're a man!"

He prodded the old man's corpse with one foot, then turned around and casually walked away, arm-in-arm with his comrade, whistling a little love song that was popular at the time.

I had not moved. It was the first time I had witnessed a murder. I felt empty. Empty of all thought. And my mouth was full of the bitterest bile. I could not take my eyes off the old man's body. His blood mingled with the snow. As soon as the large flakes touched the ground, they were tinged with red, like notched petals of an unknown flower. Once again, the sound of footsteps made me jump. Someone was approaching. I thought they had decided to come back and kill me too.

"Get the hell away, Brodeck!"

It was the voice of the student who spent hours gazing at constellations and galaxies reproduced on the pages of immense books. I raised my eyes to him. He was looking at me without hatred, but with a kind of contempt. He spoke calmly. "Get the hell away! I won't always be there to save you."

Then he spat on the ground, turned, and walked away.

27

The following day, rumour put the number of corpses recovered from the streets at sixty-seven. It was said that the police had made no effort to prevent criminal activity, even when it was in their power to do so. A new demonstration was scheduled to take place that very afternoon. The city was on the verge of going up in flames.

I rose at dawn after a sleepless night, during which my memory continually recalled the faces of the murderous child and his aged victim; and I heard again the boy's shouting, the old man's droning, the dull, thumping sound of the blows, and the sharper crack of breaking bones. I made a bundle of my few belongings, returned my room keys to the landlady, Fra Haiternitz, who accepted them without a word, and whose only response to my few words of farewell was a somewhat contemptuous, rotten-toothed smile. She was browning some onions and bacon in a skillet. Her cubbyhole was filled with greasy smoke that stung my eyes. She hung the key on a nail and then acted as though I no longer existed.

I walked quickly through the streets. There were few people about. Many areas still showed signs of the previous night's vandalism. Some men with frightened faces were talking among themselves, snapping their heads around at the slightest noise. The doors of several buildings were painted with the inscription *"Schmutz Fremdër"*, and in many places the road was still covered with a glass carpet which crunched under my feet and made me shiver.

In case I failed to find Ulli Rätte in his room, I had written him a goodbye letter, but the precaution was unnecessary. He was there, but he had got so drunk that he had fallen asleep with all his clothes on. He was still holding a half-full bottle in his hand, and he stank of tobacco, sweat, and cheap grain alcohol. The right sleeve of his jacket was torn and striped with a large stain. It was blood. I thought my friend might be wounded, but when I pulled up his sleeve I could see that he was unharmed. Suddenly I felt very cold. I did not want to think. I forced myself to stop thinking. Ulli slept on, open-mouthed and snoring loudly. I slipped my letter of farewell into his shirt pocket and left the room.

I never saw Ulli Rätte again.

Why did I just write that sentence when it is not the whole truth? I did see Ulli Rätte – or rather, I am pretty certain I saw him – once again. In the camp. On the other side. I mean, he was on the side of those who guarded us, not on our side, the side of suffering and sub-mission.

It was a frosty morning. I was Brodeck-the-Dog. Scheidegger, my master, was walking me. I was wearing the collar, and attached to the collar was the leash. I had to scramble about on all fours. I had to snort like a dog, eat like a dog, piss like a dog. Scheidegger strutted beside me, looking like a prim office worker. That day, we went all the way to the camp infirmary. Before going in, Scheidegger tied the leash to an iron ring embedded in the wall. I curled up in the dust, laid my head on my hands, and tried to forget the bitter cold.

That was when I thought I saw Ulli Rätte. When I did see Ulli Rätte. When I heard his laugh, his very particular laugh which sounded like a combination of high-pitched bells and rasping wooden rattles. He was standing with two other guards a few paces away, with his back turned to me. All three were trying to keep warm by pounding their hands together, and Ulli, or his phantom double, was saying, "Yes, I'm telling you, it's a little slice of paradise right here on earth, not one league from this shitty place. They've got a lovely stove that purrs and whistles, and they serve their beer cold, with a thick head of white foam. The waitress is as round as a ham, and not at all shy! You can sit there and smoke your pipe for hours, dreaming away, and forget all about the grubby vermin here that's ruining our lives!"

He finished his speech with a loud laugh, which was taken up by the others. Then he began to turn round, and I buried my face in my hands. It was not that I was afraid he would recognize me. No, it wasn't that. It was me. I did not want to see him. I did not want to meet his eye. What I wanted was to preserve, deep inside my mind, the illusion that this tall, stout man, so comfortable in his role as torturer, this man who was standing so close to me but who actually lived in a different world from mine, the world of the living, could be someone other than Ulli Rätte, my Ulli, with whom I had spent so much time in former days, with whom I had shared crusts of bread and dishes of potatoes, happy hours, dreams, and countless arm-in-arm promenades. I preferred doubt to the truth, even the thinnest, most fragile doubt. Yes, that is what I preferred, because I believed the truth might kill me.

Life is funny. I mean the currents of life that bear us along more than we follow them and then, after a strange journey, deposit us on the right bank or the left. I do not know how the student Ulli Rätte became a camp guard, one of those perfectly oiled and obedient cogs in the great

168

death machine we were being fed to. I do not know what trials he had endured or what changes he had been forced to undergo in order to fetch up where he was. The Ulli I had known would never have hurt a fly. How could he have become the servant of a system that crushed people, that reduced them to the lowest form of existence?

The only advantage of the camp was its vast size. I never saw the guard who could have been Ulli Rätte, or heard his laugh, again. Had that frozen morning scene been nothing but one of the many nightmares that visited me, and not a memory at all? Perhaps so, but that particular nightmare seemed very real indeed. So much so that on the day the camp was liberated, I wandered all over it, going from one mound of corpses to another. There were so many of them. The dead were mostly prisoners, but there were a few guards as well. I turned their bodies over one by one, thinking that maybe I would come upon Ulli, but he was not among them. I found only the remains of *Die Zeilenesseniss*. I contemplated them for a while as one might contemplate an abyss or the memory of unspeakable suffering.

On the morning that followed what later came to be called *Pürische Nacht*, after I had slipped my letter into the unconscious Ulli's pocket, I hurried to Emélia's. She was sitting calmly near the window of her room, absorbed in her embroidery. Her friend Gudrun Osterick was similarly occupied. They both looked at me in surprise. They had stayed inside for the past two days, just as I had asked them to, working steadily in order to finish an important commission on time, a large linen tablecloth destined for a bridal trousseau. Across the white background, Emélia and her friend had scattered hundreds of tiny lilies mingled with large stars, and when I saw those stars I felt my body go numb. Gudrun and Emélia said they had clearly heard the noises of the crowd, the shrieking and howling, but their neighbourhood was some distance from the Kolesh quarter, the scene of most of the murders and devastation. The two women knew nothing about the violence that had taken place.

I took Emélia in my arms and held her tight. I told her that I was going away, I was going away and never coming back. Above all, I told her that I had come for her, that I wanted to take her with me to my home, to my village in the mountains. It was another world there, I said, we would be protected from everything; that landscape of crests and pastures and forests would be for us the safest of bulwarks. And I told her I wanted her to be my wife.

I felt her shivering against me, and it was as though I held a trembling bird in my arms. Her tremors seemed to reach into the deepest part of my body and make it more vibrant and alive. She turned her beautiful face to me, smiled, and gave me a long kiss.

An hour later we left the city. We walked quickly, hand in hand. We were not alone. Men, women, children, old people, entire families were fleeing too, bringing with them a great deal of baggage. Some carried suitcases crammed to overflowing and impossible to close, exposing the linen and crockery they contained. Others pushed carts loaded with trunks and poorly tied bundles. Everyone looked serious, fearful, uncertain. Nobody spoke. We all marched along in great haste, as if compelled to put as much distance as possible between ourselves and what we were leaving behind.

But what was actually driving us away? Other men, or the course of events? I am still a young man, still in my prime, and yet, when I think about my life, it's like a bottle too small to hold everything that has been poured into it. Is this the case with every human life, or was I born into a time that has abolished all limits, that shuffles human lives like cards in a great game of chance?

For myself, I did not ask for much. I would have liked to remain in the village and never leave. The mountains, the forests, our rivers – all that would have been enough for me. I would have liked to stay far from the noise of the world, but people in these parts have killed one another in large numbers throughout history. Many nations have died and are now nothing but names in books. Some countries have devoured others, eviscerated them, violated them, defiled them. And that which is just has not always triumphed over that which is filthy.

Why did I, like thousands of others, have to carry a cross I had not chosen, a cross which was not made for my shoulders and which did not concern me? Who decided to come rummaging around in my obscure existence, invade my grey anonymity, my meagre tranquillity, and bowl me like a tiny ball in a great game of skittles? God? Well, in that case, if He exists, if He really exists, let Him hide His face. Let Him put His two hands on His head, and let Him bow down. It may be, as Peiper used to teach us, that many men are unworthy of Him, but now I know that He is unworthy of most of us, and that if a creature has been able to concoct horror, it is only because his Creator has suggested to him the recipe.

28

I have just read through my account from the beginning. I am not talking about the official Report; I mean this whole long confession. It lacks order. I go off in all directions. But I do not have to justify myself. The words come to my mind like iron filings to a magnet, and I shake them onto the page without worrying too much about what becomes of them. If my tale looks like some monstrous body, that is because it is made in the image of my life, which I have been unable to contain, which is going to rack and ruin.

On 10 June, the day of the *Schoppessenwass* in honour of the *Anderer*, everyone in the village and quite a few people from outside gathered in the market square and waited in front of the little platform *Zungfrost* had built. As I have said, it had been a long time since I had gazed upon such a dense concentration of humanity in so restricted a space. I saw only merry, laughing, peaceful folk, but I could not help thinking about the crowds I had seen back in the days when the Capital was seized by madness, just before *Pürische Nacht*, and with that thought in mind I perceived the tranquil countenances around me as masks that hid bloody faces, gaping mouths, demented eyes.

Viktor Heidekirch's accordion was playing every tune we knew, and in the warm, soft air of that late afternoon, various strong aromas – of fried food, of grilled sausages, of doughnuts, of waffles and *Wärmspeck* – mingled with the more delicate perfumes given off by the hay drying in the fields that surrounded the village. Poupchette inhaled them all with delight and clapped her hands at every old song that issued from Heidekirch's squeezebox. Emélia and Fédorine had stayed at home. The sun was in no hurry to disappear behind the crests of the Hörni. It appeared to be taking its time, extending the day a little so as not to miss the party.

Then all at once it seemed as though the ceremony was about to begin. Something like a wave ran through the crowd, gently moving it like the leaves of an ash tree stirred by the breeze. Viktor Heidekirch, perhaps at a signal, silenced his instrument. You could still hear a few voices, a few laughs, a few shouts, but gradually they died down and faded into a great silence. That was when I was aware of the smell of henhouse. I turned and saw Göbbler standing two steps away. He raised his peculiar beret of woven straw by way of greeting. "Coming along to the show, neighbour?"

"What show?" I asked.

With a slight wave of his hand Göbbler indicated everything around us. Then he sniggered. I did not respond. Poupchette was pulling my hair: "Black curls, Papa, black curls!" Suddenly, about ten paces away on my right, there was movement, the sound of shuffling and shoes scraping the ground as people stepped aside. We could see Orschwir's great bulk cleaving the crowd, and behind him, following in his wake, a hat, a hat we had come to know over the course of the previous two weeks: a sort of black, shiny bowler of no particular age or time, unconnected to places or any person, for it appeared to float freely in the air, as if there were no head below it. The Mayor reached the platform and mounted it without a moment's hesitation; then, as it were from on high, he made a ceremonious gesture, inviting whoever it was beneath the hat, which was all we could see, to join him.

Very cautiously, and accompanied by creaking sounds from the green wood, the *Anderer* hoisted himself up and stood at Orschwir's side. The platform was no more than three metres high and the staircase that *Zungfrost* had nailed together was made up of only six steps, but to watch the *Anderer* clamber from one to the next, you might have thought he was scaling the highest peak of the Hörni mountains, so slow and effortful was his progress. When finally he reached the Mayor's side, the crowd uttered a murmur of surprise, because it must be said that many of those present were seeing for the first time the person they had heard so much about – seeing him in the flesh. The platform was neither very wide nor very deep. *Zungfrost*, who was as thin as a lath, had

173

made a guess as to the appropriate dimensions, probably basing his estimates on his own person. But Orschwir was something of a giant, tall and broad, and the *Anderer* was as round as a barrel.

The Mayor was dressed in his fanciest outfit, which he generally wore only three times a year for the grandest occasions – the village festival, St Matthew's Fair and All Souls' Day. The only feature that distinguished this outfit from his everyday attire was a green braided jacket fastened by six frogged buttons. In order to survive in our parts, it is better to blend in rather than stand out too far, to be as simple and crude as a block of granite in a stubble-field. This is a truth long since understood by Orschwir. He keeps the pomp to a minimum.

As for the *Anderer*, well, he was something else altogether. He had dropped from the moon or somewhere even further away, and he knew nothing about our ways or what went on inside our heads. Maybe if he had worn less perfume and pomade, and fewer ribbons, we would have found him less unsettling. Maybe if he had been dressed in coarse cloth and corduroy and an old woollen overcoat, he would have blended in better with our walls and then, little by little, the village would have, if not exactly accepted him – acceptance requires at least five generations – at least tolerated him, as one might tolerate certain cats or dogs that pop up out of nowhere, from the depths of the forest most likely, and give new hope to our streets with their silent wanderings and their modest refrains.

But the *Anderer*'s toilette, especially on that day, did everything but blend in: white jabot frothing between two black satin lapels; watch chain, key chain, and chains for I do not know what else, covering his paunch with golden hardware; dazzling cuffs and matching buttons; navy-blue frock coat, woven belt, impeccable sash-*poche*, braided trousers; polished shoes and garnet gaiters; not to mention the rouge on his

cheeks – his fat cheeks, as full as perfectly ripe apples – his shiny moustache, his brushed side whiskers, or his rosy lips.

He and the Mayor, squeezed together on the little platform, made
an odd couple, better suited to a circus big top than to a village square.
the *Anderer* was smiling. He had doffed his hat and was holding it with
both hands. He smiled at nothing and looked at no-one. People around
me began to whisper: "*Teufläsgot*! What kind of a queer duck is this?"

"Is it a man or a ballon?"

"A big ape, I'd say!"

"Maybe that's the fashion where he comes from."

"He's a *Dumkof*, that's what he is. Off his rocker!"

"Quieten down, the Mayor's about to speak!"

"Let him speak. We can still admire the prodigy next to him!"

With great difficulty, Orschwir had extracted from one of his pockets
two pieces of paper, each folded four times. He smoothed them out for
a moment, trying to adopt an air of self-assurance, because it was
obvious to his audience that he was somewhat overwhelmed and even
uneasy. The speech he read was worth its weight in gold, and I am going
to reproduce it in its entirety. It is not that I remember it *verbatim*. It is
that a few days ago I simply asked Orschwir for it, because I know he
files away everything relating to his office. He said, "What do you want
it for?"

"For the Report."

"Why are you going back so far? We didn't ask you to do all that."

He made that last observation in a mistrustful tone, as if he
suspected a trap. I said, "I just thought it would be a good idea to show
what a friendly welcome our village gave him."

Orschwir pushed his ledger aside, took the pitcher and the two
glasses that the blind girl handed him, poured two glasses of beer and

pushed one over to me. It was plain that my request had upset him. He hesitated for a while, but in the end he said, "If you think it would be good for us, then do it."

He took a small piece of paper, slowly wrote a few words on it, and held it out to me: "Go to the village hall and show that to Hausorn. He'll find the speech and give it to you."

"Did you write it?"

Orschwir put down his beer glass and gave me a look that managed to be both irritated and sympathetic. Then he spoke to *Die Keinauge* in a gentle voice I had never heard him use before: "Leave us, Lise, will you?"

The little blind girl inclined her head in a slight bow and left the room. Orschwir waited until she had closed the door behind her. "You see that child, Brodeck? Her eyes, as you know, are dead. She was born with dead eyes. Of all the things you see around you – the sideboard, that clock, this table my great-grandfather made, the edge of the Tannäringen forest you can glimpse through the window – of all that she can see nothing. Of course she knows it all exists because she can feel it, she inhales it, she touches it, but she cannot see it. And even if she should ask to see it, she wouldn't be able to see it. So she doesn't ask. She doesn't waste her time making such a request, because she knows that no-one can fulfil it."

He stopped and took a long pull from his beer.

"You ought to make an effort to be a little more like her, Brodeck. You ought to content yourself with asking for what you can have and for what can serve your purpose. The rest is useless. All it can do is distract you and put I don't know what kinds of ideas into your head and set them boiling in your brain, and all for nothing! I'm going to tell you something. The night you agreed to write the Report you said you would use 'I', but that 'I' would mean all of us. You remember saying that, don't you? Well, tell yourself that all of us wrote that speech. Maybe I read it out, but we all thought it up together. Be content with that, Brodeck. Another glass?"

At the village hall, Caspar Hausorn made a face when I handed him the Mayor's note. He was about to say something, but he restrained himself at the last moment. He turned his back to me and opened two large drawers. After he had moved several registers aside, he took out a dark-brown, cardboard box containing dozens of sheets of paper in various sizes. He glanced through them quickly one by one until he came to the pages with the speech, which he handed to me without a word. I took them and was about to stick them in my pocket when he stopped me brusquely. "The Mayor's message says you have the right to read the pages and copy them, but not to go off with them."

With a movement of his head, Hausorn indicated a chair and a small table. Then he adjusted the eyeglasses on his nose and returned to his desk and whatever he had been working on. I sat down and began to copy the speech, taking great care to record every word. From time to time, Hausorn raised his head and gazed at me. The lenses of his glasses were so thick that if you looked through them they made his eyes seem disproportionately large, the size of pigeons' eggs, and although he was a man whose fine, well-modelled features had always been appreciated by women, when I saw him like that I was put in mind of an enormous insect, a kind of giant, furious fly attached to the neck of a decapitated human body.

"My dear friends, both those from our village and those visiting from elsewhere in the vicinity, and you, my dear sir, Monsieur . . . It is with great pleasure that we welcome you within our walls."

Before I reproduce the rest of what Orschwir said on this occasion, standing on the platform and speaking in the twilight of a mild day so far removed from the cold and the feeling of terror on the night of the *Ereigniës*, I must allude to the Mayor's moment of confusion and embarrassment when, early on in his speech, he said, "Monsieur . . .," and then paused, looked at the *Anderer*, and waited for him to supply his name, the name that nobody knew. But the *Anderer* said nothing at all, smiling without parting his lips, so that the Mayor, after repeating "Monsieur . . . Monsieur . . .?" several times in a gently questioning tone, was obliged to go on with his speech without having obtained any sort of answer.

"You are the first, and for the time being the only, person to visit our village since those long, grievous months when the war held this part of the world in its atrocious grip. In former days, and for centuries, our region was traversed by travellers who came up from the great plains of the south and took the mountain route on their way to the distant northern coasts and the port cities. Such travellers always found this village a pleasant and auspicious stopping place, and the old chronicles refer to it by the ancient name *Wohlwollend Trast*, 'Kindly Halt'. We do not know whether such a halt is the purpose of your stay here. But be that as it may, you honour us with your sojourn in the bosom of our modest community. You are, as it were, the first sign of a springtime of humanity, returning to us after too long a winter, and we hope that others will come after you to visit us, and that we will thus gradually reestablish our connection with the community of mankind. Please, my dear Monsieur . . ." – and here, once again, Orschwir stopped and looked at the *Anderer*, giving him the opportunity to say his name, but that name was not forthcoming, and Orschwir, after clearing his throat one more time, returned to his text – "my dear sir, please don't judge us too severely or too soon. We have gone through much adversity, and our isolation has no doubt reduced us to living on the margins of civiliza-

178

tion. Nevertheless, to those who really know us, we are better than we might appear to be. We have known suffering and death, and we must learn again how to live. We must also learn not to forget the past but to overcome it, by banishing it far from us and making sure that it no longer overflows into our present and even less into our future. In the name of every man, woman, and child, and in the name of our beautiful village, which I have the honour to administer, I therefore bid you welcome, my dear" – and this time the Mayor did not pause – "sir, and now I shall yield the floor to you."

Orschwir looked at the crowd, refolded his pages, and shook the *Anderer*'s hand as the applause rose up to the pink and blue sky, where some apparently drunken swallows were challenging one another to speed trials along indeterminate tracks. The applause gradually died down and silence fell once again, heavily. The *Anderer* smiled, but no-one could have said at whom or what he was smiling. At the country folk crowded into the first row, who had not understood much of the speech and could not wait to drink the wine and beer? At Orschwir, whose mounting anxiety grew more and more palpable as the silence persisted? At the sky? Maybe at the swallows. He had yet to pronounce a single word when there came a sudden, violent gust of wind, of very balmy, even hot wind, the kind that makes animals nervous in their stalls and sometimes agitates them so much that they begin to kick wildly at the walls and doors. The wind assailed the welcome banner, tore it in half and wrapped itself around the two parts, twisting and tearing off large sections which were carried away towards the birds, the clouds, the setting sun. The wind departed as it had come, like a thief. What was left of the banner hung down. Only two words remained: "*Wi sund*", "We are". The rest of the sentence had disappeared into thin air, vaporized, forgotten, destroyed. Once again I was aware

179

of a chicken smell very close to me. Göbbler was at my side, and he spoke into my ear. "*We are!* What are we, Brodeck? This is what I ask myself . . ."

I did not reply. Poupchette hummed as she sat on my shoulders. She had clapped very hard during every round of applause. The incident with the banner had distracted the crowd for a few seconds, but now it had calmed down again, and it was waiting. Orschwir was waiting too, and if you knew him even slightly, you would know that he would not be able to wait much longer. Maybe the *Anderer* could sense that as well, for he moved a little, rubbing and stretching his cheeks with both hands; then he brought them down in front of him, joined them as if he were going to pray, nodded his head to left and right, smiling all the while, and said, "Thank you." That was it: "Thank you." Then he bowed ceremoniously three times, like an actor at the end of a play. People looked at one another. Some of them opened their mouths so wide that a round loaf of bread could have been slipped in without difficulty. Some elbowed their neighbours and exchanged questioning looks. Others shrugged or scratched their heads. Then someone began to applaud. It was as good a way as any to ease the embarrassment. Others followed suit. Poupchette was happy again. "Fun, Papa, fun!"

As for the *Anderer*, he replaced his hat, climbed down the steps as slowly as he had climbed up them, and disappeared into the crowd before the eyes of the Mayor who stood there dumbfounded and unmoving, his arms hanging at his sides, while the surviving fragment of the banner brushed against the fur of his cap. Soon the people at his feet abandoned him, moving briskly towards the trestle tables laden with the mugs, the glasses, the pitchers, the sausages and the brioches.

29

Someone has been in the shed! Someone has been in the shed! It is Göbbler, I know it! I would swear to it! It could not be anybody but him! Besides, there are tracks, footsteps in the snow, big, muddy tracks going in the direction of his house! He did not even try to hide! They think they are so powerful, they do not even bother to hide the fact that they are all spying on me, that they've got their eyes on me every moment of the day.

I was away for barely an hour; I went to buy three balls of wool for Fédorine in Frida Pertzer's little shop, which offers a little of everything – gold braid, needles, thread, gossip, buttons, cloth by the metre – and that gave him enough time to get into the shed and rummage through everything! Everything is upside down! Everything has been overturned, opened, moved! He didn't even try to put things back in order after he went through them! And he forced the desk drawer open, the one in Diodème's desk – he broke the drawer and left it on the floor! What was he looking for? He wanted what I am writing, that is certain. He hears the typewriter too much. He suspects I am writing something other than the Report! But he did not find anything. He could not find anything! My hiding place is too secure.

A short while ago, when I discovered what had happened, I was furious. I did not stop to think. I saw the tracks, I rushed over to Göbbler's, and I banged on his door with the flat of my hand. It was quite late at night and the village was sleeping, but there was a light in

Göbbler's house and I was pretty certain he was not asleep. His wife answered the door. She was wearing a nightgown, and when she saw that it was me, she smiled. Against the light I could distinguish the outlines of her big hips and her immense breasts. She had taken down her hair.

"Good evening, Brodeck," she said, passing her tongue back and forth over her lips.

"I want to see your husband!"

"Aren't you feeling well? Are you sick?"

I shouted his name at the top of my voice. I kept on shouting it. There was movement upstairs, and before long Göbbler made his appearance, with a candle in his hand and a nightcap on his head.

"Why, Brodeck, what's going on?"

"You tell me! Why did you ransack my shed? Why did you break the desk drawer?"

"I assure you, I haven't done any—"

"Don't take me for a simpleton! I know it was you! You're always spying on me! Did the others put you up to it? The footprints lead to your house!"

"The footprints? What footprints? Brodeck . . . Do you want to come in and have some herb tea? I think you're—"

"If you ever do it again, Göbbler, I swear I'll . . ."

"You'll what?"

He stepped close to me. His face was a few inches from mine. He was trying to see me through the whitish veil that covers his eyes a little more each day. "Be reasonable," he said. "It's nighttime. Take my advice and go to bed. Take my advice."

All of a sudden Göbbler's eyes frightened me. There was nothing human about them any more. They looked like ice eyes, frozen eyes, like eyes I saw once when I was eleven years old and a caravan of men from the village had gone to collect the bodies of two foresters from the hamlet of Froxkeim, who had been carried off by a snowslide on the Schnikelkopf slopes. The villagers had brought down the mortal remains in large sheets suspended from poles. I saw them pass not far from our cabin while I was out getting water from the stream. I noticed that the arm of one of the corpses was hanging out of the sheet and beating time on the ground, and I glimpsed the other man's head through a tear in the cloth. His stare was fixed and white, with a flat, full whiteness as if all the snow that had killed him had poured itself into his eyes. I cried out, dropped the water jug, and went running back to the cabin to fling myself against Fédorine.

"Don't you ever tell me what to do, Göbbler."

I left without giving him time to reply.

I have spent the last hour putting the shed back in order. Nothing has been stolen, and there is a good reason for that: there is nothing to steal. My manuscript is too well hidden; no-one will ever be able to find it. I am holding the pages in my hands. They are still warm, and when I bring them up to my face and inhale, I smell paper, ink, and another scent, the scent of skin. No, no-one will ever find my hiding place.

Diodème had a hiding place too; I have just discovered it, completely by chance, when I was trying to fix the desk drawer. I turned the desk over and laid it on the floor with its legs in the air, and that is when I saw, on the underside of the desktop, a large envelope. It was glued there, just above the drawer that was supposed to hide it. When the desk was upright, the drawer was empty, but glued above it and impossible to find was the envelope.

To tell the truth its contents were rather a jumble. I have just sorted through them. To begin with, there is a long list in two columns, one headed "Novels Written" and the other "Novels to be Written". The first list includes five titles: *The Girl by the Water, The Amorous Captain, Flowers in Winter, Mirna's Bouquets,* and *Agitated Hearts.* Not only do I recognize those titles, but I also know all about the novels themselves, because Diodème used to read to me from them. We would sit in his little house, which was cluttered with books, registers and loose sheets of paper liable at any moment to catch fire from the candles, and I would always have to struggle not to fall asleep. But Diodème was so enraptured by his own stories and words that he would not even notice my frequent dozes.

I smiled as I read the list, for those titles reminded me of all the times I had spent in his company, and I could picture his handsome face – like something on an old coin – and the way it became animated when he read. When I perused the other part of the list, the "Novels to be Written", I could not help bursting into laughter at the thought of what I had escaped. Diodème had put down the names of more than sixty novels-to-be! Most of the titles resembled one another and gave off a distinct whiff of rose water. But two of them stood out, and Diodème had underlined them both several times: *The Treason of the Just* and *Remorse.* This last title, in fact, had been copied out four times, each time in bigger letters, as if his pencil had stammered.

On another sheet of paper he had drawn up a kind of genealogical tree of his family. There were the names of his parents, his grandparents and his great-grandparents, along with their dates and places of birth. There were also uncles, aunts, cousins and distant ancestors. But alongside these there were some great voids, some holes, some lines that stopped suddenly at a blank space or a question mark. Thus the tree contained both full, abundant branches, almost cracking under their load of names, and naked limbs, reduced to a simple line that died out unadorned. I thought about the strange forests of symbols and dead lives that our trees would create if they were all lined up together side by side. My tree would disappear under the suffocating branches of so many families that for centuries have safeguarded their memory as their most precious inheritance. In fact, mine would not be a tree at all, just a puny trunk. Above my name there would be only two stems, cut very short, bare, leafless and resolutely mute. But I might still find a place for Fédorine, as one sometimes grafts a sturdy plant onto a sickly one in order to give it some of the other's strength and sap.

The envelope also contained two letters. They had been read and reread so often that the paper on which they were written was reduced to a thin film about to fall apart at the creases. They were signed "Magdalena" and had been sent to Diodème a long time ago, well before he came to settle in the village. Both were love letters, but the second spoke of the end of love. It spoke of it in simple terms, without grand phrases, without mawkish expressions or affectations. It spoke of the end of love as a universal truth, an actuality which cannot be striven against and which forces man to bow his head and accept his fate.

I do not wish to transcribe here all or even part of those two letters. They do not belong to me. They are not part of my story. As I read them, I thought that perhaps they had been the cause of Diodème's arrival among us, the reason why he put so much distance between his former existence and the daily life he then built for himself, little by little, in the village. I do not know if he succeeded in healing his wound, or even if he really wanted to. Sometimes you love your own scars.

I was holding in my hands fragments of Diodème's life, small but essential pieces which, if put together, offered insights into his departed spirit. And as I thought about his life, about mine and Emélia's and

Fédorine's, and also about the *Anderer*'s – about which, to tell the truth, I knew almost nothing, and which I only imagined – the village appeared before me in a new light. I suddenly saw it as the end place, arrived at by those who leave the night and the void behind them; not the place for new beginnings, but rather the place where everything may end, where everything must end.

But there was something else in the large brown envelope.

There was another letter, a letter addressed to me. I seized upon it with great curiosity, for it is not often you can hear a dead man speak to you. Diodème's letter began with these words: *"Forgive me, Brodeck, please forgive me . . ."* and ended with the same words.

I have just finished reading that long letter.

Yes, I have just read it.

I do not know if I will be able to give any sense of what I felt as I read the letter. Besides, I am not certain I felt anything. Still, I can swear that there was no suffering. I did not suffer as I read Diodème's letter, which is in fact a long confession, because I am missing the organs essential for experiencing suffering. I do not possess them any more. They were taken from me, one by one, in the camp. And – alas – they have not grown back since.

30

I am sure Diodème assumed that I would end up thoroughly detesting him after reading the letter he wrote to me. Diodème believed that I was still a participant in the human order, but he was mistaken.

Yesterday evening, after tidying up the shed and accidentally finding Diodème's hiding place and going through the contents of the brown envelope, I joined Emélia in bed. It was late. I nestled myself against her. I embraced her warmth and the shape of her body and fell asleep very quickly. I did not even think about what I had just read. My heart felt curiously light, while my body was heavy with weariness and disentangled knots. I fell asleep happily, as one does every night of one's childhood. And I had dreams. Not the dreams that usually torment me; the black crater of the *Kazerkswir* with me circling around it, circling and circling – no; my dreams were peaceful.

I encountered the student Kelmar again. He was very much alive and wearing his beautiful, white linen shirt with the embroidered front. The immaculate shirt set off his suntanned skin and his graceful neck. We were not on the road to the camp. Nor were we in the railway wagon where we spent so many days and nights, crammed in with the others. We were in a place that reminded me of nothing that I knew; I could not even say whether it was inside a house or outdoors. I had never known Kelmar like this. He bore no trace of any blow. His cheeks were fresh and clean-shaven. His clothes smelled good. He was smiling. He talked to me. He talked to me at length, and I listened without interrupting him. After some time he stood up, and I understood, without his having to tell me, that he had to go. He looked at me and smiled, and I have a clear memory of the last words we exchanged.

"After what they did to us in the wagon, Kelmar, I should have stopped like you. I should have stopped running and sat on the road."

"You did what you thought you should do, Brodeck."

"No, you were right. It's what we deserved. I was a coward."

"I'm not sure I was right. The death of one man never makes up for the sacrifice of another, Brodeck. That would be too simple. And it's not up to you to judge yourself. Nor to me, either. It's not up to men to judge one another. They're not made for that."

"Kelmar, do you think it's time for me to join you now?

"Stay on the other side, Brodeck. Your place is still over there."

Those are the last words I remember him saying. Then I tried to get close to him, I wanted to take him in my arms and hold him tight, but I embraced only the wind.

Contrary to what some claim, I do not believe that dreams foreshadow anything at all. I only think they come at the right moment, and they tell us, in the hollow of the night, what we perhaps do not dare to admit to ourselves in the light of day.

I am not going to reproduce Diodème's entire letter. For one thing, I no longer have it. But I am aware of what it must have cost him to write it.

I did not leave for the camp of my own accord. I was arrested and transported there. The *Fratergekeime* had entered our village barely a week before. The war had begun three months before that. We were cut off from the world, and we did not know much about what was happening. The mountains often protect us from commotion and turmoil, but at the same time, they isolate us from a part of life.

We saw them coming one morning, a lengthy, dusty column marching up the road from the border. Nobody attempted to slow their progress, and in any case such an effort would have been futile; furthermore, I think the deaths of Orschwir's two sons were on our minds, and if there was one thing everyone wanted to avoid, it was any further deaths.

Besides, the most important point, and one that was essential for understanding the rest, was that those troops on their way to our village – helmeted, armed, and emboldened by the crushing victories they had inflicted on every opposition they had encountered – were much closer to the inhabitants of our region than the great majority of our own country's population. As far as the men around here were concerned, our nation barely existed. It was a little like a woman who occasionally reminded them of her presence with a gentle word or a request, but whose eyes and lips they never really saw. The soldiers entering our village as conquerors shared our customs and spoke a language so close to our own that it only required a minimum of effort for us to understand and use it. The age-old history of our region was mingled with that of their country. We had in common legends, songs, poets, choruses, a way of preparing meat and making soups, an identical melancholy, and a similar propensity to lapse into drunkenness. When all is said and done, borders are nothing more than pencil strokes on maps. They slice through worlds, but they do not separate them. Sometimes borders can be forgotten as quickly as they are drawn.

The squad that broke into the village comprised a hundred or so men under the command of a Captain Adolf Buller. I did not come to know him well. I remember him as a man of small stature, very thin, and afflicted with a tic that caused him to jerk his chin abruptly to the left every twenty seconds or so. That day he was riding a filthy, mud-covered horse, and he never let go of his hunting crop, which was short and had a braided tip. Orschwir and Father Peiper had stationed themselves at the entrance to the village, both to welcome the conquerors and to implore them to spare its inhabitants and houses, while doors and shutters were closed and locked everywhere and everyone in the village held their breath.

Captain Buller listened to Orschwir's stammering without getting off his horse. A soldier at his side carried a lance bearing a red and black standard. The following day that standard replaced the flag that flew above the village hall. You could read the name of the company's regiment, *Der unverwundbare Anlauf* – "The Invulnerable Surge" – as well as its motto, *Hinter uns, niemand* – "After us, no-one".

Buller did not answer Orschwir. He jerked his chin twice, gently moved the Mayor aside with his hunting crop, and advanced, followed by his soldiers.

We all thought he was going to demand that his men be given beds and warm lodging within the thick walls of the houses, but he did no such thing. The troops moved into the market place, unpacked some large tents, and pitched them in the twinkling of an eye. Then the soldiers knocked on every door with orders to collect and confiscate all weapons, which mostly turned out to be hunting rifles. They did so without the least brutality and with the greatest politeness. On the other hand, when Aloïs Cathor, a crockery mender who was always trying things on, told them there were no weapons in his house, they aimed their own at him, ransacked the rabbit cage he lived in from top to bottom, and eventually discovered an old rifle. They waved it in front of his nose and brought Cathor and the rifle before Captain Buller, who was sipping an *eau-de-vie* outside his tent while an orderly stood behind him with the flask, poised to supply a refill. The soldiers explained what had happened and Cathor adopted a mocking tone. Buller sized him up from head to foot, drained his glass, twitched with his little nervous tic, pointed with his hunting crop to summon a pink-skinned lieutenant with straw-coloured hair, and whispered a few words in his ear. The young man nodded, clicked his heels, saluted and left, taking with him the two soldiers and their prisoner.

A few hours later, a drummer passed through the streets calling out an announcement: the entire population, without exception, was to gather in front of the church at seven o'clock in order to witness an event of the greatest importance. Attendance was obligatory, under pain of sanctions.

Shortly before the stipulated hour, everyone left his house. In silence. The streets were soon filled with a strange procession; no-one said a word and people did not dare to raise their heads, to look around them, to meet anyone else's eye. We walked along together, Emélia and I, holding hands tightly. We were afraid. Everyone was afraid. Captain Buller was waiting for us, hunting crop in hand, on the square in front of the church. He was flanked by his two lieutenants, the one I have already mentioned and another who was squat and dark-haired. When the small church square had filled up, and everyone was quite still and silent, he spoke:

"Villagers, ladies and gentlemen, we have not come here to defile or to destroy. A man does not defile or destroy what belongs to him – what is his – unless he is afflicted with madness. And we are not mad. As of today, your village has the supremely good fortune to form a part of the Greater Territory. You are in your homeland here, and this homeland is our homeland too. We are henceforth united for a millennial future. Our race is the first among races, immemorial and unstained, and so will yours be if you consent to rid yourselves of the impure elements which are still to be found among you. Thus it is imperative that we live in perfect mutual understanding and total frankness. Lying to us is not good. Attempting to deceive us is not good. One man has made such an attempt today. We trust that his example will not be followed."

Buller had a delicate, almost feminine voice, and the curious thing was that the uncontrolled chin movement that made him look like a robot with a screw loose disappeared when he spoke. He had hardly finished his speech when, with flawless protocol, as if everything had been rehearsed numerous times, Aloïs Cathor was led into the square escorted by the two soldiers who had him in their charge, and brought before the Captain. Another soldier followed close behind them, carrying something heavy that we could not quite identify. When he placed it on the ground, we could see that it was a timber log, a section about a metre high cut from the trunk of a fir tree. Then everything passed very rapidly: the soldiers grabbed Cathor, forced him to his knees, laid his head on the log and stepped back. They were immediately replaced by a fourth soldier, whom no-one had until then seen. A big apron of dark leather was strapped to his chest and legs. In his hands he held a large axe. He came very close to Cathor, raised the axe and – before anyone even had time to catch his breath – brought the blade hurtling down on the pottery mender's neck. The cleanly-severed head hit the ground near the block and rolled a little. A great stream of blood gushed from Cathor's body, which jerked about spasmodically for several seconds, like a decapitated goose, before all movement ceased and the corpse lay inert. Cathor's head looked at us from the ground. His eyes and mouth were wide open, as if he had just asked a question that none of us had yet answered.

It had happened so fast; this awful scene had transfixed us all. It was the sound of the Captain's voice that cleared our heads, only to plunge us into an even greater stupor: "This is what happens to those who play games with us. Think about it, villagers! Ladies and gentlemen, think about it! And in order to assist your reflections, the head and body of this *Fremdër* will remain here! You are forbidden to bury him, unless you wish to suffer the same fate! One further word of advice: cleanse your village! Do not wait for us to do it for you. Cleanse it while there's still time! And now disperse, go back to your houses! I wish you a good evening!"

His chin gave a little jerk to the left, as if to shoo a fly. He smacked his hunting crop against the seam of his trousers, did an about-turn and left, followed by his lieutenants. Emélia was trembling at my side and sobbing. I held her to my chest as best I could. In a very soft voice she kept repeating, "It's a bad dream, isn't it? Isn't it just a bad dream, Brodeck?" She stared at Cathor's headless body slumped against the block.

"Come on," I said, putting my hand over her eyes.

Later, when we were already in bed, someone knocked at our door. I felt Emélia flinch. I knew she was not asleep. I kissed her on the nape of her neck and went downstairs. Fédorine had already admitted the visitor; it was Diodème. She was extremely fond of him. She called him the *Klübeigge*, which means "scholar" in her old language. He and I sat at the table. Fédorine brought two cups and poured us some tea that she had just prepared with wild thyme, mint, lemon balm and fir tree buds.

"What do you intend to do?" Diodème asked me.

"What do you mean, what do I intend to do?"

"I don't know. Look, you were there, you saw what they did to Cathor!"

"Yes, I saw it."

"And you heard what the officer said."

"That it's forbidden to touch the body? It reminds me of a Greek story Nösel used to tell back at the University, about a princess who—"

"Forget Greek princesses! That's not what I came here to talk about," Diodème blurted out, interrupting me. He had not stopped wringing his hands since he sat down. "When he said we have to 'cleanse the village', what do you think he meant?"

"Those people are madmen. I watched them at work when I was in the Capital. Why do you think I came back to the village?"

"They may be mad, but they are nevertheless the masters, ever since they deposed their Emperor and crossed our borders."

"They will leave, Diodème. In the end they will leave. Why would they want to stay with us? There's nothing here. This is the ends of the earth. They wanted to show us who's in charge now. They've shown us. They wanted to terrorize us. They've done that. They're going to stay for a few days and then they'll go somewhere else, somewhere further along."

"But the captain threatened us. He said we were supposed to 'cleanse the village'."

"So? What do you propose we do? Get a bucket of water and a broom and tidy up the streets?"

"Don't joke, Brodeck! You think they're joking? There wasn't anything innocent about what he said. He chose every word, he did not use those words by mere chance. Like the word '*Fremdër*' he used to refer to poor Cathor."

"That's the word they use when they talk about anyone they don't like. They're all *Fremdër*, all 'gangrene'. I saw that word painted on many a door during *Pürische Nacht*."

"As you well know, it means 'foreigner' too!"

"Cathor wasn't a foreigner! His family is as old as the village!"

Diodème loosened his shirt collar, which seemed to be strangling him. He wiped his sweaty forehead with the back of his hand, gave me a fearful look, turned his eyes to his cup, took a quick sip, looked at me furtively once more, cast his eyes down again and said almost in a whisper, "But you, Brodeck? You?"

31

I know how fear can transform a man.

I have not always know it, but I have learned it. In the camp. I saw men scream, beat their heads against stone walls, hurl themselves onto wire with barbs as sharp as razors. I saw them vomit, soil their trousers, empty their bowels entirely, expel all the liquids, all the humours, all the gases their bodies contained. I saw some pray, while others renounced the name of God, heaping it with obscene insults. I even saw a man die of it – of fear, I mean. One morning the guards played their little game and picked him as the next to be hanged, but when one of them stopped in front of him, laughed and said, *"Du!"* the man did not move. His face betrayed no emotion, no distress, no thought. And as the guard's smile began to vanish and he lifted his club, the man fell down dead, just like that, before the guard even laid a finger on him.

The camp taught me this paradox: Man is great, but he can never measure up to his full greatness. It is an impossibility inherent in our nature. When I made my vertiginous journey, descending one by one the rungs of the sordid ladder that carried me ever deeper into the *Kazerkswir*, I was moving not only towards the negation of my own person, but at the same time proceeding towards a complete awareness of my tormentors' motivations and an awareness of the motivations of those who had delivered me into their hands. And thus, somehow, towards a rough outline of forgiveness.

It was the fear felt by others, much more than hatred or some other emotion, that had made a victim of me. It was because fear had seized some of them by the throat that I was handed over to torturers and executioners, and it was also fear that had turned those same torturers, who had once been men like me, into monsters; fear that had caused the seeds of evil, which we all carry within us, to germinate.

There is no doubt that I severely misjudged the consequences of Aloïs Cathor's execution. I had grasped its horror, its odious cruelty, but I had not envisioned the inroads it would make in people's minds. Nor had I understood the extent to which Captain Buller's words, examined and sifted through dozens and dozens of brains, would distress them; I had not considered that those words could induce the others to arrive at a judgment whose victim would be me. And there was also, of course, Cathor's body, his head lying on the ground a couple of metres from the rest of him, with the sun shining down and all the ephemeral insects which in those days of early autumn were born in the morning, died at night, and spent the hours of their brief existence zooming around the corpse, revelling in the banquet, whirling, zigzagging, buzzing, driven wild by the great mass of flesh putrefying in the heat.

The nauseating smell permeated the whole village. The wind seemed to be on Buller's side. It arrived at the church square, loaded itself with the exhalations of decaying carrion, and then rushed gusting and swirling down every street, dancing a jig, slipping under doors, penetrating ill-fitting windows and dislodged tiles, and delivering to all of us the fetid spoor of Cathor's death.

During this time the soldiers behaved with the utmost propriety, as if everything were normal. There was no thieving, no plundering, no violence, no demands. They paid for whatever they took from the shops. Whenever they encountered women, young or old, they raised their caps. They chopped wood for elderly widows. They joked with the children, who became frightened and ran off. They saluted the Mayor, Father Peiper, and Diodème.

Captain Buller, always flanked by his two lieutenants, never without his tic, took a walk through the village streets on his short, thin legs every morning and every night. He walked fast, as if he were expected somewhere, and paid no attention to those he passed on his way. Sometimes he flailed the air with his hunting crop to drive off bees.

The villagers were all dazed. There was very little in the way of conversation. Communication was kept to a minimum. Heads were bowed. We weltered in our astonishment.

After Diodème left my house on the night of the execution, I never saw him again. I learned everything I am about to write from the long letter he left me.

On the evening of the third day of the *Fratergekeime*'s presence in the village, Buller summoned Orschwir and Diodème. Orschwir was no doubt sent for because he was the Mayor, but Diodème was a surprising choice. Anticipating a question Diodème would never have dared to ask, Buller observed that the village teacher must necessarily be less stupid than everyone else and could even be capable of understanding him.

Buller received the two men in his tent. It contained a camp bed, a desk, a chair, a sort of travelling chest, and a canvas wardrobe with a slipcover beneath which there appeared to hang a few articles of clothing. On the desk was some paper printed with the regimental letterhead, along with ink, pens, blotting paper and a framed photograph showing a thickset woman surrounded by six children ranging in age from about two to about fifteen.

Buller sat with his back to Orschwir and Diodème and was writing a letter. He took his time finishing it, read it through, slipped it into an envelope, sealed it, and placed it on the desk. Only then did he turn to face his guests, who were of course still on their feet and had not moved a muscle. Buller gazed at them in silence for some time, apparently trying to divine something about the men he would be dealing with. Diodème felt his heart beating as though it would burst, and his palms were clammy with sweat. He wondered why he was there and how long the ordeal would last. Buller's tic made his chin jerk at regular intervals. He picked up his hunting crop which lay to hand on the bed beside him and stroked it slowly, gently, as if it were a pet. Finally he said, "Well?"

Orschwir opened his mouth wide, found no reply and looked at Diodème, who could not even swallow, much less speak.

"Well?" Buller said again, without showing any real impatience.

Gathering all his courage, Orschwir managed to ask in a strangled voice, "Well what, Captain?"

This question elicited a smile from Buller, who said, "The cleansing, Monsieur le Maire! What else would I be talking to you about? How much progress have you made with the cleansing?"

Once again Orschwir stared at Diodème, who lowered his head and tried to avoid his companion's eyes. Then the Mayor, who is ordinarily so sure of himself, whose words can sting like whips, whom nothing impresses, who naturally behaves like the rich, powerful man he is, began to stammer and fall to pieces in the face of a uniformed creature little more than half his size, a minuscule fellow afflicted with a grotesque tic, who sat there caressing his hunting crop like a simpering woman. "The thing is, Captain," Orschwir said. "The thing is we . . . we didn't entirely . . . understand. Yes. We didn't understand . . . what you . . . what you meant."

Orschwir drooped, his shoulders sagging, like a man who has made too great an effort. Buller laughed softly, stood up and began to walk around inside the tent, pacing back and forth as if deep in thought. Then he came to a stop in front of his two visitors. "Have you ever observed butterflies closely, Monsieur le Maire? Or you, Monsieur Schoolmaster? Yes, butterflies, any sort of butterflies at all. No? Never? That's a shame . . . a great shame! I have dedicated my life to butterflies, you see. Some people focus on chemistry, medicine, mineralogy, philosophy, history; in my case, my entire existence has been devoted to butterflies. They fully deserve such devotion, but not many people are able to see that. It's a sad state of affairs, because one could learn some lessons of extraordinary importance to the human race by contemplating these splendid, fragile creatures. Consider this, for example: the earliest observers of one species of Lepidoptera, known by the name of *Rex flammae*, noted certain behaviour that seemed groundless at first; after further observation, however, it proved to be perfectly logical. I do not hesitate to use the word 'logical' when speaking about butterflies, as they are endowed with remarkable intelligence. The *Rex flammae* live in groups of about twenty individuals. It is believed that some sort of solidarity exists among them; when one of them finds a quantity of food large enough to nourish the entire group, they all gather for the feast. They frequently tolerate the presence among them of butterflies of a different species, but if a predator suddenly appears, it seems that the *Rex flammae* warn one another in who knows what form of language and hide themselves. The other butterflies that were integrated with the group an instant earlier apparently fail to receive the information, and they are the ones that get eaten by the bird. By providing their predators with prey, the *Rex flammae* guarantee their own survival. When everything is going well for them, the presence of one or more foreign individuals in their group does not bother them. Perhaps they even profit from it in some way. But when a danger arises, when it is a question of the group's integrity and survival, they do not hesitate to sacrifice an individual of a different species."

Buller stopped talking and resumed his pacing, but he did not take his eyes off Orschwir and Diodème, who were sweating profusely. Then he spoke again: "Narrow-minded individuals may find the conduct of these butterflies lacking in morality, but what is morality, and what use does it have? The single prevailing ethic is life. The dead are those who have got it wrong."

The Captain sat at his desk and paid no more attention to the Mayor and Diodème, who silently left the tent.

A few hours later, my fate was sealed.

De Erweckens'Bruderschaf – "The Brotherhood of the Awakening" I spoke of earlier – held a meeting in the little room reserved for it at the back of Schloss' inn. Diodème was there too. In his letter he swears to me that he was not a member of the brotherhood and that this was the first time they had ever invited him to a meeting. I do not see why that is important. First time, last time, what does that change? Diodème does not give the names of those who were present, just their number: there were six of them, not counting him. He does not say it, but I believe that Orschwir must have been one of them, and that it was he who reported Adolf Buller's monologue on butterflies. The group weighed the captain's words. They understood what there was to understand, or rather, they understood what they were willing to understand. They convinced themselves that they were the *Rex flammae*, the brilliant butterflies the captain had talked about, and that in order to survive they would have to remove from their community those who did not belong to their species. Each of them took a piece of paper and wrote down the names of the alien butterflies. I presume that it was the Mayor who gathered up the papers and read them.

Each piece of paper bore two names: Simon Frippman's and my own. Diodème swears he did not write my name, but I do not believe him. And even if that were true, the others could not have had much difficulty persuading him to add my name to his list in the end.

Frippman and I had much in common: neither of us had been born in the village, we did not look like people from around here (hair too black, skin too swarthy), and we came from far away, from an obscure past and a painful, itinerant, age-old history. I have written about my arrival in the village, riding in Fédorine's cart having made my way amid ruins, among the already dead, orphaned of my parents and orphaned of my memory. As for Frippman, he had arrived ten years ago, babbling a few words of the local dialect mixed with the old language Fédorine had taught me. Since many found him impossible to understand, I was asked to act as interpreter. It seemed likely that Frippman had suffered a severe blow to the head. He kept repeating his last name followed by his first, but apart from that he did not have much to say for himself. As he appeared to be a gentle sort, he was not driven away. Instead, a bed was found for him in a barn attached to Vurtenhau's farm. Frippman was full of heart. He did day labour for various farmers – haymaking, ploughing, milking, woodcutting – without ever seeming to grow tired, and he received his wages in food. He did not complain. He whistled tunes we had never heard before. The village adopted him, and he let himself be tamed without difficulty.

Simon Frippman and I were thus *Fremdër* – the "gangrene" and the "foreigners" – the butterflies that are tolerated for a while when everything is going well and offered as expiatory victims when everything is going badly. What was odd was that the men who decided to turn us over to Buller – that is, to send us to our deaths, though they could not have known that – agreed to spare Fédorine and Emélia, even though they were alien butterflies too. I do not know that one should speak of courage when referring to this omission, to this wish to spare the two women. I think rather that the gesture was an attempt at expiation. Those who denounced us needed to keep an area of their conscience pure and intact, a portion that would be free from the taint of evil and would therefore allow them to forget what they had done or at least enable them to live with it, in spite of everything.

The soldiers kicked in the door of our house shortly before midnight. Not long before that, the men who had participated in the meeting of the brotherhood had gone to see Captain Buller to give him the two names. Diodème was there. In his letter he says that he was crying. He was crying, but he was there.

Before I realized what was happening, the soldiers were already in our bedroom. They grabbed me by the arms and dragged me outside while Emélia screamed, clung to me, tried to beat them with her girl's fists. They paid her no heed. Tears were running down Fédorine's old cheeks. I felt as though I had become the little lost boy again, and I knew that Fédorine was thinking the same thing. Out in the street I saw Simon Frippman, his hands tied behind his back, waiting between two soldiers. He smiled at me, wished me a good evening as if nothing were amiss, and remarked that it was rather chilly. Emélia tried to embrace me, but someone pushed her away and she fell to the ground.

"You will come back, Brodeck! You will come back!" she screamed, and her words made the soldiers burst out laughing.

32

I do not feel any hatred towards Diodème. I bear him no grudge. As I read his letter, I imagined his sufferings more vividly than I remembered my own. And I understood too. I understood why he had been so assiduous in taking care of Fédorine and Emélia, visiting them every day, endlessly doing things for them, all the more so after Emélia entered into the great silence. And I also understood why, once he had recovered from his initial astonishment, he greeted my return from the camp with such an explosion of joy, hugging me, making me dance, spinning around with me in his arms, laughing all the while and wheeling me faster and faster, until in the end I passed out. I had returned from the dead, but he was the one who could now live again.

Brodeck, all my life I have tried to be a man, but I haven't always succeeded. It's not God's forgiveness I want; it's yours. You'll find this letter. I know if something happens to me, you'll keep my desk, and that's why I'm going to hide the letter in it. I know you'll keep the desk because you talk about it so much – it must be lovely to write at that desk, you say, and I write all the time. So sooner or later you'll find this. And you'll read it, all of it. All of it. About Emélia too, Brodeck. I found out everything; I owed you that much. And now I know who did it. It wasn't only soldiers – Dörfermesch, men from the village, were in on it too. Their names are written on the back of this sheet. There's no possibility of a mistake. Do what you want with this information, Brodeck. And forgive me, Brodeck, forgive me, I beg you . . .

I read the end of the letter several times, bumping up against those last words, unable to do as Diodème asked; I could not turn the page to look at the names. The names of men I inevitably knew, because our village is very small. Emélia and Poupchette were asleep only a dozen metres or so from where I sat. My Emélia, and my adorable Poupchette.

I am thinking all of a sudden of the *Anderer*. It was to him that I told the story. It was two weeks after I had come upon him sitting on the Lingen rock, contemplating the landscape and making sketches. I was on my way home from a long trek I had made to check the state of the paths that connected the pastures in the high stubble. I had left at dawn and walked a long way, and now I was hungry and thirsty and glad to be back in the village. I encountered him just as he was leaving Solzner's stable, where he had gone to visit his horse and donkey. We greeted each other. I went on my way, but when I had gone a few steps I heard him speak: "Would this be an appropriate time for you to accept my recent invitation?"

I was on the point of telling him I was exhausted and eager to get home to my wife and daughter, but I looked at him as he stood there expectantly, a broad smile on his round face, and I found myself saying the exact opposite. My response seemed to please him, and he beckoned me to follow.

As we entered the inn, Schloss was rinsing down and scrubbing the floor. There were no customers. The innkeeper was about to ask me what I was having, but then he realized I was following the *Anderer* up the stairs to his lodging. Schloss leaned on his mop and gave me a funny look, and then, seizing the handle of his bucket as if in anger, he violently flung the rest of the water onto the wooden floor.

A suffocating smell of incense and rose water pervaded the air in the *Anderer*'s room. Some open trunks stood in one corner, and I could see that they contained a quantity of books with gold-embossed bindings as well as a variety of fabrics, including silks, velvets, brocades and gauzes. Other textiles hanging on the walls hid the drab, cracked plaster and gave the place an Oriental flair, like a nomad encampment. Next to the trunks were two big, bulging portfolios, each apparently containing a great deal of material, but the ribbons that bound them were intricately knotted and their contents invisible. On the small table that served as a desk, some old, coloured maps were spread out; they depicted elevations and watercourses unknown to me and appeared to have nothing to do with our region. There was also a large copper compass, a telescope, a smaller compass and another measuring instrument that looked like a theodolite, but of a miniscule size. His little black notebook lay closed on the table.

He invited me to sit in the only armchair in the room after he had removed from it three volumes of what I imagined to be an encyclopedia. From an ebony case he took two extremely delicate cups, probably of Chinese or Indian workmanship, decorated with motifs of warriors armed with bows and arrows, and kneeling princesses. He placed the cups on matching saucers. On the bedstand was a large, silver-plated samovar with a neck like that of a swan. The *Anderer* took the samovar, poured boiling water into our cups and then added some dry, shrivelled, very dark brown leaves. They unfolded into a star shape, floated for an instant on the surface of the water, and then slowly sank to the bottom of the cup. I realized that I had watched this as if it were a magic trick, and I also realized that my host had been observing me with a look of amusement in his eyes.

"A lot of effect for not much," he said, handing me one of the cups. "You could fool entire populations with less." Then he sat facing me on the desk chair. It was so small that his broad buttocks hung over both sides of its seat. He brought the cup to his lips, breathed on the brew to cool it, and drank it in little sips with apparent delight. Then he put down his cup, rose to his feet, rummaged around in the largest trunk, the one that contained the biggest books, and returned with a folio volume whose worn covers suggested that it had been handled a great deal. Of all the volumes in the trunk, books that gleamed with gold and brilliant colours, the one in his hand was the dullest by far. The *Anderer* held it out to me. "Have a look," he said. "I am sure it will be of interest to you."

I opened it and I could not believe my eyes. The book was the *Liber florae montanarum* by Brother Abigaël Sturens, printed at Müns in 1702, illustrated with hundreds of colour engravings. I had searched in all the libraries of the Capital without ever finding it. Later I learned that only four copies were believed to be in existence. Its market value was immense; wealthy men of letters would have given a fortune to possess it. As for its scientific value, it was inestimable, because it listed all mountain flora, including the rarest and strangest species that have since disappeared.

The *Anderer* obviously perceived my bewilderment, which I made no effort to conceal. "Please," he said, "feel free to examine it. Go on, go on . . ."

Then, like a child who has just had a marvellous toy placed in front of him, I took hold of the book, opened it, and began to turn the pages.

It was like plunging into a treasure trove. Brother Abigaël had made his inventory with exceptional precision, and the extensive notes on each flower, each plant, not only recapitulated all the known lore, but also added details I had never read anywhere else.

But the most astonishing aspect of the work, and the main reason for its extraordinary reputation, was to be found in its illustrations; in the beauty and delicacy of the plates that accompanied the commentaries.

Mère Pitz's herbaria were a precious resource that had often helped me to revise or complete my reports, and sometimes even to focus and direct them. All the same, what I found there had lost all life, all colour, all grace. Imagination and memory were required to envision that entombed, dry world as it once had been, full of sap and suppleness and colour. Here, on the other hand, in the *Liber florae*, it seemed as though an intelligence combined with a diabolical talent had succeeded in capturing the very essence of flowers. The disturbing exactitude of lines and hues made it seem as though each subject had been picked and placed on the page only a few seconds before. Summer snowflake, lady's slipper orchid, snow gentian, healing wolfsbane, coltsfoot, amber lily, iridescent bellflower, shepherd's spurge, genepy, lady's mantle, fritillary, potentilla, mountain avens, stonecrop, black hellebore, androsace, silver snowbell – they danced before me in an endless round and made my head spin.

I had forgotten the *Anderer*. I had forgotten where I was. But suddenly the spinning stopped short. I turned a page, and there before my eyes, as fragile as gossamer, so tiny that it seemed almost unreal, its blue, pink-edged petals surrounding and protecting a crown of golden stamens, was the valley periwinkle.

I am certain I cried out. There in front of me, in the ancient, sumptuous volume lying across my knees, was a painting of that flower, a testament to its very existence, and there was also, peering over my shoulder, the face of the student Kelmar, who had told me so much about the valley periwinkle and made me promise to find it.

"Interesting, isn't it?"

The *Anderer*'s voice drew me from my reverie. "I've been looking for this flower for such a long time . . ." I heard myself saying in a voice I did not recognize as my own.

The *Anderer* looked at me with his thin smile, the other-worldly smile that he always wore. He finished his cup of tea, set it down, and then said in an almost light-hearted tone, "Things in books don't always exist. Books lie sometimes, don't you think?"

"I hardly ever read them any more."

A silence fell that neither of us sought to break. I closed the book and clasped it to me. I thought about Kelmar. I saw us getting down from the railway car. I heard the uproar again, the cries of our companions in misery, the bellowing guards, the barking dogs. And then Emélia's face appeared before me, her beautiful, wordless face, her lips humming their never-ending refrain. I felt the *Anderer*'s kindly eyes upon me. And then it all came out of its own accord. I began to talk to him about Emélia. Why did I speak of her to him? Why did I tell him, whom I knew not at all, things I had never acknowledged to anyone? No doubt I needed more than I was willing to admit to talk, admit even to myself; I needed to relieve the burden that was weighing down my heart. Had Father Peiper not since the end of the war turned into an *eau-de-vie*-soaked scarecrow, would I perhaps have confided in him? I am not so sure.

I have suggested that the *Anderer*'s smile did not seem to belong to our world. But then he himself did not seem to belong to our world. He was not part of our history. He was not part of History at all. He came out of nowhere, and today, now that there is no more trace of him, it is as if he never existed. So who better for me to tell my story to? He was on no particular side.

I told him about my departure, about being led away by the two soldiers as Emélia lay on the ground behind me, sobbing and scream-ing. I also told him about Frippman's good humour, his unawareness of what was happening to us and of our inevitable fate.

We left the village that same evening on foot, bound by the hands to the same tether, under the watchful eyes of the two soldiers on horseback. The journey took four days, during which the guards gave us nothing but water and the remains of their meals. Frippman was far from despair. He kept talking about the same things as we trudged along, doling out advice about sowing, the phases of the moon and cats, which, he declared, often chased him through the streets. He told me all this in his gobbledygook, a mélange of dialect and the old language. It was only over the course of those few days I spent with him that I realized he was simple-minded; before I had just considered him weird. Everything filled him with wonder: the movements of our guards' horses, the sheen of our guards' polished boots, the glint of their uniform buttons in the sunlight, the landscape, the birdsong.

The two soldiers did not mistreat us. They hauled us along like bundles. They never addressed a word to us, but nor did they beat us.

When we reached S., it was in chaos. Half the city had been destroyed; its streets were filled with rubble and charred ruins. For a week we were penned up in the train station with all sorts of other people – men, women, children, entire families – some of them poor, some still wearing the signs of their former riches and looking down on the others. There were hundreds of us. We were all *Fremdër*. In fact, that name had become our name. The soldiers never called us anything but that. Little by little, we were no longer existing as individuals. We all had the same name, and we had to obey whenever that name – which was no name – was spoken. We did not know what awaited us. Frippman stayed close by me. He never left my side. He sometimes held on to my arm for many long minutes at a stretch, squeezing it between his hands like a frightened child. I let him do it. Facing the unknown is always easier when you are with someone else. One morning the camp authorities carried out a selection process. Frippman was put in the column on the left, and they assigned me to the one on the right.

"Schussa Brodeck! Au baldiegeï en Dörfe!" – "Goodbye, Brodeck! See you soon in the village!" – Frippman called out, his face beaming, as his column was marched away. I could not reply. I simply waved; I gave him a little wave of my hand so he would suspect nothing, and especially not the great nothing I had a premonition of. I was sure we would both be heading there, him first and me later, forced along by cudgel blows. He turned and walked away at a good pace, whistling.

I never saw Frippman again. He did not return to the village. Baerensbourg the road-mender inscribed his name on the monument. Unlike mine, there was no need to rub it out.

Emélia and Fédorine remained alone in the house. The rest of the village avoided them, as if they had all of a sudden caught some kind of plague. Diodème was the only person who concerned himself with them, out of friendship and out of shame, as I have said. In any case, he took care of them.

Emélia hardly ever received commissions for her embroidery any more, but even though she no longer spent much time working on trousseaus and tablecloths and curtains and handkerchiefs, she was never idle. She and Fédorine had to have food and warmth. I had shown Emélia all the useful things that could be found in the woods and fields: branches, roots, berries, mushrooms, herbs, wild salads. Fédorine taught her how to trap birds with birdlime and string, how to snare rabbits, how to station herself under a tall fir tree, lure down a squirrel, and stun it with a rock. They did not go hungry.

Every evening Emélia jotted down in a little notebook – which I have since found – some words meant for me. Her sentences were always simple and sweet, and she wrote about me, about us, as if I were going to come back any moment. She recounted her day and began every entry the same way: "My little Brodeck . . ." There was never any bitterness in what she wrote. She did not mention the *Fratergekeime*. I am sure she omitted them on purpose. It was an excellent way of denying their existence. I still have her notebook, of course. I often reread passages from it. It is a long, touching account in which those days of my absence unspool, one after another. It is our story, Emélia's and mine. Her words are like lights, counterpoints to all my vast darkness. I want to keep them for myself, for myself alone, the last traces of Emélia's voice before she stepped into the night.

Orschwir did not bother to visit them. One morning he had half a pig delivered to them; they found it outside the door. Peiper came to visit two or three times, but Fédorine found him almost unbearable. He would sit for hours next to the stove, emptying the bottle of plum brandy she brought out for him, while his speech became steadily more confused. One evening she ended up chasing him out of the house with a broom.

Adolf Buller and his troops continued to occupy the village. A week after Frippman and I were arrested, Buller finally gave his authorization to bury Cathor. The deceased had no family apart from Beckenfür, who had married his sister, and so Beckenfür took charge of the burial. "A filthy job, Brodeck, let me tell you . . . Not pretty, not pretty at all . . . His head was twice its former size, like some strange balloon, with the skin all black and splitting, and then the rest, my God, the rest – let's not talk about it any more . . ."

Aside from Cathor's execution and our arrest, the *Fratergekeime* behaved most civilly towards the villagers, to the extent that the two events were soon forgotten, or rather, people did all they could to forget them. It was during this time that Göbbler returned to the village with his fat wife. He moved back into the house he had left fifteen years before, and was received with open arms by the whole village, and by Orschwir in particular; the two of them had been conscripts together.

It was Göbbler's counsels, I would be prepared to swear, which gradually sent the village over the edge. He remarked to everyone how advantageous it was to be occupied by foreign troops, how there was nothing hostile about the occupation, no, quite the opposite; it guaranteed peace and security, and it ensured that the village and its surroundings would be spared any massacre. Admittedly, it was not hard for him to convince people that it was in everyone's interest for Buller and his men to stay in the village for as long as possible. Undoubtedly a hundred men eating and drinking and smoking and having their clothes washed and mended bring a community a considerable infusion of money.

Göbbler became a sort of Deputy Mayor, with the consent of the whole village and Orschwir's blessing. He was often seen in Buller's tent. In the beginning, the Captain had viewed him with suspicion, but then, seeing the benefits to be derived from the feckless fellow and the rapprochement he championed, Buller began to treat him almost like a comrade. As for Boulla, she opened her thighs wide to the whole troop and distributed her favours to officers and to the rank and file alike.

"Well, what can I say? We got used to it," Schloss told me the day he came over to my table and sat opposite me and got all tearful. "It became quite natural for them to be here. After all, they were men like us, cut from the same block. We spoke about the same things in the same language, or close to it. In the end we knew most of them by their first names. A lot of them did odd jobs for the old people, and others played with the kids. Every morning ten of them cleaned the streets.

Others maintained the roads and the paths, cut wood and cleared away the piles of dung. The village has never been so clean, not before nor since! What can I say? When they came in here, I filled their glasses – I certainly wasn't going to spit in their faces! How many of us do you think wanted to end up like Cathor, or vanish like you and Frippman?"

The *Fratergekeime* stayed in the village for nearly ten months. There were no notable incidents, but the atmosphere worsened during the final weeks. Later, the reason for this became clear. Both the location and the mood of the war were shifting. Like a fire in spring, when the acrid smoke, agitated by the wind, panics and abruptly changes direction, military success was abandoning one side and going over to the other. No news came to the village – at least not to the villagers. If they were kept ignorant, they could not become dangerous. But Buller knew everything, of course. I like to imagine his face, increasingly ravaged by his tic as messages arrive with their tidings of defeat, of disaster, of the collapse of the Greater Territory, which was meant to extend its sway over the whole world and last for thousands of years.

The occupying troops, like dogs, sensed their Captain's confusion and became more and more nervous. The masks fell. The old reflexes revived. Brochiert the butcher was beaten before Diodème's eyes for teasing a corporal about his fondness for tripe. Limmat was jostled by two soldiers having neglected to salute them on the street, and only the intervention of Göbbler, who happened to be passing at that moment, saved him from a severe clubbing. A dozen incidents of this kind made everyone realize that the monsters had never left them, that they had simply fallen asleep for a while, and that now their slumbers were over. Then the fear returned, and with it a desire to keep it at bay.

One afternoon – in fact, it must have been the day before the troops' departure – some *Dörfermesch*, some "men of the village", who had gone

213

off with a sledge to the Borensfall forest to bring in some timber, made a discovery near Lichmal clearing: beneath a mass of fir branches arranged to form a sort of shelter were three panic-stricken young girls, adolescents who clung to each other when they saw the men coming. They wore clothes that were not the same as those worn by peasant women, nor were their shoes anything like clogs or boots. The girls had one small suitcase between them. They had come from far away, very far away. They had obviously been on the run for weeks, and then – God knows how – they had arrived in that forest in the middle of a strange universe in which they were completely lost.

The *Dörfermesch* gave them something to eat and drink. They flung themselves on the food as though they had not had a bite for days. Then they followed the men trustingly to the village. Diodème thought that the men did not know at that stage what they were going to do with those girls. I would like to believe him. In any case they realized that the girls were *Fremdër*, and they knew that each step, each metre along the path that led to the village would bring them closer to their fate. As I have said, Göbbler had become an important man, the only person in the village whom Captain Buller had really accepted, and so the men brought the three girls to Göbbler's house. It was he who convinced the *Dörfermesch* that they should hand the three over to the *Fratergekeime* as a means of currying their favour, appeasing them, taming them. The three young girls waited outside Göbbler's house as he dispensed this advice. They were still waiting when rain suddenly came down in torrents.

The Gods make play with us. I have often thought that if the rain had not beaten down on the roof tiles so hard, Emélia might never have looked out of her window. In which case she would not have seen the three drenched, trembling, thin and exhausted young girls. She would

214

not have gone outside and invited them to come and sit by the fire. She would not have been out there with them when the two soldiers, alerted by one of the *men from the village*, appeared and took hold of the girls. Therefore, she would not have protested. She would not have screamed at Göbbler that what he was doing was inhuman, as I am sure she did, and she would not have slapped his face. The soldiers would not have seized her too. They would not have taken her away with the three girls. And it follows that she would not have taken that first step towards the abyss.

Rain. Just rain, pelting the roof tiles and the windowpanes.

The *Anderer* listened. From time to time he poured hot water into his glass and added a few tea leaves. As I talked, I clutched the old *Liber florae montanarum* in my arms as if it were a person. The *Anderer's* benevolent silence and his smile encouraged me to continue. It soothed me to talk about all that for the first time, to speak of it to that stranger, with his odd looks and his odd clothes, and in that place, which so little resembled a mere room.

The rest I told him in a few words. There was not much left to say. Buller and his men were breaking camp, and despite the driving rain, there was a great deal of feverish activity in the market square. The air was filled with orders, shouts and the sound of shattering glass as dozens of drunken men, laughing, stumbling and exchanging insults, drank their bottles dry and dashed them to the ground. Buller, his head jolted by his tic with ever-increasing frequency, stood as rigid as a picket just inside the flap of his tent and observed the whole tumult. At that paradoxical moment, the *Fratergekeime* were still the masters, even though it was already clear to them that they had lost. They were fallen gods, mighty warriors with a premonition that soon they would be stripped of their arms and their breastplates. They were still clinging on to their dream, but they knew they were hanging upside down.

Such was the scene when the little procession arrived: the three girls and Emélia, escorted by the *Dörfermesch* and the two soldiers. Very soon Emélia and the girls became prey; all four were surrounded, shoved, touched, groped. To the sound of great outbursts of laughter, they disappeared into the centre of a circle that closed behind them, a circle of inebriated, violent men who drove them towards Otto Mischenbaum's barn shouting obscenities and filthy jokes. Mischenbaum, a farmer who was nearly a hundred years old, had never had children – *"Hab nie Zei gehab, nieman Zei gehab!"* ("Never had the time, never ever had the time!") – and spent most of the day shut up in his kitchen.

They vanished into the barn.

They were swallowed up in there.

And then, nothing.

The next day the square was deserted, but littered with innumerable shards of glass. The *Fratergekeime* were gone. All that remained of them was the sour stench of wine, brandy vomit and thick beer, which lay in puddles all over the square. After that sickening night during which some soldiers and a few *men from the village*, with Buller's mute blessing, had done great harm to bodies and souls, the doors of all the houses remained shut. Nobody yet dared to go outside. And old Fédorine went knocking, knocking, knocking at all those doors. Until she came to the barn.

"I went inside, Brodeck." That's old Fédorine, telling me the whole story while she feeds me with a spoon. My hands are covered with sores. My lips hurt so much. My broken teeth hurt so much, as if their fragments were still cutting into my gums. I have just come back after almost two years away from the world. I left the camp. I walked along highways and byways, and now I am home again, but I am still half dead. I am so weak. A few days earlier at last I had pushed open the door of my house. I found Fédorine there, and the sight of me made her drop the big earthenware dish she was drying. Its pattern of red flowers was scattered to all four corners of the room. I found Emélia too, more beautiful than ever, yes, even more beautiful than she was in all my memories, and those are not empty words. Emélia was sitting by the stove, and despite the noise of the breaking dish, despite the sound of my voice calling her name, despite my hand on her shoulder, she did not look up at me but kept humming a song that pained my heart, "*Schöner Prinz so lieb / Zu weit fortgegangen*", the song of our first kiss. And as I said her name, as I said it once more with the great joy I felt at seeing her again, as my hand patted her shoulder and stroked her cheek and her hair, I saw that her eyes did not see me, I understood that she did not hear me, I understood that Emélia's body and Emélia's wonderful face were there before my eyes, but that her soul was wandering somewhere else, I did not know where, it was in some unknown place, but I swore to myself that I would go to that place and bring her back, and it was at that precise moment, at the moment when I made that vow, that I heard for the first time a little voice I had never heard before and did not know, a child's voice, coming from our bedroom and rubbing the syllables against one another the way you rub flint to make sparks fly, and producing a joyous, free, disorderly cascade of melody, a playful babbling that I now know must be the closest thing to the language of the angels.

"I went into the barn, Brodeck. I went inside. It was completely silent and very dark. I saw some shapes on the floor, little shapes lying in a heap, not moving. I knelt beside them. I know death too well not to recognize it. They were the young girls, so young – not one of them twenty – and all three had their eyes wide open. I closed their eyelids.

And there was Emélia. She was the only one still breathing, but weakly. She had been left for dead, but she did not want to die, Brodeck, she did not want to die because she knew you would come back one day, she knew it, Brodeck . . . After I went over to her, while I was kneeling with her face pressed against my belly, she began to hum that song she has not stopped humming since . . . I rocked her in my arms, I rocked her and rocked her for a long, long time . . ."

There was no more water in the samovar. Gingerly, I put the *Liber florae* down beside me. It was almost dark outside. The *Anderer* opened a window. A scent of hot resin and humus permeated the room. I had been talking for a long time, probably for hours, but he had not interrupted me. I was on the point of apologizing for having opened my heart to him like that, without shame and without his permission, when chimes sounded directly behind me. I spun around as if someone had fired a shot. It was a peculiar, old-fashioned clock, the size of a large watch, made in days gone by to be hung inside carriages. I had not noticed it before. Its delicate golden hands indicated eight o'clock. The casing was made of ebony and gold, and the numerals marking the hours were of blue enamel on an ivory background. Beneath its centre the watchmaker, Benedik Fürstenfelder, whose name was engraved at the base of its frame, had inscribed a motto in fine, slanted, intertwining letters: "*Alle verwunden, eine tödtet*" – "They all wound, one kills."

As I stood up, I read the motto aloud. The *Anderer* also got to his feet. I had talked a great deal. Too much, perhaps. It was time for me to go home. Somewhat confused, I told him he must not think that . . . He interrupted me by swiftly raising a small, chubby hand, like the hand of a slightly overweight woman. "Don't apologize," he said, his voice almost as imperceptible as a breath. "I know that talking is the best medicine."

33

I do not know whether the *Anderer* was right.

I do not know if it is possible to be cured of certain things. Maybe talking is not such good medicine after all. Maybe talking has the opposite effect. Maybe it only serves to keep wounds open, the way we keep the embers of a fire alive so that when we want it to, when we are ready for it, it can blaze up again.

I burned Diodème's letter. Of course I burned it. Writing had been no cure at all, not for him. And it would not have done me any good to turn over the last page and read the names of the *Dörfermesch* he had written there. No good at all. I have no spirit of revenge. Some part of me will always remain Brodeck-the-Dog, a creature that prefers to lie in the dust than to bite, and maybe it is better that way.

That evening I did not go straight home. I made a long detour. The night air was soft. In the light that was vanishing, the stars in the sky were like silver nails hammered into the deepening blackness. There are hours on this earth when everything is unbearably beautiful, with a beauty whose scope and sweetness only serve to emphasize the ugliness of our condition. I walked to the bank of the Staubi, and then upstream from the Baptisterbrücke until I came to a grove of white willows. Baerensbourg tortures these trees every January, cutting off all their branches. That is where the three young girls are buried. I know, because Diodème told me so. He showed me the exact spot. There is no grave marker, no cross, nothing at all. But I know the three girls are there, beneath the grass: Marisa, Therne and Judith. Names are important, and those are their names. The names I have given them. Because in addition to having killed them, the *Dörfermesch* made every trace of them disappear so thoroughly that no-one knows what their names were, or where they came from, or who they really were.

That stretch of the Staubi is so beautiful. Its clear waters roll over a bed of grey pebbles. It murmurs and babbles, almost like a human voice. To those willing to lend an ear and sit for a moment on the grass, the Staubi proffers a subtle music.

The *Anderer* would often sit on that grassy bank, making notes in his little notebook and drawing. I think some of the people who saw him there in that exact spot, so close to the young girls' mute graves, persuaded themselves that he was not dallying in that place purely by chance. And it was no doubt during these sojourns by the willow grove that the *Anderer*'s doom, unbeknownst to him, began to be sealed, that the *Dörfermesch* gradually resolved upon his death. One must never, not even inadvertently, not even against one's will, exhume horror, for then it revives and spreads. It bores into brains; it grows; and it gives birth to itself again.

Diodème also met his death not far from there. "Met his death" – a strange expression when you think about it, but I think it is quite fitting for Diodème: In order to meet something you must seek it, and I do believe that Diodème sought his own end.

I know he left his room. I know he left the village. I know he walked along the banks of the Staubi, and I know that as he made his way upstream, in the opposite direction to the current, his thoughts flowed backwards, against the current of his life. He thought about our long walks, about all the things we had said to each other, about our friendship. He had just finished writing his letter, and as he walked along the riverbank, his mind was on what he had written. He passed the white willows, he thought about the young girls, he walked on, he kept walking, he tried to drive out the ghosts, he tried to talk to me one last time, I am sure of it, yes, I am certain he spoke my name; he climbed up to the top of the Tizenthal rocks, and that very short ascent did him good, because the higher he climbed, the lighter he felt. When he reached the summit, he looked at the roofs of the village, he looked at the moon's reflection on the edges of the river, he looked one last time at his life, he felt the night breeze caressing his beard and his hair. He closed his eyes; he let himself drop. He fell, and fell. Maybe, wherever he is now, he is falling still.

On the night of the *Ereigniës*, Diodème was not at Schloss' inn. Together with Alfred Wurtzwiller, our hare-lipped postmaster, Diodème had gone to S. with some important papers, sent there by Orschwir. I believe the Mayor gave Diodème this mission deliberately, to get him out of the way. When he came back to the village three days later, I tried to tell him what had happened, but he quickly cut me off: "I don't want to hear it, Brodeck. You can keep all that to yourself. Besides, you don't know anything for sure. Maybe he left without saying anything to anyone. Maybe he tipped his hat and bowed and went off the way he came. You didn't see anything, you said so yourself! Did he even exist, this *Anderer* of yours?"

His words took my breath away. I said, "But Diodème, you can't possibly—"

"Shut up, Brodeck. Don't tell me what I can and cannot do. Leave me alone! There's enough trouble in this village as it is!"

Then he hurried away, leaving me at the corner of Ruelle Silke. I think it was that very evening that Diodème began to write his letter to me. The *Anderer*'s death had stirred up too many things, more things than he could bear.

I repaired the desk and its broken drawer. I did a good job, I think. Then I rubbed it with beeswax, which made it smell good and gleam in the candlelight. And here I am, sitting at the desk and writing again. It is cold in the shed, but the pages hold the heat from Emélia's belly for a long time. I hide all these words I have written against Emélia's belly. Every morning I wash and dress Emélia, and every evening I undress her. Every morning, after I have been writing for most of the night, I slip the pages into a finely woven linen pouch and tie it around her stomach, under her shirt. Every night, when I put her to bed, I remove the pouch, which is warm and impregnated with the smell of her.

I tell myself that Poupchette grew in Emélia's belly, and that, in a way, the story I am writing comes out of it too. I like this analogy; it gives me courage.

I have almost finished the Report that Orschwir and the others are waiting for. I have just a few more things to say and then it's done. But I do not want to give it to them before I have finished my own story. I still have certain avenues to go down. I still have several pieces to put together. I still have a few doors to open. So they will not be getting their Report yet, not right away. First I have to go on describing the days that led up to the *Ereigniës*. Imagine a bowstring being pulled tauter and tauter, every hour a little more. Such an image gives a good sense of the weeks which led up to the *Ereigniës*; the entire village was drawn like a bow; but no-one knew which arrow it would let fly, nor what its exact target would be.

The summer heat was baking us like an oven. The old people said that they could not remember such a heatwave. Even in the heart of the forest, where in mid-August among the rocks the cool breath of buried

222

glaciers usually rises from the depths, the only breezes were searingly hot. Insects whirled madly above the dry mosses, rubbing their elytra together with an unnerving sound like an orchestra of out-of-tune violins, so filling woodcutters' brains, as to put them all day in a foul temper. Springs dried up. The wells were at their lowest level. The Staubi turned into a narrow, feeble stream in which brown trout, brook trout and char died by the score. Cows panted for air, their withered teats yielding only small amounts of thin, bitter milk. The animals were brought back to their sheds and only let out again at nightfall. They lay on their sides with their big eyelids lowered over shiny eyes, and their tongues which were as white as plaster, lolling. Anyone in search of a cool spot had to climb up to the highest stubble-fields, and the happiest creatures of all were undoubtedly the flocks of sheep and goats, and the shepherds and goatherds on the heights, heartily drinking in the fresh wind. Below, in the streets and houses, all conversation revolved around the blazing sun, which we watched in despair as it rose every morning and quickly climbed to its zenith in a blue, absolutely unclouded sky and so it stayed the whole day long. We moved very little. We turned things over in our minds. The smallest glass of wine went to people's heads, and they needed no further pretext to fly off the handle. No-one is to blame for a drought. No-one can be condemned for it. And so anger builds and it must be taken out on something, or someone.

Let the reader make no mistake. I am not saying that the *Ereigniës* occurred because we had scorching weather in the weeks preceding it and heads were on the boil like potatoes in a pot on a good fire. I think it would have happened even at the end of a long wet summer. In that case, for sure, it would have taken more time. There would not have been the violent haste, the tautened bow I mentioned earlier. The thing would have happened differently, but it would still have happened.

People are afraid of someone who keeps quiet. Someone who says nothing. Someone who just looks and says nothing. If he remains mute, how can we know what he is thinking? No-one was happy about the *Anderer*'s scant, two-word reply to the Mayor's speech. The next day, once the joy of the celebration – the free wine, the dancing – was past, people talked about the stranger's attitude, about his smile, his attire and the pink cream on his cheeks, about his donkey and his horse, about the various nicknames he had been given, about why he had come to our village, and why he was still here.

And it cannot be said that the *Anderer* made up any lost ground over the course of the following days. I have no doubt that I am the person he talked to most – apart from Father Peiper, but in that regard I have never been able to determine which of them talked more than the other, and about what. And one may judge the *Anderer*'s verbosity from the fact that I have already recorded in these pages every word he ever said to me. A sum of about ten lines, scarcely more. It is not that he ignored people. If he passed someone, he would raise his hat, incline his large head (upon which the remaining hair was sparse, but very long and frizzy), and smile, but he never said a word.

And then, of course, there was his black notebook and all the notes people saw him taking, all the sketches and drawings he made. That conversation I overheard between Dorcha, Pfimling, Vogel, and Hausorn at the end of one market day – I did not invent it! And those four were not the only people who were aggravated by that notebook! Why was he doing all that scribbling and scratching? What was the purpose of it? What would it lead to?

We would eventually learn the answers to those questions. On 24 August.

And that day, for him, was really the beginning of the end.

34

On the morning of 24 August, there was a little card under the door of each house in the village. The cards were fragrant with the essence of roses, and written on them, very elegantly and in violet ink, were the following words:

This evening, at seven o'clock,
at Schloss' Inn,
portraits and landscapes

More than one villager examined his card from every angle, turning it over and sniffing it, reading and rereading the brief text. By seven in the morning the inn was already awash with people. With men. Only men, obviously, but some of them had been sent by their wives to see what they could find out. There were so many extended arms and empty glasses that Schloss had trouble keeping everyone served.

"So, Schloss, tell us what this carnival is all about!"

Elbow to elbow, they were all knocking back wine, *schorick* or beer. Outside, the sun was already beating down hard. Schloss' customers pressed against one another and pricked up their ears.

"Did your lodger fall and bang his head?"

"What's he up to?"

"Is it *Scheitekliche* or what?"

"Come on, Schloss, say something! Tell us!"

"How long is this braggart going to be hanging around here?"

"Where does he think he is, with his smelly little card?"

"Does he take us for tyros?"

"What's a tyro?"

"How should I know? I didn't say it!"

"For God's sake, Schloss, give us an answer! Tell us something!"

It was worse than a machinegun fire of questions. And Schloss took them all for inoffensive pellets. His only perceptible response was a little smile, full of malice, on his fat face. He said nothing. He let the tension mount. It was good for business, all this. Talking about it made people thirsty.

"Come on, Schloss, out with it! Fuck it, you're not going to leave us hanging on until this evening, are you?"

"Is he upstairs?"

"Can't you shove over?"

"Well, Schloss?"

"Alright, alright, shut up! Schloss is going to speak!"

Everyone held their breath. The two or three who had not noticed this and were going on with their private conversation were swiftly called to order. All eyes – some of them already a bit out of focus – converged on the innkeeper, who was enjoying his little show and taking his time. At last he said, "Since you insist, I'm going to tell you . . ."

A general murmur of approval and relief greeted these opening words.

"I'm going to tell you everything I know," Schloss said.

Necks were twisted round and craned as far as possible in his direction. He slapped his towel on the bar, put both hands flat on top of it, and stared at the ceiling for a long time amid absolute silence. Everyone else followed suit, and had anyone came into the inn at that moment, he would surely have wondered why some forty men were standing there mute, with their heads tilted back and their eyes fixed on the ceiling, staring intently at the filthy, sooty, blackened beams as though asking them some question of great moment.

"This is what I know," Schloss went on in a confidential tone. His voice was very low, and everyone drank his words as if they were the finest *eau-de-vie*. "What I know is . . . well . . . it is that, well, I don't know very much!"

Another rumble rose from the gathering, but this time it was full of disappointment and a touch of anger, and it was accompanied by the crash of fists striking the bar, several choice insults, and so forth. Schloss raised his arms in an attempt to calm everyone down, but he had to shout to be heard: "He just asked me for permission to have the room to himself, from six o'clock, so he can make his preparations."

"Preparations for what?"

"I have no idea! One thing I can tell you is that he's going to pay for everyone's drinks."

The crowd recovered their good humour. The prospect of quenching their thirst at little or no expense sufficed to sweep away all their questions. Slowly but surely the inn emptied out. I was on the point of leaving myself when I felt a hand on my shoulder. It was Schloss.

"Brodeck, you didn't say anything."

"I let the others talk—"

"But what about you? Don't you have any questions to ask? If you don't have any questions, maybe that's because you know the answers. Maybe you're in on the secret."

"Why would I be?"

"I saw you go up to his room the other day and stay there for hours. You must have found some things to talk about during all that time, yes?"

Schloss' face was very close to mine. It was already so hot that his skin was perspiring all over, like a slice of bacon in a hot skillet.

"Leave me be, Schloss. I've things to do."

"You shouldn't talk to me like that, Brodeck. You shouldn't!"

At the time, I considered his words a threat. But after the other day, when he sat at my table and got all maudlin talking about his dead infant son, I am not so sure any more. Some men are so maladroit that you take them for the opposite of what they really are.

The only thing I had learned at Schloss' inn that morning was that the *Anderer*'s little perfumed cards had succeeded in focusing everyone's attention on him yet more closely. It was barely seven o'clock in the morning, and the last breath of air was already gone. The swallows in the sky looked exhausted and flew slowly. High aloft, one very small, almost transparent cloud in the shape of a holly leaf drifted alone. Even the animals were quiet. The cocks had not crowed. Silent and unmoving, trying to stay cool, hens languished in holes dug in the dusty earth of farmyards. Cats dozed in the shade of carriage entrances, lying on their sides with their limbs outstretched and their pointy tongues lolling out of half-open mouths.

As I was passing Gott's forge, I heard a great commotion inside. The diabolical racket was being made by Gott himself, who was putting the place in some sort of order. He noticed me, waved at me to stop and came towards me. His forge was at rest. No fire burned in it, and the blacksmith was freshly bathed, clean-shaven and combed. He was not wearing his usual leather apron, nor were his shoulders bare; instead he had on a clean shirt, high-waisted trousers and braces.

"So what do you think about all this, Brodeck?"

Not taking any chances, I shrugged, as in truth I did not know what he was talking about: the heat, the *Anderer*, his little rosewater-scented card, or something else altogether.

"If you ask me it's going to blow up all of a sudden, and it's going to be violent, I swear it is!"

As he spoke, Gott clenched his fists and his jaw. His cleft lip moved like a muscle, and his red beard made me think of a burning bush. He was three heads taller than me and had to stoop to speak in my ear.

"It can't go on like this, and I'm not the only one who thinks so! You're educated, you know more about things like this than we do. How is it going to end?"

"I don't know, Gott. We just have to wait until this evening. Then we'll see."

"Why this evening?"

"You got a card like everyone else. We're all invited for seven o'clock."

Gott stepped back and scrutinized me as if I had lost my wits. "Why are you talking to me about a card? I mean this fucking sun! It's been grilling our skulls for three weeks! I'm just about suffocating, I can't even work any more, and you want to talk to me about a card!"

A moan from the depths of the forge made us turn our heads. It was *Ohnmeist*, skinnier than a nail, stretching and yawning.

"He's still the happiest one," I said to Gott.

"I don't know if he's the happiest, but he's certainly the idlest!"

And as if wishing to concur with the blacksmith, with whom he had chosen for the time being to make his home, the dog laid his head on his forepaws and went back to sleep.

It was yet another of those unbearably hot days, yet it seemed peculiar, hollowed out, as if its centre and its hours were unimportant and only the evening was worth thinking about, waiting for, yearning towards. As I recall, after I returned from the inn that day, I did not leave the house again. I worked at organising notes I had made over the

229

past several months. My scribblings covered a variety of subjects: the exploitation of our forests; sections already felled and earmarked to be felled; assessments for each parcel of land; replanting; sowing; timber-land most in need of clearing next year; distribution of firewood-cutting permits; payments of dues. Hoping to find relief from the heat, I had chosen the cellar for my workplace, but even there, where an icy perspiration usually dampens the walls, I found nothing but heavy, dusty air, scarcely cooler than that in other rooms in the house. From time to time I heard the sound of Poupchette's laughter above my head. Fédorine had placed her in a large wooden basin filled with fresh water. She stayed in there for hours, tirelessly pretending to be a little fish while Emélia sat at the window near her, hands flat on her knees, staring out at nothing and intoning her melancholy refrain.

When I came up from the cellar, Poupchette, rubbed, dried and pink all over, was having a big bowl of clear soup, a broth of carrots and chervil. She called to me as I was getting ready to go out: "Leave, Papa? Leave?" She let herself down from her chair and ran to throw herself in my arms.

"I'll be back soon," I said. "I'll come and kiss you in bed. Be good!"

"Good! Good! Good!" she repeated, laughing and spinning around as if dancing a waltz.

O little Poupchette, some may tell you that you are nobody's child, a child of defilement, a child begotten in hatred and horror. Some may tell you that you are a child of abomination conceived in abomination, a tainted child, a child polluted long before you were born. Do not pay any attention to them, my little sweetheart, please do not listen to them; listen to me. I say you are my child and I love you. I sometimes say that out of horror, beauty and purity and grace are born. I say I am your father for ever. I say the loveliest rose can bloom in contaminated soil. I say you are the dawn, the light of all my tomorrows, and the only thing that matters is the promise you represent. I say you are my luck and my forgiveness. My darling Poupchette, I say you are my whole life.

Göbbler and I shut our doors behind us at the same moment, and we were both so surprised that we simultaneously looked heavenwards. Our houses, designed for winter, are naturally dark, and we often have to burn one or two candles even on bright, sunny days to be able to see. When I stepped out of the dim interior, I expected to find, as soon as I crossed my threshold, the leonine sun that had roared down at us unremittingly for the past few weeks. But it was as if an immense, drab, greyish-beige blanket, streaked with black, had been cast over the whole sky. On the eastern horizon, the crests of the Hörni were fading into a thick, metallic magma, speckled with fleecy blotches, which gave the suffocating impression of gradually sinking lower, as if it would eventually crush the forests and stave in the roofs of houses. Irregular patches of brightness mottled the dense mass here and there with a false, yellowish light, like aborted flashes of lightning. The heat had grown sticky and took hold of our throats like the hands of criminals, slowly but surely strangling us.

After our initial surprise had passed, Göbbler and I began to walk at the same time, in the same tempo, side by side. We trudged like a pair of robots down the dusty road which, bathed in that strange light, looked as though it were covered with birch ashes. The smell of chicken feathers and chicken droppings floated around me, a sickening, corrupt odour like that of flower stems rotting in vases, neglected for days.

I had no desire to talk to Göbbler, and the silence disturbed me not at all. I expected him to start a conversation at any moment, but he said nothing. We walked through the streets like that, mute, like two men

231

on their way to a funeral who know that all words are useless in the face of death.

The closer we drew to the inn, the more silhouettes joined us, gliding out of side streets and lanes, slipping out of alleyways and doorways, and walking beside us, as unspeaking as we were. It may be that the general silence was due not to the prospect of discovering what we were going to be shown in the inn, but to the sudden change in the weather, to the thick metallic cloak still covering the sky which had brought the afternoon to a dark, winterish end.

There was not one woman among that stream of men, which swelled at every turn. We were all men, nothing but men, men among men. And yet there are women in the village, as there are everywhere else, women of every sort, young, old, pretty and very ugly women, all of whom know things, all of whom think. Women who have brought us into the world and who watch us destroy it, who give us life and often have occasion to regret it. I do not know why, but that is what I was thinking about at that moment, as I walked along without saying a word to anyone, in the midst of all those men who were walking along without saying anything either, and I thought especially about my mother. About the woman who does not exist, whereas I exist. Who has no face, whereas I have one.

Sometimes I look at myself in the little mirror that hangs above the stone sink in our house. I observe my nose, the shape and colour of my eyes, the colour of my hair, the outline of my lips, the formation of my ears, the shade of my skin. And with all these features I attempt to compose a portrait of my absent mother, of the woman who one day saw the little body emerge from between her thighs, who cradled it to her breast, who caressed it, who gave it her warmth and her milk, who talked to it, who gave it a name, and who no doubt smiled a smile of happiness. I know what I am doing is futile. I will never be able to compose her features or draw them out of the night she entered so long ago.

Everything had been turned inside out in Schloss' inn. The place was unrecognizable. It was as if it had put on a new skin. We went in on tiptoe, almost not daring to enter at all. Even those who were ordinarily incapable of keeping their mouths shut remained speechless. Many turned towards Orschwir, apparently under the impression that the Mayor was different from them and would show them what was to be done, how they should behave, what to say and not to say. But Orschwir was like everybody else. No smarter, not any wiser.

The tables had been pushed against one wall, covered with clean cloths, and laden with dozens of bottles and glasses lined up like soldiers before a battle. There were also big platters piled with sliced sausages, pieces of cheese, strips of lean bacon, slices of ham, loaves of bread and brioches, enough to feed a regiment. At first, all eyes were attracted by that array of food and drink, which was lavish to a degree that is rarely seen among us, except at certain weddings where well-to-do peasants unite their progeny and seek to impress their guests. And so it was a while before we noticed the twenty or so cloths hanging on the walls, covering what appeared to be about twenty picture frames. Members of the company indicated these objects to one another, pointing their chins, but there was no time to say or do anything else, because the staircase steps began to creak and the *Anderer* appeared.

He did not have on any of the bizarre clothing that people had over time grown accustomed to – no frilly shirt, no jabot, no frock coat, no stovepipe trousers. Instead he was wearing a sort of large, ample robe, which covered his entire body, even to his feet, baring his thick neck in a way that made it look disembodied, as though an executioner had neatly lopped off his head.

The *Anderer* walked down a few steps. He made a most odd impression, for his robe was so long that even his feet were hidden; he seemed to glide along a few inches above the floor, like a ghost. No-one said a word, and he precluded any reaction by beginning to speak himself in his discreet, slightly reedy voice:

"I have long searched for a way to thank you all for your welcome and your hospitality. In the end I decided that I should do what I know how to do: to look, to listen and to capture the souls of people and things. I have done much travelling, all over the world. Perhaps that is the reason why my eyes see more and my ears hear better. I believe, without presumption, that I have understood you yourselves to a great degree, and likewise this landscape which you inhabit. Accept my little works as homages. Look for nothing more in them. Monsieur Schloss, if you please!"

The innkeeper had been standing to attention, awaiting only this signal before going into action. At the double, he covered the perimeter of his inn's main room, whisking away the cloths that covered the pictures. As if the scene were not strange enough, this was the moment when the first thunderclap sounded, loud and sharp, like a whip cracking on an old nag's rump.

The perfumed card had told the truth: there were *portraits*, and there were *landscapes*. They were not, properly speaking, paintings, but rather ink drawings, sometimes composed in broad brushstrokes, sometimes in extremely delicate lines jostling, covering and criss-crossing one another. We passed before them in procession, following a peculiar Way of the Cross, to see the pictures up close. Some in attendance, such as Göbbler and Lawyer Knopf, who were both as blind as bats, all but pressed their noses against the pictures; others did the opposite, backing away to take the full measure of a drawing and falling behind the rest of the company. The first cries of surprise and nervous laughs came when some of the men recognized themselves or others in the portraits. The *Anderer* had made his selection. How? This was a mystery, but the subjects he had chosen were Orschwir, Hausorn, Father Peiper, Göbbler, Dorcha, Vurtenhau, Röppel, Ullrich Yackob the verger, Schloss and me. The landscapes included the church square and the low houses at its perimeter, the Lingen, Orschwir's farm, the Tizenthal rocks, the Baptisterbrücke with the grove of white willows in the background, the Lichmal clearing, and the main room in Schloss' inn.

What was really curious was that although we recognized faces and places, no-one could have said that the drawings were perfect likenesses. It was almost as though they called forth familiar echoes, impressions and resonances to complete in our minds the portraits which were merely suggested in the pictures before us.

Once everyone had completed his little round, things began to get serious. The company turned its back on the drawings as though they had never existed. There was a general movement towards the laden tables. You would have thought that most of the men in the inn had neither eaten nor drunk for years on end. Savages. In no time at all, everything that had been put out had disappeared, but Schloss must have had orders to provide a steady supply of fresh bottles and platters, because the buffet never seemed to empty entirely. Cheeks grew flushed, foreheads began to sweat, conversation became louder, and the first expletives reverberated off the walls. Many in the group had doubtless already forgotten why they had come, and no-one was looking at the pictures any more. The only thing that mattered was what they could get down their throats. As for the *Anderer*, he had disappeared. It was Diodème who pointed this out to me: "Right after his little speech he went back up to his room. What do you think about that?"

"About what?"

"About this whole affair . . ." Diodème waved a hand at the exposition on the walls. I believe I shrugged. "It's funny," he said. "Your portrait, I mean. It doesn't look very much like you, and yet it's absolutely you. I don't know how to describe it. Come and have a look."

Not wanting to be disagreeable to Diodème, I followed him. We manoevred past the bodies in our way, with their smells, their sweat, their beery or vinous breath. Voices were growing heated, and so were heads; many of the company were talking very loudly. Orschwir had removed his velour hat. Lawyer Knopf was whistling. *Zungfrost*, who normally drank only water, had downed three glasses under compulsion and was starting to dance. Three laughing men were restraining Lulla Carpak, a vagrant with yellow hair and the complexion of a radish, who as soon as he got drunk always felt a burning desire to punch someone in the face.

"Take a good look," Diodème said. We were standing in front of my portrait. I looked at it, as he had suggested, for a long time. At first I did not pay particularly close attention to the lines the *Anderer* had traced there, but then, little by little, and without understanding why or how, I went deeper and deeper into the drawing.

The first time I had seen it a few minutes earlier I had not noticed anything. My name was written under it, and maybe I felt a bit embarrassed at having been portrayed, because I had quickly turned my head away and hurried on to the next picture. But when I saw it again, when I stood in front of it and considered it properly, it was as if it had sucked me in, as if it had come alive, and what I saw were no longer lines and curves and points and little blots, but fragments of my life. The portrait

236

the *Anderer* had composed was, so to speak, alive. It was my life. I was confronted with myself, with my sorrows, my follies, my fears, my desires. I saw my extinguished childhood, my long months in the camp. I saw my homecoming. I saw my mute Emélia. I saw everything. The drawing was an opaque mirror that threw back into my face all that I had been and all that I was. Diodème once again brought me back to reality.

"Well?"

"It's peculiar," I said.

"If you look, if you really look, it's like that with all of them: not exactly faithful, but very true."

Maybe it was Diodème's passion for novels that made him always peer into the deepest folds of words and caused his imagination to run ten times faster than he did. But on that particular occasion, what he said to me was by no means stupid. I made one more tour of the room, studying the pictures the *Anderer* had put up on the walls of the inn. The landscapes, which had at first struck me as run-of-the-mill, came to life, and the faces in the portraits told of secrets, of torments, of heinousness, of mistakes, of confusion, of baseness. I had touched neither wine nor beer, and yet I tottered and my head spun. In Göbbler's portrait, for example, there was a mischievousness in the execution which caused the viewer, if he looked at the image from the left, to see the face of a smiling man with faraway eyes and serene features, whereas if he looked at it from the right, the same lines fixed the expressions of the mouth, eyes and forehead in a venomous scowl, a sort of horrible grimace, haughty and cruel. Orschwir's portrait spoke of cowardice, of dishonourable conduct, of spinelessness and moral flaw. Dorcha's insinuated violence, bloody actions, unpardonable deeds. Vurtenhau's displayed meanness, stupidity, envy, rage. Peiper's suggested abdication, shame, weakness. It was the same for all the faces; the *Anderer*'s portraits acted like magical expositions that brought their subjects' hidden truths to light. It was like a gallery of the flayed.

And then there were the landscapes! It might not seem like much, a landscape. It has nothing to say. At best it sends us back to ourselves, nothing more. But in these sketches by the *Anderer*, landscapes could talk. They recounted their history. They carried traces of what they had known. They bore witness to events that had unfolded there. In the church square, on the ground, an ink stain, drawn in the very spot where the execution of Aloïs Cathor had taken place, evoked all the blood that had flowed out of his beheaded body, and in the same drawing, if you looked at the houses around the square, all their doors were closed. The picture showed only one open door, the one to Otto Mischenbaum's barn. I am not inventing this, I swear it! Also, if you tilted your head a little while looking at the drawing of the Baptisterbrücke, you could see that the roots of the white willows formed the shapes of three faces, the faces of three young girls. In the same way, if you squinted slightly when you looked at the picture of the Lichmal clearing, you could make out the girls' faces in the oak branches. And if I was unable at that moment to discover what was to be seen in some of the other drawings, that was simply because the events they alluded to had not yet taken place. At the time, for example, the Tizenthal rocks were just that, ordinary rocks, neither pretty nor ugly, playing no part in either history or legend, but it was in front of the *Anderer*'s drawing of those very rocks that I found Diodème. He was planted in front of it like a milestone in a field. Transfixed. I had to say his name three times before he turned a little to look at me.

"What do you see in this one?" I asked.

"Several things," he said dreamily. "Several things . . ."

He did not elaborate. Later, when he was dead, I had time to reflect. I thought about the *Anderer*'s drawing again.

I suppose it could be said that I have a short temper and a cracked brain. That the whole story with the drawings made no sense. That an unsound mind and deranged senses would be required for someone to see in those primitive scribbles everything that I saw. And that it is of course easy to bring all this up for consideration now, when there is no proof of anything, when the drawings no longer exist, when they have all been destroyed. Yes, that's right, they were all destroyed! That very evening, no less! If that is not proof, then what is? The drawings were ripped into a thousand pieces, scattered to the four winds, or reduced to ashes because they said, in their fashion, things that should never have been said, and they revealed truths that had been carefully smothered.

As for me, I had had more than enough.

I left the inn as the drinking was proceeding at a gathering pace and men were bellowing like beasts – but they were still happy beasts, carousing merrily. Diodème, on the other hand, stayed until the end, and I got my account of what happened from him. Schloss brought out pitchers and bottles for about an hour after I left, and then, suddenly, the ammunition having run out, hostilities were suspended; evidently the sum agreed between him and the *Anderer* had been reached. From this point on, everything went sour. At first there were words followed by a certain amount of weight being thrown about, but nothing really nasty as yet – just general grumbling, the odd breakage, nothing more serious. But then the nature of the grumbling changed, as when a calf is separated from its mother's teats; at first it whimpers, but then it resigns itself and looks around for another amusement, some small *raison d'être*. The change came when everyone remembered why they were there in the first place. They turned back to the pictures and considered them again. Or differently. Or with the scales fallen from their eyes, if you will. In any case, they took another look at the pictures and saw themselves. Exposed. They saw what they were and what they had done. They saw in the *Anderer*'s drawings everything that Diodème and I had seen. And of course they could not bear it, of course. Who could have borne it?

"It was a real mess! I never quite worked out who started it, and in any case that's not important, because everyone joined in, and nobody tried to restrain anyone else. The priest had long since passed out. He was asleep under a table sucking on a bit of his cassock, like a child sucking his thumb. The older fellows had gone home shortly after you did. As for Orschwir, he didn't take part in the spectacle; he just watched, but he had a satisfied smile on his face, and when young Kipoft threw his portrait into the fire, Orschwir looked downright happy, believe me! And the whole thing happened so fast! Before I had time to blink, everything on the walls was gone. The only person who looked a bit peeved was Schloss."

Diodème gave me this account two days after that festive evening at Schloss' inn. The rain had not stopped falling; it was as if the heavens needed to do a big wash, to launder men's dirty linen since they were apparently not up to doing it themselves. The walls of our houses seemed to be weeping, and in the streets, rivulets of water turned brown by earth and stable dung streamed between the cobblestones, ferrying along small pebbles, bits of straw, sundry vegetable peelings, flecks of dirt. What's more, it was an odd kind of rain, a continuous deluge that fell from a sky we could not even see, so thick, leaden and waterlogged was the blanket of clouds that kept it persistently hidden. We had waited for that rain for weeks. For weeks the village had baked in the heat, and along with the village the bodies of the villagers, their nerves, their muscles, their desires, their hearts, and then this storm came, this great splashing havoc of a storm, which corresponded on a gigantic scale to the human gushing, the unleashing of all that was pent up inside Schloss' inn, for precisely at the moment when that minor rehearsal for the *Ereigniës* was going on, when effigies were being burned as a preliminary to killing the man, the overloaded sky split in two along its entire width, from east to west, and torrents of grey rain spilled out of it as from bowels, as from intestines, an immense downpour of water as greasy and heavy as dishwater.

Schloss threw everyone out, including the Mayor, and the whole jolly crew waded home through the storm, occasionally illuminated by lightning. Some of them lay down in puddles and pretended to swim, shouting like schoolboys off the leash, throwing handfuls of mud at their companions' faces, as if they were snowballs.

I like to think that the *Anderer* stood at his upstairs window and contemplated the scene. I imagine his little smile. The heavens were vindicating him, and everything that he saw down below – creatures soaked to the skin, vomiting and trading insults, their laughter and their slurred words interspersed with their streams of piss – could but make his demolished portraits seem even truer to life. It was, in a way, something of a triumph for him. The consecration of a master of the game.

But down here it is better never to be right. That is one thing you always end up paying dearly for.

35

The next day was the morning after hangover day, when the skull pounds away like a drum of its own accord, and one is not sure whether what one remembers was dreamed or lived. I believe that most of those who had gone wild the previous night must have felt like great fools once they had sobered up; they might have felt relief, but they also knew they had been damned stupid. Not that they were ashamed of their treatment of the *Anderer*, no; in that regard their minds were set, and nothing could change them. But when they thought about it, their furious attack on plain scraps of paper could not have seemed especially manly.

The rain suited them. They did not have to leave their houses or encounter one another or converse or see in the eyes of others what they themselves had done. Only the Mayor braved the storms that came sweeping over the village in rapid succession, as if it were April and not August. That evening he left his house and went directly to the inn. He was soaked to the skin by the time he arrived. Schloss was quite surprised when his door opened, since it had remained insistently shut all day long. Moreover, he had not in truth spent the day hoping for customers. It had taken him hours to clean up after the intemperance of the night and wash everything, including the floor, and at the same time maintain a roaring blaze in the hearth to dry the tiles and consume the rancid air. He had just finished the job. Everything – the room, the tables, the walls – was at last back to normal, as if nothing had happened the previous evening. And at this point Orschwir made his entrance.

Schloss looked at him as if he were a monster, a monster that had taken on a great deal of water, but a monster all the same. The Mayor removed the big shepherd's cloak he had rigged himself out in and hung it on a nail near the fireplace. He took out a crumpled and rather dirty handkerchief, wiped his face with it, blew his nose, folded it up again, stuffed it in his pocket, and finally turned to Schloss, who was leaning on his broom, waiting.

"I have to talk to him. Go and get him."

This was clearly an order. No need for Schloss to ask Orschwir to specify who "him" was; there were only two people at the inn, Schloss and the *Anderer*. As he did each morning, Schloss had placed a breakfast tray – round brioche, raw egg, pot of hot water – outside his guest's door. A little later he had heard, as he did each morning, footsteps on the stairs, followed by the sound of the little back door opening and closing. That was the door his guest used when he went to visit his horse and donkey in Père Solzner's stable, which adjoined the inn. Shortly thereafter, Schloss had heard the little door open again and the stairs creak, and then that was all.

The Mayor is somebody, in a village like ours. No innkeeper is going to argue with him about what he is being told to do. So Schloss went upstairs and knocked on the door of his guest's room. Almost at once he found himself face to face with the *Anderer*'s smile and relayed Orschwir's request. The *Anderer* smiled a little more, made no reply, and closed the door. Schloss went back downstairs and said, "I think he's coming."

Orschwir replied, "Very good, Schloss. Now, I suppose you have enough work to keep you busy in the kitchen, yes?"

The innkeeper, who was no fool, mumbled a yes. The Mayor drew a complex and finely-worked silver key from his pocket and opened the door to the smaller of the two public rooms in the inn, the one reserved for *De Erweckens' Bruderschaft*.

When Schloss told me all this, I asked him, "You don't have a key to that door?"

"Of course I don't! I've never even gone into that room! I don't even fucking know what it looks like. I don't know how many keys there are or who has them, apart from the Mayor and Knopf, and most probably Göbbler, but I'm not even sure about him."

Schloss came to our house not long ago. He waited until the night was black as pitch and scratched at the door like an animal. I imagined he had crept along the walls of houses along the way, careful to make no noise and above all trying to avoid being seen. It was the first time he had ever stepped over our threshold; I wondered what in the world he could want. Fédorine looked at him as if he were rat droppings. She does not like him. As far as she is concerned, he is a thief who buys a few provisions cheap and then sells them at a very high price. She calls him *Schlocheikei*, which in her ancient language is an untranslatable pun that combines the innkeeper's name with a word that means "profiteer". Soon after he arrived, she made an excuse about having to put Poupchette to bed and left us alone. When she said the word Poupchette I saw a sad light glimmer in the innkeeper's eyes, and I thought about his dead infant son; then, very quickly, the light went out.

"I wanted to talk to you, Brodeck. I have to talk to you. I have to try once more to make you see that I'm not your enemy, I'm not a bad man. I know you didn't really believe me that other time. I'm going to tell you what I know. You can do what you want with it, but I warn you, don't say you heard it from me, because if you do, I'll deny everything. I'll say you're lying. I'll say I never told you that. I'll even say I never came to your house. Understand?"

I did not reply to Schloss. I had not asked him for anything. He had come of his own accord. It was up to him to say his piece, without trying to obtain anything from me.

Eventually, he told me, the *Anderer* came downstairs and the Mayor showed him into the room used by the brotherhood. Then he closed the door behind them.

"As for me, I stayed in my kitchen as Orschwir told me to. But here's the thing: the cupboard where I keep the brooms and buckets is built into the wall, and the back of the cupboard is nothing but planks of wood. I don't think they were nailed up straight in the first place, and over the years the gaps have grown as wide as eyes. Now, the cupboard backs onto their little room. Gerthe knew this too. I'm certain she listened to what was said and done in there some evenings, even if she never would admit it to me. She knew very well I'd be furious."

So on the day in question, Schloss did what he had never before allowed himself to do. Why? Men's actions can be very bizarre; you can torture yourself endlessly about human behaviour without ever getting to the bottom of it. Perhaps Schloss believed that eavesdropping might be the way for him to become a man, by defying a prohibition, and thereby passing a test, by changing camps definitively to do what he thought was just, or was he merely satisfying a curiosity too long suppressed? Whatever his motive, he wedged his large body in among brooms, shovels, buckets and old dusting rags and glued his ear to the planks.

"Their conversation was peculiar, Brodeck, believe me! Most peculiar . . . At the beginning you might have thought they understood each other very well; they didn't need a lot of words; they spoke the same language. The Mayor began by saying that he hadn't come to apologize. What had happened the previous evening was of course regrettable, but it was quite understandable, he said. The *Anderer* didn't move.

245

"'The people here are a little uncouth, you see,' the Mayor went on. 'If they have a wound and you throw pepper in it, they're going to kick your backside hard, and they'll keep kicking it. And your drawings were big handfuls of pepper, weren't they?'

"'The drawings are of no importance, Monsieur le Maire. Don't give them another thought,' the *Anderer* replied. 'Had your people not destroyed them, I would have done so myself . . .'"

At this moment in his tale, which he was reciting as if he had learned it by heart, Schloss paused: "One thing you have to know, Brodeck, is that their conversation was full of long silences. When one of them asked a question, it was a good while before the other replied, and vice versa. I'm sure they were sizing each other up, those two. They reminded me of chess players and the little games they play between moves. I don't know if I make myself clear."

I made a noncommittal movement with my head. Schloss looked at his hands, which were pressed together, and went on with his story. It was Orschwir who posed the question: "May I ask you what it was, exactly, that you intended to do when you came to this village?"

"Your village appeared to me to be worthy of interest."

"But it is far away from everything."

"Perhaps that was the very reason. I wished to see what sort of people live far away from everything."

"The war brought its ravages here as it did elsewhere."

"'*War ravages and reveals . . .*'"

"What do you mean?"

"Nothing, Monsieur le Maire. It is a verse translated from a very ancient poem."

"There's nothing poetic about war."

"No, indeed; no indeed."

"I think it would be best for you to leave the village. You stir up – whether you do it intentionally or not – you wake up things that have gone to sleep. No good can come of that. Leave the village, please . . ."

Schloss could not remember the rest word for word, because Orschwir abandoned his clipped phrases and lost himself in a series of interminable ramblings, so confused that he often lost his way. But I know that Orschwir is too crafty to rattle on blindly. I am sure he weighed his thoughts and his words, one by one. He was merely affecting hesitations and confusion.

"It was quite sly," Schloss said. "In the end, everything he said was a veiled threat, but it could also have been taken to mean just the opposite. And if the *Anderer* had ever objected to being threatened, Orschwir could always have claimed he had been misunderstood. Their little encounter lasted a while longer, but I was going numb in the cupboard and I needed air. My ears were buzzing. I felt as though bees were flying around me. I have too much blood in my head, and sometimes it gets too much. In any case, at some point I heard them get up and walk towards the door. Before he opened it, the Mayor said a few other things and then he asked one final question, the one that had the most effect on me, because his voice changed when he asked it. I know that not much gets to him, but I could detect a hint of fear in his tone. But before that he said, 'We don't even know your name.'

"'How can that be important now?' the *Anderer* said. 'A name is nothing. I could be nobody or everybody.'

"Several moments passed before Orschwir continued: 'I wanted to ask you one more question. It is something that has preyed on my mind for a good while now.'

"'I am at your service, Monsieur le Maire.'

"'Were you sent here by someone?'

"The *Anderer* laughed, you know, his little laugh, almost like a woman's. Then, after a long, long pause, he finally said, 'It all depends on your beliefs, Monsieur le Maire, it all depends on your beliefs. I'll let you be the judge . . .'

"And then he laughed again. And that laugh – I tell you, Brodeck, it sent a chill down my spine."

Schloss was spent. He looked exhausted, but at the same time relieved to have let me in on his secret. I went and got two glasses and a bottle of *eau-de-vie*.

As I was filling the glasses, he asked, with a hint of anxiety, "Do you believe me, Brodeck?"

"Why wouldn't I believe you, Schloss?"

He bowed his head very low and sipped his drink.

Whether Schloss told me the truth or not, whether the conversation he reported took place or not, in the exact terms that I have transcribed or in other more or less similar terms, the indubitable fact is that the *Anderer* did not leave the village. What is also certain is that, five days later, when the rain stopped and the sun reappeared and people began to come out of their houses and talk to one another, you could hear the last bit of the exchange between the Mayor and the *Anderer* repeated everywhere. Those words were worse than the driest tinder, waiting to burst into flames! If we had had a priest with a functioning brain, he would have thrown buckets of holy water on that blaze; he would have put it out with some well-chosen words and a little common sense. But instead, Peiper poured a little more oil on the fire the following Sunday with his drunken raving during his sermon, babbling something about the Antichrist and the Last Judgment – in connection with what, I do not know. Nor do I know who spoke the word "Devil" first, whether it was the priest or someone else, but it suited most of the congregation, and they seized upon it. Since the *Anderer* had not wanted to give his name, the village had found one for him. A name that was made to measure. A name which has been put to much use over the centuries, but which never wears out. A name that is always striking. Effective. Definitive.

Stupidity is a sickness that goes very well with fear. They nurture each other, creating a gangrene that seeks only to propagate itself. Peiper's sermon and the things the *Anderer* was supposed to have said combined to make a fine concoction indeed!

And yet he suspected nothing. He continued to take his little walks until Tuesday, 3 September. He did not seem surprised when people no longer returned his greetings or crossed themselves in self-defence when they passed him. Not one child followed him any more. Having been sternly warned at home, the children took to their heels as soon as they saw him a hundred metres off. Once the cheekiest of them even threw a few stones at him.

Every morning as usual he went to the stable to visit his horse and donkey. But despite his arrangement with Père Solzer and the money he had paid the stable owner in advance, the *Anderer* noticed that his animals had been left to themselves. Their drinking trough was empty. Their mangers too. He did not complain; he performed the necessary chores himself, rubbed down his two beasts, groomed them, whispered in their ears, reassured them. Mademoiselle Julie showed him her yellow teeth and Monsieur Socrate bobbed his head up and down, flicking his short tail. This happened on Monday evening; I witnessed the scene myself on my way home from a day in the forest. Since I was behind the *Anderer*, he did not see me. I was on the point of stepping into the stable or coughing or saying something, but I did nothing. I stood quite still in the doorway. Unlike their master, the animals saw me. Their big soft eyes rested on me. I stayed there for a moment, hoping that one of them would react to my presence – with a little kicking, perhaps, or a grunt or two. But they did nothing. Nothing at all. The *Anderer* kept on stroking them with his back to me. I went on my way.

36

It was Diodème who came on the following day, to collect me. Out of breath, his shirt unbuttoned, his trousers askew, and his hair dishevelled. "Come! Come quick!"

I was busy carving some clogs for Poupchette out of blocks of black fir. It was eleven o'clock in the morning.

"Come on, I said! Come and see what they've done!"

He looked so panic-stricken that there was no room for discussion. I put down my gouge, brushed off the wood shavings that had fallen on me like down from a plucked goose, and followed him.

Along the whole way, he said not a word. He hurried on as if the fate of the world depended on his speed, and I had trouble matching my strides with those of his long legs. I saw that we were heading towards the sharp bend in the Staubi, where it curves around the fields of vegetables belonging to Sebastian Uränheim, the biggest producer of cabbages, turnips and leeks in our valley, but I did not understand why. As soon as we got past the last house, I saw. I saw the big crowd on the riverbank, close to a hundred people, I think, men, women and children, all of them facing away from us and looking in the direction of the water.

A surge of panic made my heart beat faster, and I thought, rather stupidly, of Poupchette and Emélia. I say "rather stupidly" because I knew they were at home. A few minutes earlier, I thought, when Diodème came to get me, they were there in the house. Therefore they cannot have been involved in whatever misfortune has just taken place out here. I made myself see reason and joined the silent crowd.

Nobody spoke, nor was there any expression on anyone's face as slowly I pushed my way to the front. The scene was utterly strange: the expressionless features, the staring, unblinking eyes, the closed mouths, the bodies I nudged standing aside to let me pass, and me going through them as if they were insubstantial. After I had passed through, the crowd regained its shape and people popped back into their original positions, like rocking toys.

I was perhaps three or four metres from the water's edge when I heard the moaning, a sad one-note song without words that got into your ears and froze your blood, though God knows it was hot that morning; after the great deluge and the carnival of cloudbursts and lightning, the sun had reclaimed its rights. I had come almost all the way through the crowd. In front of me there were only the eldest Dörfer boy and his little brother Schmutti, who is simple-minded and carries on his rather feeble shoulders a disproportionately large head, as big as a pumpkin and as hollow as the trunk of a dead tree. I gently pushed them aside, and then I could see.

The crowd had gathered at the spot where the Staubi runs deepest. It cannot be much less than three metres to the bottom, but it is a little difficult to gauge as the water is so clear and pure that the riverbed looks as though you could touch it with your finger.

In my life I have seen many men weep. I have seen many tears flow. I have seen people crushed like nuts between stones until nothing was left but debris. That was part of the daily routine at the camp. But despite all the sorrow and tragedy I have witnessed, if ever I had to choose one from among the infinite gallery of faces in my memory who have expressed suffering, of all the people who have suddenly realized that they have lost everything, that everything has been taken from them, that they have nothing left, it would be the face of the *Anderer* as it looked that morning, that morning in September on the banks of the Staubi, which would make the deepest impression on me.

He was not weeping. He was not gesticulating. It was as though he had been divided in two. One part was his voice, his unceasing lament which resembled a song of mourning, something beyond words, beyond all language, rising from the depths of the body and soul: the voice of grief. And then there was the other part, the trembling, the shuddering, his round head which turned from the crowd to the river and back again, and his body wrapped in a luxurious brocade dressing gown which was totally alien to the landscape; its dripping skirts, saturated with mud and water, swayed against his short legs.

I did not understand at first why the *Anderer* was in such a state, why he looked like an automaton doomed perpetually to repeat gestures of madness. I stared at him so hard, hoping to discover something in his face, in his partially open mouth, in his plenipotentiary's bathrobe, that I did not immediately notice his right hand, which was clutching something that looked like a tress of long, slightly faded blond hair.

It was the hair of his horse's tail, which emerged from the Staubi like a mooring line with one end still attached to the quay and the other to an irretrievably sunken vessel. I could see two large masses below the surface of the water, calm, ponderous bulks stirring gently in the river currents. The sight was unreal and almost peaceful: the big horse and the smaller donkey, both drowned, floating underwater with wide-open eyes. Due to some unknown phenomenon, the donkey's coat was decorated with thousands of minuscule air bubbles, as polished and shiny as pearls, and the horse's full, flowing mane mingled with the algae which in that place grew in thick scarves. It was like looking at two mythological creatures performing a fantastic dance. An eddy made them execute a circular movement, a slow waltz, without any music apart from the intrusive and suddenly obscene song of a blackbird, which soon resumed poking its brown beak into the soft soil of the bank to pull out long red worms. At first I thought that some final reflex had made both horse and donkey curve their bodies and gather their legs so that all four hoofs were nearly touching, the way one might curl up and roll oneself into a ball in order to present nothing but a rounded back to danger or to the cold. But then I saw the ropes and realized that in fact the beasts' legs were hobbled and solidly bound together.

I did not know what to do or say. And even if I had spoken, I am not sure that the *Anderer*, enclosed in his lamentation, would have heard me. He was trying to drag the horse out of the water – without success, of course, because the animal's weight was so disproportionate to his own strength. Nobody helped him. Nobody made a move in his direction. The only movement of the assembled multitude was a backwards surge. The crowd had seen enough. Here and there, people began to leave. Soon no-one remained except the Mayor, who had arrived after everyone else, accompanied by *Zungfrost*, driving a team of oxen. *Zungfrost* contemplated the scene without showing the least surprise, either because he had already seen it, or because he had been told about it, or because he was in on it. As for me, I had not moved. Orschwir looked at me suspiciously and addressed me without even acknowledging the presence of the *Anderer*.

"What do you think you're going to do, Brodeck?"

253

I did not see why the Mayor was asking me that question, or how I could reply to it. I was on the verge of saying, "A horse and a donkey don't tie their legs together all by themselves," but I decided to keep silent.

"You'd best do like the others, Brodeck, and go home," Orschwir continued.

Basically, he was right, so I started to do as he said, but before I had taken three paces he called me back: "Brodeck! Please take him back to the inn."

Zungfrost had succeeded, I do not know how, in making the *Anderer* release his grip on Mademoiselle Julie. Now he stood perfectly still on the riverbank, his hands hanging at his sides, and watched as the stammerer tied the horse's tail to a thick leather strap whose other end was attached to the oxen's yoke. I put my hand on the *Anderer*'s shoulder, but he did not react. Then I slipped my arm through his, turned and began to walk away. He let himself be led like a child. His keening had stopped.

A man could not have done away with those beasts on his own. Nor could two men have managed it. A job like that would require several men. And besides, what an expedition! To get into the stable – at night, no doubt – would not be hard. Nor was getting the animals out, because they were docile and good-natured, anything but wild. But then, on the river bank (because it can have happened nowhere else), to make the animals lie on their sides, maybe by pushing them over, to seize their legs, hold them together and bind them solidly, and then to carry or drag them to the water and throw them in – that was quite a feat. After careful consideration, I believe there could have been no fewer than five or six of them, five or six beefy fellows who, on top of everything else, had to be unafraid of getting kicked or bitten.

The cruelty of the animals' death did not seem remarkable to anyone.

254

Some villagers declared that such beasts could be nothing less than demonic creatures. Some even murmured that they had heard the beasts talking. But most people said that what had happened was perhaps the only way to get rid of the *Anderer*, the only way to compel him to clear out of our village and go back to where he came from, that is, to a far-off place nobody even wanted to think about. This imbecile savagery was, among other things, somewhat paradoxical, since by killing the *Anderer*'s mounts in order to make him understand that he had to go, they had deprived him of his only swift means of leaving the village. But murderers, whether of animals or of men, rarely reflect on their deeds.

37

I have never killed donkeys or horses.

I have done far worse.

Yes, far worse.

At night, I do not only walk along the rim of the *Kazerkswir*.

I see again the wagon.

I live again the six days I spent in the wagon.

I live again the six nights too, and especially, like a never-fading nightmare, the fifth of those nights.

They made us board the wagons at the train station in S., after we were separated into two columns as I have already said. We were all *Fremdër*. Some rich, some poor. Some from the city, others from the country. Such distinctions were soon blurred. We were shoved into big, windowless freight wagons. There was a little straw, already soiled, on the wooden floor. Under normal conditions, each wagon would have had space for about thirty people to sit very close together. The guards pushed more than double that number into our wagon. There were cries, moans, protests, tears. An old man fell down. Some people next to him tried to lift him up, but the guards thrust in still more prisoners, causing erratic, abrupt and violent shifts among those already inside. The old man was trampled by the very people who had tried to save him.

He was the first to die in our wagon.

A few minutes later, having loaded their freight, the guards slid the big iron doors shut and bolted them. We were plunged into darkness. The only light of day came through a few small cracks. The train started to move. There was a great lurch, which had the effect of pressing us even more tightly together. The journey began.

It was in these circumstances that I made the acquaintance of the student Kelmar. Chance had placed us side by side. Kelmar was on my right, while on my left was a young woman with a child in her arms, a baby of a few months. She held the child close the whole time. We were aware of everything of the next person, their heat, all their smells, of their skin, of their hair, of their perspiration, of their clothes. You could not move without making your neighbour move. You could not stand up or shift position. The occasional jolts of the train threw us yet more one against the other. People spoke in low voices at first; later, they did not speak at all. There was some weeping, but very little. Sometimes a child hummed a tune, but most of the time there was silence, nothing but silence, and the sound of the axles and the pounding of the iron wheels on the rails. Sometimes the wagon rolled along for hours without stopping; sometimes it remained at a standstill, but we never knew where or why. Over the course of six days, the big door was opened only once, the morning of the fifth day, not with any intention of letting us out; but only to have hands with no faces behind them douse us with several buckets of tepid water.

Unlike some of our more provident companions, Kelmar and I had brought nothing to eat or drink. But strangely enough – at least for the first few days – we did not suffer much from that. We talked softly to each other. We called to mind memories of the Capital. We discussed the books we had read, our friends at the University and the cafés I used to pass with Ulli Rätte, the same cafés in which Kelmar, who came from a well-to-do family, used to meet his friends to drink *eaux-de-vie flambées* and beer, and large creamy hot chocolates. Kelmar told me about his family: about his father, who was a fur merchant; about his mother, who spent her days playing piano in their great house on the banks of the river; and about his six sisters, who ranged in age from ten to eighteen. He told me their names, but I cannot remember them. I talked to him about Emélia and Fédorine, about our village and the countryside round about, its springs, its forests, the flowers and the animals.

Thus for three days our food and drink were words, and we nourished each other with them in the stinking heat of the wagon. Sometimes at night we would manage to sleep a little, but when we could not, we continued our conversations. The child that the young woman held tight to her made no sound. He took her breast when she offered it to him, but he never asked for it. I watched him with the nipple in his little mouth, creasing his cheeks in his effort to draw out some milk, but his mother's breasts looked flaccid and empty, and the baby soon grew tired of sucking in vain. Then his mother produced a glass demijohn enclosed in wickerwork and poured a little water into his mouth. Others in the wagon had similar treasures – a piece of bread, a hunk of cheese, some biscuits, some sausage, and some water, which they jealously guarded under their clothes, next to their skin.

At the beginning, I was very thirsty. My mouth burned. I felt as though my tongue was growing huge and dry, like an old stump, filling my mouth to the point of bursting. I had no more saliva. My teeth were like coals, piercing with their little daggers into my gums. I thought at one point that they were bleeding, but then I passed my fingers over them and saw that it was only an illusion. Gradually, bizarrely, my thirst disappeared. I felt weaker and weaker, but I was no longer thirsty. Hardly hungry. The two of us, Kelmar and I, kept on talking.

The young woman paid no attention to us. She must have heard us, however, and I know she could feel me as I felt her, her hip against mine, her shoulder, sometimes even her head, striking my head or leaning on me in sleep. She never said a word to us. She held her baby close, and likewise her equally precious demijohn, rationing the water methodically and sparing only a little at a time for herself and her child.

All of us, as many as we were, were losing the sense of time and place. I do not mean the immediate place we were in, the constricting dimensions of the wagon, but the land through which our train was slowly lumbering. In which direction were we travelling? What was its destination? What regions, what countries were we crossing? Did they exist on any map?

Today I know that they existed on no map and only came into being as our wagon rolled over them. Our wagon and all the other wagons like it – in which, as in ours, dozens of women, children and men, gasping for air, consumed by thirst, fever and hunger, were pressed against one another, sometimes the dead against the living – the wagon and all the other wagons were inventing, from one minute to the next, a land of inhumanity, of the negation of all humanity, and the camp was going to be that land's heart. That was the journey we were making, the likes of which nobody had ever made before, at least not such a methodical, thorough, efficient journey as ours, which left no leeway for the unforeseen.

We had stopped counting the hours, the nights, the appearances of the sun through the cracks. In the beginning, such calculations had helped us, as had our efforts to orient ourselves, to say that we were travelling east, or rather south, or now in a northerly direction. But then we gave it up when it became a source of sorrow. We made no more estimates and had no idea where we were. I do not even think we hoped to arrive anywhere. The desire to do so had abandoned us.

Only much later when I thought about that terrible journey, when I tried to remember it and relive it, did I come to the conclusion that it lasted six days and six nights. And since reaching that conclusion, I have often thought that such a period of time was no accident. Our tormenters believed in God. They were well aware that, according to the Scriptures, it had taken Him six days to create the world. I am sure they told one another that they needed six days to start destroying it. Destroying it in us. And if the seventh day was a day of rest for Him, for us, when the guards opened the doors of the wagons and drove us out with their truncheons, it was for us the end.

But for me and for Kelmar, there had also been the fifth day. That morning, the door of the wagon was opened a little and buckets of water were thrown at us – lukewarm, muddy water which splashed over our filthy, jumbled, and in some cases dead bodies, and which, instead of refreshing and soothing us, did the opposite; it burned us and scalded us. That stale water brought back memories of all the pure, clear, limpid water we had drunk so avidly in days gone by.

The thirst came back. But this time, no doubt because our bodies were nearing extinction and our enfeebled minds were abandoning themselves to delirium, the thirst we felt made madmen of us. But let no-one misunderstand me: I am not seeking to excuse what we did.

The young woman beside me was still alive, and her baby too. They were breathing rather feebly, but they were breathing. It was their demijohn of water that had kept them alive, and in that demijohn, which seemed to Kelmar and me inexhaustible, there was still some water. We could hear it lapping against the sides of the bottle at every movement of the wagon, making a beautiful and unbearable music reminiscent of little streams, of flowing springs, of the melodies of fountains. The exhausted young woman closed her eyes more and more frequently and let herself drop into a sort of thick sleep out of which she would awaken abruptly with a start a few minutes later. In a few days her face had aged ten years, and so had her baby's, which took on the strange features of a little old man reduced to the proportions of an infant.

Kelmar and I had long since stopped talking. Each of us was coping as best he could with the shocks and aftershocks in his brain. We were both trying to reconcile, if it were possible, our past history and our present state. The wagon stank of enervated flesh, of excrement and sour humours, and when it slowed, it was assailed by countless flies which abandoned the peaceful countryside, the green grass and the fallow soil, to penetrate between the planks and fall upon us, rubbing their wings together as if to comment on our agony.

I believe we saw what we saw at the same instant. Then we turned our heads towards each other with the same movement, and that exchange of looks contained everything. The young woman had fallen asleep once again, but unlike the previous times, her weakened arms had loosened their grip on her child and her large glass bottle. The baby, who weighed very little, remained attached to his mother's body, but the demijohn had slipped onto the floor by my left leg. Kelmar and I understood each other without saying a word. I do not know if we gave the matter any thought. I do not know if there was anything to think about, or even if we were still capable of thinking. I do not know what it was deep down inside us that made the decision. Our hands grasped the demijohn at the same time. There was no hesitation. Kelmar and I exchanged one last look, and then we drank in turn, he and I, we drank the warm water from its glass container, we drank it to the last drop, closing our eyes, swallowing greedily, drinking as we had never drunk water before in the certainty that what was flowing down our throats was life, yes, life, and the taste of that life was putrid and sublime, bright and insipid, happy and sorrowful, a taste I believe I shall remember with horror until my dying day.

Towards evening, after screaming for a long time, the young woman died. Her child, the baby with the pale, wrinkled little body, the worried brow, and the swollen eyelids, survived her by a few hours. Before she died, she called the people around her thieves and murderers and struck out at everyone within her reach. Her fists were so small and weak that I felt her blows as caresses. I pretended to be asleep. So did Kelmar. The little water we had drunk had given us back much of our strength and cleared our heads as well – cleared them enough for us to regret what we had done, to find it abominable. We kept our eyes shut, not daring to open them to look at her, or to look at each other. The young woman and her baby would doubtless have died in any case, but this thought, however logical it may have been, did not suffice to erase the ignominy of the crime we had committed. That crime was our tormenters' great triumph, and we knew it. Kelmar even more than I perhaps at that moment, since shortly afterwards he chose not to go on. He chose to die quickly. He chose to punish himself.

As for me, I chose to live, and my punishment is my life. That is the way I see things. My punishment is all the suffering I have endured since. It is Brodeck-the-Dog. It is Emélia's silence, which sometimes I interpret as the greatest reproach of all. It is my constantly recurring nightmares. And more than anything else, it is this perpetual feeling of inhabiting a body I stole long ago thanks to a few drops of water.

38

When I left the shed yesterday evening, I was drenched with sweat despite the cold, the mist and the *Graufrozt* – the light frost, not white but grey, that occurs only around here – that had settled on the roofs of all the houses. I had only about ten metres or so to cover before I would find Fédorine in her kitchen, Poupchette in her little bed and Emélia in ours, but the distance seemed vast to me. In Göbbler's house there was a light burning. Was he by any chance watching me? Had he been outside the shed, listening to the sporadic clacking of my typewriter? I could not have cared less. I had travelled my road once again. I had returned to the wagon. I had written it all.

In our bedroom I wrapped my pages in the linen pouch, as I do every evening, and then I slipped into the warm bed; and this morning, as I do each morning, I tied my linen-wrapped confession around Emélia's waist. I have been doing this for weeks and weeks. Emélia never puts up any resistance or pays any attention to what I am doing, but this morning, just as I was about to remove my hands from her stomach, I felt her put one of her hands on one of mine and squeeze it a little. It was not for long, nor did I see it because it was still dark in the room. But I was not dreaming. I am sure it happened. Was it an involuntary movement, or could it have been something like a caress, like the beginning or the renewal of a caress?

It is now a little after noon, in the middle of a colourless day. Night has yet to clear completely. The day is too lazy to hold on to its light, and frost is still covering the gables and the treetops. Poupchette is pulling the skin of Fédorine's face into grotesque shapes, and Fédorine smiles and lets her do it. Emélia is in her seat at the window, looking out. She is humming.

I have just finished the Report. In a few hours I am going to submit it to Orschwir and the thing will be over and done with – at least I hope so. I have kept it simple. I have tried to tell the story faithfully. I have not made anything up. I have not altered anything. I have followed the trail as closely as possible. The only gaps I have had to fill occurred on the *Anderer*'s last day, the one that preceded the *Ereigniës*. Nobody wanted to talk to me about it. Nobody wanted to tell me anything.

On that infamous morning when the drowned carcasses of the donkey and the horse were found, I accompanied the *Anderer* back to the inn. Schloss opened the door for us. We looked at each other without exchanging a word, Schloss and I. The *Anderer* went up to his room. He did not come out of it all day. He did not touch a thing on the tray Schloss brought up.

One and all resumed their usual activities. The diminished heat made it possible for the men to go back into the fields and forests. Even the animals raised their heads a little. A pyre was constructed on the riverbank, and upon it were burned the carcasses of Monsieur Socrate and Mademoiselle Julie. Some of the village children watched the spectacle all day long, occasionally casting branches into the flames, and returned home with their hair and clothes reeking of cooked flesh and burned wood. And then night fell.

One hour after sunset we heard the first cries. A slightly high-pitched voice, filled with distress but perfectly clear, was shouting outside the door of each house: "Murderers! Murderers!" It was the voice of the *Anderer*. Like some strange nightwatchman he was shouting out in the street, reminding the villagers of what they had done or what they had not prevented. No-one saw him, but everyone heard him. No-one opened their door. No-one opened a shutter. People stopped their ears. People burrowed into their beds.

The following day, in the shops, in the cafés, at the inn, on the street corners, and in the fields, the cries in the night were the subject of some conversation. Some, but not much; people quickly passed on to other subjects. The *Anderer* remained out of sight, shut up in his room. It was as though he'd vanished into thin air. But again that second evening, two hours after sunset, the same mournful refrain echoed in every street, before every door: "Murderers! Murderers!"

Myself, I prayed he would stop. I knew how it was all going to end. The horse and the donkey would only be the preamble. Killing his animals would suffice to cool the hotheads for a time, but if he got on their nerves again, they would get some new ideas, and those ideas would be conclusive. I tried to tell him so. I went to the inn. I knocked at the door of his room. There was no response. I held my ear to the wood. I heard nothing. I tried the handle. The door was locked. But it was here that Schloss saw me.

"What are you up to, Brodeck? I didn't see you come in!"

"Where is he?"

"Where's who?"

"The *Anderer*!"

"Stop, Brodeck. Please stop . . ."

That day, those were the only words that Schloss addressed to me.

Then he turned his back and went away.

That evening, at the same hour as on the other evenings, the round began again, the crying out as before. This time shutters were banged open, and stones and insults flew through the air. But this did not discourage the *Anderer* from continuing on his way or prevent him from shouting into the darkness, "Murderers! Murderers!" I had trouble falling asleep. In nights like that I have learned that the dead never abandon the living. They find one another even if they were strangers. They gather. They come and sit on the edge of our bed, on the edge of our night. They gaze upon us and haunt us. Sometimes they caress our forehead; sometimes they stroke our cheeks with their fleshless hands. They try to open our eyelids, but even when they succeed, we do not always see them.

I spent the whole following day brooding, without moving. I did not move much. I thought about History with a capital H, and about my history, our history. Do those who write the first know anything about the second? Why do some people retain in their memory what others have forgotten or never seen? Which is right: he who cannot reconcile himself to leaving the past in obscurity, or he who hurls into obscurity everything that does not suit him? To live, or to go on living – can that be a matter of deciding that the real is not entirely so? Perhaps it is a matter of choosing another reality when the one we have known becomes too heavy to bear? After all, is that not what I did in the camp? Did I not choose to live in my memory of Emélia, to make her my present, to cast my daily existence into the unreality of nightmare? Could History be a greater truth made up of millions of individual lies, sewn one to another like the old quilts Fédorine used to make so that she could buy food for us when I was a child? They looked new and splendid with their rainbow of colours, and yet they were sewn

265

together from fabric scraps of differing shapes, indeterminate quality and unknown origins.

When the sun went down, I was still sitting in my chair. In the dark; Fédorine had not lit a candle. The four of us were there, in the dark and in silence. I was waiting. I was waiting for the *Anderer*'s cries, for his lugubrious recriminations to ring out again into the night, but no sound came. Outside it was night. All was silent. And then I became afraid. I felt fear come upon me and pass into my stomach, under my skin, inside my whole being, in a way that had not happened in a long time. Poupchette was humming softly. She had a touch of fever. Fédorine's syrups and herbal teas were not helping to bring it down, so she tried to calm the child by telling her stories. She had just got started on *Bilissi and the Poor Tailor* when she interrupted herself and asked me to fetch her some butter from Schloss' inn, so that she could make some little short-breads for Poupchette to dip in her milk at breakfast. For a few seconds I did not react. I had no desire to leave the house, but Fédorine insisted. At last I got up from my chair. I took my coat and I left as the old woman was starting the story again, and my Poupchette, all pink and glowing with fever, stretched out her little hands to me and said, "Papa, come back Papa, come back!"

It is an odd tale, the tale of Bilissi. It is the one that fascinated me the most when I was little and Fédorine would tell me stories; as I listened to it, I had the feeling that the earth was slipping away from beneath my feet, that there was nothing for me to hold on to, and that maybe what I saw before my eyes did not altogether exist.

"*Bilissi is a small tailor and very poor, who lives with his mother, his wife and his little daughter in a crumbling shack in the imaginary town of Pitopoï. One day, three knights pay him a visit. The first knight comes forward and orders a suit of red velvet from Bilissi for his master the King. Bilissi carries out the order and* produces the most beautiful suit he has ever made. When the knight collects the suit, he says to Bilissi, 'The King will be happy. In two days, you shall receive your reward.' Two days later, Bilissi sees his mother die before his eyes. 'Is this my reward?' Bilissi thinks, and he is filled with sadness.

"The following week, the second knight returns and knocks on Bilissi's door. He orders a suit of blue silk from Bilissi for his master the King. Bilissi carries out the order and produces the most beautiful suit he has ever made, much more beautiful than the suit of red velvet. When the knight comes to collect the suit, he says to Bilissi, 'The King will be happy. In two days, you shall receive your reward.' Two days later, Bilissi sees his wife die before his eyes. 'Is this my reward?' Bilissi thinks, and he is filled with sadness.

"The following week, the third knight returns and knocks on Bilissi's door. He orders a suit from Bilissi for his master the King, a suit of green brocade. Bilissi hesitates, tries to refuse, says that he has too much work, but the knight has already drawn his sword from its sheath. In the end, Bilissi accepts the order. He produces the most beautiful suit he has ever made, much more beautiful than the suit of red velvet, and much more beautiful even than the suit of blue silk. When the knight returns to pick up the suit, he says to Bilissi, 'The King will be happy. In two days, you shall receive your reward.' But Bilissi replies, 'Let the King keep the suit, but I want none of his reward. I am very happy as I am.'

"The knight looks at Bilissi in surprise. 'You are wrong, Bilissi. The King has the powers of life and death. He wishes to make you a father by giving you the little daughter you have always desired.'

"'But I already have a little daughter,' Bilissi replies, 'and she is the joy of my life.'

"The knight looks at the tailor and says, 'My poor Bilissi, the King took from you what you had, your mother and your wife, and you did not grieve overmuch, but he wishes to give you what you do not have, a daughter, for the little girl whose father you believe yourself to be is naught but an illusion, and you are all bereft. Do you really think that dreams are more precious than life?'

"The knight does not wait for Bilissi's reply, nor does the tailor make any. He tells himself that the knight has sought to deceive him. He goes back into his house, takes his child in his arms, sings her a song, gives her some nourishment, and then kisses her, without realizing that his lips touch only air and that he has never, ever, had a child."

I will not go back over events I have already described at the beginning of this long account: my arrival at Schloss' inn, the mute gathering of all the men in the village, their faces, my fright, my terror when I understood what they had done. Then, the circle of their bodies closing in upon me, their request and my promise to write the Report on my old typewriter.

The Report is finished, as I have said. I have therefore performed the task assigned to me. All I have to do now is to deliver it to the Mayor. Let him do with it what he will, it is no longer my problem.

39

Yesterday – but was it really yesterday? – I delivered the Report to Orschwir. I tucked the pages under my arm and went to his house without letting him know I was coming. I walked across the village. It was very early, and I saw nobody except for *Zungfrost*: "Not too . . . hot . . . hot, Brodeck!"

I greeted him and continued on my way.

I came to Orschwir's farm. I passed his farm hands and I passed his pigs. Nobody paid any attention to me. Neither the men nor the animals so much as looked at me.

I found Orschwir sitting at his big table, just as he had been when I came to see him the morning after the *Ereigniës*. But yesterday morning he was not in the middle of his breakfast. He was just sitting there. His hands were joined on the table in front of him, and he seemed to be lost in thought. When he heard me, he looked up and smiled at me a little. "There you are, Brodeck," he said. "How are you? You may not believe it, but I've been waiting for you. I knew you'd come this morning."

On another occasion I might have asked him how he could possibly have known such a thing, but oddly enough, I found that I was indifferent to, or rather, detached from a great many questions and their answers. Orschwir and the others had played with me enough. The mouse had learned to pay no more attention to the cats, so to speak, and if they needed entertainment, they had only to scratch one another with their sharp claws. They could stop counting on me to amuse them. They had given me an assignment and I had done it. I had told the story.

I laid before the Mayor all the pages on which I had set down the facts in question. "Here is the Report which you and the others asked for."

Orschwir picked up the sheets absent-mindedly. I had never seen him so distant, so thoughtful. Even his face lacked the brutal features it normally presented to the world. A kind of sadness had erased a little of his ugliness.

"The Report . . ." he said, scattering the pages.

"I want you to read it straight away, right here in front of me, and tell me what you think. I have the time. I will wait."

Orschwir smiled at me and said simply, "If you wish, Brodeck, if you wish . . . I've got time too . . ."

Then the Mayor began to read from the beginning, from the first word. My chair was comfortable and I settled myself down. I tried to

269

discern what Orschwir might be thinking by scrutinizing his facial expressions, but he read without betraying even the smallest reaction. Nevertheless, from time to time he passed one big hand over his forehead, rubbed his eyes as if he had not slept, or pinched his lips harder than he seemed to realize.

From outside came the sounds of the large farm waking up. Footsteps, cries, squeals, bucketfuls of water striking the ground, voices, the screech of axles – the noises of a way of life resuming its course, beginning a day which would be, all in all, like every other, during which some people would be born into the world and others would die, in a kind of perpetual motion.

The reading took a few hours – I could not say exactly how many. My mind seemed to be at rest. I let it roam as after a great effort, free to relax a little, to loaf, to go where it would.

The clock struck. Orschwir had finished his reading. He cleared his throat three times, gathered up the pages, shuffled them into an orderly stack and brought his big, heavy eyes to bear on me.

"Well?" I asked.

He waited a while before answering me. He rose to his feet without a word and began to walk slowly around the big table, rolling up the papers until they formed a kind of sceptre. Then he spoke: "Brodeck, I am the Mayor, as you know. But I do not think you know what that fact means to me. You write well, Brodeck – we were not wrong to choose you – and you love images, maybe a little too much, but still . . . I'm going to talk to you in images. You know our shepherds well; you have often observed them in the stubble-fields and the meadows. I have no idea whether or not they love the animals entrusted to them. Besides, how they feel about them is none of my business, and I do not think it is any of theirs either. The animals are placed in the shepherd's care.

270

He must find them grass in abundance, pure water, and sheepfolds sheltered from the wind. He must protect his flock from all danger and steer it away from excessively steep slopes, from rocks where the animals could slip and break their backs, from certain plants which would cause them to swell up and die, from various pests and predators which might attack the weakest of them, and from the wolves, of course, that come prowling near the flock. A good shepherd knows and does all that, whether he loves his animals or not. And what about the animals, you may ask. Do they love their shepherd? I put the question to you."

As a matter of fact, Orschwir did not put any such question to me. He did not even look at me once. He continued to walk around the big table, talking all the while, keeping his head down, tapping his left hand with the rolled-up Report which he held in his right.

"The animals, moreover, do they know they have a shepherd who does all that for them? Do they know? I don't believe so. I believe they are interested only in what they can see at their feet and right in front of their eyes: grass, water, straw to sleep on. That's all. A village is a small thing, and a fragile one at that. You know that. You know it well. Ours nearly did not survive. The war rolled over it like an enormous millstone, not to extract flour from it, but to smother and flatten it. All the same, we managed to deflect the stone a little. It did not crush everything. Not everything. The village had to take what was left and use it for its recovery."

Orschwir came to a stop near the enormous blue-and-green tiled stove that occupied an entire corner of the room. A small, carefully laid stack of firewood stood against the wall. Orschwir stooped, picked up a log, opened the door to the firebox, and thrust it in. Lovely flames, short and agile, danced around it. The Mayor did not close the door right away. He gazed at the flames for a long time. They made a cheerful music, like the sounds a hot wind sometimes draws from the branches of certain oaks covered with dry leaves in the middle of autumn.

"The shepherd always has to think about tomorrow. Everything that belongs to yesterday belongs to death, and the important thing is to live. I know you are well aware of that, Brodeck – you came back from a place people don't come back from. And me, my job is to act so that others can also live, so that they can see tomorrow and the day after that . . ."

That was the moment when I understood. "You can't do that," I said.

"Why not, Brodeck? I am the shepherd. The flock counts on me to protect it from every danger, and of all dangers, memory is one of the most terrible. I am not telling you anything you don't know, am I? You who remember everything, who remember too much?"

Orschwir gave me two little prods on the chest with the Report, either to keep me at a distance or to drive an idea into me, like a nail into a board: "It's time to forget, Brodeck. People need to forget."

Very gently, at these last words, Orschwir slipped the Report into the stove. In a second the pages which had been tightly wrapped around one another opened up like the petals of a strange flower, enormous, tormented. Then they writhed, became incandescent, then black, then grey, and then collapsed upon themselves, mingling their fragments in a red-hot dust that was quickly sucked into the flames. "Look," Orschwir whispered in my ear. "There's nothing left, nothing at all. Are you any unhappier?"

"You burned a stack of paper. You did not burn what is in my head!"

"You're right, it was only paper, but that paper contained everything the village wants to forget – and will forget. We're not all like you, Brodeck."

When I got home, I told Fédorine everything. She was holding Poupchette on her knee. The little one was taking her nap. The child's cheeks were as soft as peach-flower petals. Our peach orchards are in blossom now, the first to gladden our early spring with their very pale pink bloom. People here call them *Blumparadz*, "flowers of Paradise". That is a funny name when you think about it; as if Paradise could exist on this land, as if it could exist anywhere at all. Emélia was sitting by the window.

When I finished my account, I asked Fédorine, "What do you think?"

She did not reply, apart from a few disconnected words that made no sense. Then, after a few moments, finally she did say something: "It is up to you to decide, Brodeck. You alone. We will do what you decide."

I looked at the three of them, the little girl, the young woman and the old grandmother. The first was sleeping as though she had not yet been born, the second was singing as though she were absent, and the third was talking to me as though she were no longer there.

Then I said in an odd voice that did not sound much like mine, "We'll leave tomorrow."

40

I got out the old cart again. The one we had arrived with, Fédorine and I, a long time ago. I never thought we would need it again one day. I never thought there would be another going away. But maybe there can only be going aways, eternally, for those like us, for those made in our image.

Henceforth I am far away.

Far away from everything.

Far away from the others.

I have left the village.

Then again, maybe I am nowhere any more. Maybe I have left the story. Maybe I am only like the traveller in the fable, in the unlikely event that the hour of fables has come.

I left the typewriter in the house. I do not need it any more. Now I write in my brain. There can be no more intimate book. No-one will be able to read it. I will not have to hide it. It can never be found.

This morning, when I woke up very early, I felt Emélia lying against me and I saw Poupchette asleep in her little bed with her thumb in her mouth. I took both of them in my arms. In the kitchen, Fédorine was ready and waiting for us. The bundles were already made up. We left without making any noise. I took Fédorine in my arms too; she weighs nothing, she is so old and frail. Life has worn her thin. She is like a cloth that has been washed a thousand times. I start to walk, bearing my three treasures like that and pulling the cart. I think there is an old story about a traveller who left this way, fleeing his burning city and carrying his old father and his young son on his shoulders. I must have read that tale somewhere. Yes, I must have read it. I have read so many books. Could it be something Nösel told us about? Or maybe it was from Kelmar I heard it, or Diodème.

The streets were quiet and the houses asleep. So too were the people inside those houses. Our village was like unto itself, like a flock, as Orschwir had said, yes, a flock of houses pressed against one another, tranquil beneath the still black but already starless sky, and as inert and blank as every stone in their walls. I passed in front of Schloss' inn. A little light was shining in his kitchen. I passed in front of Mère Pitz's

274

café, Gott's forge and Wirfrau's bakery, and I heard the baker kneading his dough. I passed close by the covered market and the church and Röppel's ironmongery and Brochiert's butcher's shop. I passed the fountains and drank a little water as a sign of farewell. All those places were alive, intact, preserved. I stopped for a moment beside the monument to the dead and read there what I had always read: the names of Orschwir's two sons, the name of Jenkins, our policeman who died in the war, Cathor's name, Frippman's name, and mine, half effaced. I did not linger as I felt Emélia's hand on my neck. I am sure she was trying to tell me to go on; she had never liked it when we used to pass the monument and I would stop to read the names aloud.

It was a beautiful night, cold and clear, a night that seemed not to want to end, wallowing in its own darkness, turning round and round in it, as one sometimes likes to remain between warm sheets on a cold morning. I skirted the Mayor's farm. I heard the pigs moving about in their pens. I also saw Lise, *Die Keinauge*, cross the farmyard, holding a bucket that seemed to be full of milk and overflowed at every step, leaving a little white trail behind her.

I went on. I crossed the Staubi by the old stone bridge. I stopped a moment to listen to the murmur of the water one last time. It tells many stories, a river, if you know how to listen to it. But people never listen to what rivers tell them, or forests, or animals, the trees, the sky, the rocks on the mountainsides, other people. Nevertheless, there must be a time for telling as well as a time for listening.

Poupchette had not woken up yet, and Fédorine was dozing. Only Emélia had her eyes wide open. I carried the three of them along without any trouble. I felt no fatigue. Shortly after we crossed the bridge, I saw *Ohnmeist* about fifty metres away. He seemed to be waiting for me, as if he wanted to show me the way. He began to trot as I approached, and he went on ahead of me like that for more than an hour. We climbed the path towards the Haneck plateau. We passed through the great conifer woods. There were pleasant aromas of moss and pine needles. Snow formed gleaming corollas at the feet of the tall firs, and the wind swayed the tops of the trees and made their trunks pop and creak. When we reached the upper limit of the forest and had started to cross Bourenkopf's stubble-fields, *Ohnmeist* broke into a run and climbed atop a boulder. The first rays of the dawning sun shone on him then, and I perceived that he was no longer a masterless dog, no longer the *Ohnmeist* that walked down our streets and through our houses as though everything were part of his realm, but a fox, a very handsome and very old fox as far as I could judge. He struck a pose, turned his head in my direction, gazed at me for a long time, and then, with one agile, graceful bound, disappeared among the broom.

I walk tirelessly. I am happy. Yes, I am happy.

The summits around me are my accomplices. They are going to hide us. I turned around a few moments ago, near the wayside cross with the strange and beautiful Christ, to take a last look at our village. There is usually such a fine view from that place. The village looks small. The houses like tiny figurines. If you stretched out your arm, you could almost scoop them up in the palm of your hand. But this morning I saw none of that. It was no use looking; I did not see anything. There was no fog, no clouds, no mist. But down there below me there was also no village. There was no village any more. The village, my village, had completely disappeared. And with it, all the rest: the faces, the river, the living beings, the sorrows, the springs, the paths I had just taken, the forests, the rocks. It was as though the landscape and everything it contained had receded as I passed. As if, at every step, the set were being dismantled behind me, the painted backdrop rolled up, the lights extinguished. But I, for all that, I Brodeck, am not responsible. I am not guilty of that disappearance. I have not provoked it. I have not desired it, I swear it.

My name is Brodeck, and I had nothing to do with it.

Brodeck is my name.

Brodeck.

For pity's sake, remember it.

Brodeck.

FINIS

AUTHOR'S NOTE

The reader will find phrases here and there in these pages which I have consciously borrowed from other writers without asking their permission. May they pardon me and accept my thanks:

"Alle verwunden, eine tödtet" ("They all wound; one kills") is a motto inscribed on an 18th-century German carriage clock made by Benedik Fürstenfelder, a watchmaker in Fridberg, and put up for sale in a French auction house a few years ago.

"Talking is the best medicine" is a sentence from Primo Levi's story "The Molecule's Defiance".

"The hour of fables, has it not come?" is a question asked in André Dhôtel's *La Chronique fabuleuse*.

"I have learned that the dead never abandon the living" is a slightly amended version of a line I found in Fady Stephan's lovely book *Le Berceau du monde*.

"I write in my brain" is, if I remember correctly, a remark made by Jean-Jacques Rousseau in his *Confessions*.

ACKNOWLEDGEMENTS

I would like to extend my heartfelt thanks to Marie-Charlotte d'Espouy, Laurence Tardieu and Yves Léon, who through their joint efforts managed to save *Brodeck's Report* from virtual oblivion.

I would also like to mention, in connection with this book, several people who have been important to me at different moments in my life and who, having passed away during the two years I worked on this book, accompanied my thoughts as it unfolded: Marie-Claude de Brunhoff, Laurent Bonelli, Marc Vilrouge, René Laubiès, Jean-Christophe Lafaille, Patrick Berhault, Jacques Villeret.

And finally, my thanks go to the entire team at Éditions Stock, my French publisher, who, under the leadership of Jean-Marc Roberts, have honoured me with their trust and their friendship, and also to Michaela Heinz, faithful reader from the Outre-Rhin and precious counsellor.